Arden of Valray

A reimagining of the corpse-bride tale

Courtney G Hamilton

This book is for everyone who knows the true power of Redamancy~ a love returned in full. It is dedicated to anyone who has a corpse-bride sleeping beneath their feet.

And to Gregg, who did not run away in fear when mine awakened.

Foreword

Dear Reader,

It is no coincidence that you are here. I have woven a painted tapestry, where words are entwined with threads of time, creating images that dance in both light and shadow. This journey is one of death, mystery, lost love, betrayal, and revenge. But mostly, it is one of true Redamancy, resurrection, mercy, and redemption.

The characters in this layered timeline reveal that the past always influences the future. No one is immune to the sorrows that are passed down through the blood along the weary veins of ancestors. However, sometimes someone is given the chance to pass through the veil of time to untangle the knots of inherited generational heartaches. These knots, tightly wound around past loss and regrets, maintain a chokehold on a continuous cycle and prevent anyone from breaking free from the roots or bursting forth from seed to forge a new path. Occasionally, someone is allowed to gaze into the mirror of their shadow, where all patterns are revealed.

Arden was chosen for this dark, arduous, bittersweet task. Her story is alive in the present, as it remains within me, never fading into the past. As you journey with her, you will also gain insight into the restless minds of other characters—a luxury Arden never possessed until the very end, when everything was recorded and left for her in the suitcase. I have placed these notes throughout her journey at just the right moments to give you a broader perspective of how the past is woven into her present journey. I do hope that these additions both pique and quench your curiosity in just the right dose. I have also pulled from the suitcase a map of the realms and enclosed them here for you.

These beloved and complex characters are woven into this tapestry I now wear wrapped around my shoulders and my heart. This story has many layers, and I hope that you may see the threads creating the art above the loom as well as the secret knots that are formed below. To be able to see both sides of the tapestry is to experience the journey of the weaver. Come, let us begin.

Ever so I am,

~the Powers Above

Map

Zenit

Lashga

Dashel

Wincot

Valray

Vaxa

the by pass

Pallayes

Kallos

Teahn

Cleimen

Amara

Prologue

{One hundred and twenty-five years before the present}

Florin

As the remains of my body nourish the living creatures beneath this choppy water, my bones lie in darkness, awaiting discovery. Many lunar cycles have waxed and waned over the seas, but I cannot determine how many years have elapsed since my untimely fall. I wait, knowing that there must be more to life than this. There must be more; I was only seventeen, caught in the grips of fate, when I fell to this watery grave.

My father had a violent temper and could never be trusted with the truth. I learned this lesson too late. He disliked women and hated even more his desperate need for them. My mother's union with him was forced upon her when her father lost a wager to a foreigner, a debt he could only pay with her hand in marriage, which is how I came to be. Fortunately for my mother, she eventually had her position as ruler of Amara to distract her from their misery. Unfortunately for me, my father had no distraction other than the bottom of his bottle and the cards in his hands.

That night, I stood on the cliffside, watching the sunset as the waves crashed against the rocky coastline, when he closed in on me, clutching a bottle with unsteady hands, slurred speech, and fury in his eyes. He demanded to know the secret behind my mother's perpetual youth, which starkly contrasted with his own disheveled decline.

He had heard the ominous rumors about her not having the well-known pearl hair, suggesting that he was not worthy of her heart, and he seemed desperate for answers. I was unaware that my mother had kept secrets from him. I did not know she had never divulged that her power of longevity could be traded for true love or that she never believed his soul was worth such an exchange.

I was the one who revealed the truth to him. His glassy eyes ignited with a fierce rage. In that moment, I beheld the wild fury of a man who felt outwitted by a woman who had always deftly planned to outsmart and outlast him. I'll never forget the way he looked when he realized he was merely a small part of her timeline while she bided her time. His desire for revenge was palpable, and his thirst for vengeance transformed into an unhinged resolve—a tempest brewing in the void of his heart. In that final act of malice, he resolved the conflict that raged within him and thrust me, his own daughter, into the clutches of the tumultuous waves below.

One

My Dearest Rexus,

Soon. This madness will be over soon. Arden will be safe in the Wincot seat, I have made sure she will be taken care of. You and I will finally be free to be together and have the life we always dreamed of. We will finally tell Aster the truth. We must leave Valray of course. I have planned everything.

Forever yours,

Maren

Arden

It hurts to be awakened from death. My stiff bones ache, and each ghostly thought is more painful than the next, like jagged stones whipped up into a vortex inside my skull. The air changes, and I begin to feel the dirt moving and shifting around me. My mind is whirling with a new awareness of something happening above me. I have the visceral feeling that I am no longer alone; someone is digging into my grave. When the air and sunlight flood in through the dirt, my bones push up through the earth to find out who has disturbed me. At first, I cannot see anything; the light is blinding. But then, the silhouette of a face is bending over mine, and I can see daylight.

"Can you hear me?" he asks.

I try to focus on his words, but the pain of awakening lingers, pulling me into a new, unfamiliar reality. The whirling in my skull is unsettling. I am not sure if I still have a voice. I do not try to speak yet, so I nod, and my jaw bones clack with the movement.

"I have been looking for you. You are the only one that can break the spell."

He has no idea that I am no one who can do anything remarkable, especially break a spell. I am the most unremarkable person he could have dug up. I almost feel sorry for him and the disappointment he will have when he finds out I am not who he thinks I am. I feel caught between time and space.

It takes all of me to scratch out with my voice, "Me? How?" I rasp.

"Your tears. I think your tears are how," he replies.

"My tears?" The questions creak out in a hoarse whisper. "How will I cry tears for you? I am a corpse with dry bones." I lift my skeletal arms and look at them, feeling uncertain. I am still wearing my dirty wedding gown. "You pulled me from death, but I do not believe that I am alive. I am not sure what this is…" gesturing to my skeleton, "and I do not believe that I can make tears from bone."

He nods with understanding. "If you agree to help me, your life will be returned to you…and then you will once again be able to cry."

That sounds like a miserable existence. One so familiar to my grim past. My thoughts rustle around, scrambled and confused. Do I want my life to be returned to me?

"If I give you my tears, I get my life back?" I ask him, considering that tears might be worth trying to get back to my fiancé, Taryn.

But he interrupts to clarify, "a new life, one you have not lived yet."

I reconsider. "What happens to me if I decide not to help you?" I ask as I weigh my options.

"I put you back in your eternal bed, let you rest in peace, and grieve your loss for the rest of my life," he says somberly.

These new thoughts crackle against my skeleton. Do I really want to stay here in this dismal existence? This might be my last chance to escape death. He watches me with absolute attention. I have never felt more seen in all the years I was alive. Will I feel like this in my new life, seen? Maybe it is worth finding out. A second chance at life sounds better than staying underground forever. I let my bony head gently pull up and down to nod yes to him.

His face still has not come into focus, but I see it move into a smile as he says, "Thank you. I am so grateful."

I close my eyes and then begin to feel it, my soul returning to me. The sensation starts at my feet, and the warm fullness slowly rises through my body. New air lingers in my chest, filling my lungs. Warm blood courses through my now beating heart. The warmth then swirls around a few times in my head, filling my mind with memories, curiosity, and a strange new thirst for understanding. My cheeks flush, and my new skin, soft and warm, wraps gently around my bones. My life has returned to me. And then I feel his power, his strength, as he, in one fluid movement, scoops me up into his arms and carries me away from my grave.

Two

Nulfest Valray is a complicated man. He inherited the Sovran seat later in life after his father and older brother both enjoyed the Sovran benefits, both overstaying their welcome, and then both passing, leaving no other heir but him. Some would call him mad, others ambitious, some still eccentric. He was always different, experimenting and researching the edges and limits of his world, needing to understand what lay beyond them. To some, he was mysterious and charming. To others, he was thoughtless and aloof. To his family, he was an unpredictable combination of it all.

He married later in life to a woman much younger than he was. Her family had garnered power and prosperity in the furniture industry and was looking to expand a bit more. Theirs was more of an arrangement than a marriage, and daughters were a disappointment after such an extensive line of male heirs.

The Valray seat had lost its balance. It came to believe in a rigid patriarchy, forgetting the dignity and equality of women. Therefore, it had lost its enchantment. Women were no longer to be trusted after the tragic downfall of Dashel. What a bad light Vera Valray had put the Valray seat in. Fortunately, for the men, she was the last woman born into the line for nearly a century. Until his daughter, Arden, was born.

But for Nulfest, having the Sovran seat of Valray was an inconvenience that kept him from his true aspirations, ones he believed would be found in a world beyond the realms. If he could only get there.

He concluded that he would be a self-made man in the end. That he would become something great; someone his father and brother could never be. Invincible. Immortal.

He intended to unlock these powers, no matter the cost.

Nulfest had no interest in anything or anyone that did not pique his curiosity or aid his ambition, especially a daughter. So, Nulfest always had something to keep him busy, to keep him away from home, therefore, keeping him distracted from the life he did not seem to want.

And there were plenty of distractions.

Until he discovered that Arden had powers of her own. As a gambling man, he was sure there was a deal to be brokered in there somewhere.

Arden

I am sure we leave the realm and arrive at some place where I have never been, a place where everything, even the air, is different. He has set me down on soft ivory-colored cushions and gives me a few moments to adjust. I breathe in the new air; it is lighter. Everything around me is in shades of white and cream: the walls, the fabrics, the furniture, but beyond the white walls of the villa, everything else is in full color. Over the balcony, there is a sweeping landscape of lush green fields and aqua blue water all under a lavender-peach sky, with distant mountain peaks beyond.

"What is your name?" I ask, finally taking in the sight of him. The intricate gold and copper braids pulled back around his head are intertwined with gold and turquoise beads. The strands that have fallen loose tell me he has naturally curly hair, and I have never seen copper freckles like his before. His turquoise eyes have flecks of dark orange and magenta, like a distant galaxy has been captured within them, like I could fall in and lose myself there. His smile feels holy, and I do not know where to settle my eyes. I want to look at all of him at once. I can sense his strength from the size of his neck and shoulders, and he smells like the morning sun with layers of fresh cardamom and smoked clove. He is gorgeous. He is dressed in loose, fresh white pants and a matching white shirt.

"I am Kyrie, heir to the Sovran seat of the Kallos province in the Pallayes realm."

I am in a different realm. I somehow crossed the bypass. He is the heir of this faraway province. I could not dream this up even if I tried.

"Arden…" My eyes flinch as I recognize my name. He already knows my name. I wonder how he knows me. Kyrie holds out a soft cloth to me and says softly, "When the tears do come, wipe your eyes with this. It will collect and hold them safe until we know what to do with them."

I take the cloth in my hand and know that I have never felt a fabric like this before. It is soft, and I swear the cloth pulses very gently against my skin. I am not sure if I will be able to cry for him, though.

"You are known as the corpse-bride. The story of your ghost has made it all the way to my realm. Will you tell me what happened that day?" He asks gently, like I might still be breakable.

"Do you mean when I appeared after my death?" I clarify, letting the phrase corpse-bride settle in my mind. It sounds as horrible as my memory of it.

"Yes," he replies.

"How long ago did that even happen?" I begin to realize that I have so many questions.

"You appeared at Taryn and Vesta's proposal three months ago," he answers so smoothly.

The questions that were circling above are now starting to drop in. "Do you know how long I have been dead? I do not have any sense of time."

Without needing any time to consider, he answers, "Just a little over six months."

A memory falls into my mind. I was anticipating getting married and then celebrating my twenty-second birthday days later. I now suddenly realize that I spent my twenty-second birthday under dirt. How did it end? My momentary life. A poem arrives in my mind—my first one in this new life. My shadow has returned to me, and I still have this secret gift.

> Sometimes, you must pretend
> To be dead
> In order to survive.
>
> Sometimes, you must die
> A thousand deaths
> In order to live.

My shadow, my constant companion, whispers the words of truth it observes from the dark as it watches what plays out in the light. I am lost in my thoughts when I remember that he is patiently waiting for me to tell him how I came to be known as the corpse-bride. I guess I should start at the beginning. I am amazed that I still have my memory. I begin. "My mother decided it was time for me to get married. She chose a groom for me, Taryn, heir to the Wincot province. She hoped the betrothal would create some sort of alliance, but she never told me what it was exactly. Taryn and I had never met before. He had only sent me letters, and one day, one of the letters included a song he wrote titled, Come to Me. He said that he would sing it to me on our wedding day." I swallow, remembering his words.

"It was the power of that song that pulled my corpse out of the ground and caused me to levitate. With no effort of my own, completely spellbound by it, the song made me travel towards the sound of it, my feet landing far away from my grave in the rose garden of a small cottage. And there he was, down on his knee."

Kyrie's eyebrows raise, and he nods for me to continue. But first, my shadow needs to whisper to me.

> When they buried the corpse-bride
> They never thought
> She would find the groom again,

But she heard him calling.
She knew his song,
And she thrust herself
From the grave
Towards the sound of him.

"When I saw Taryn for first time, I felt a longing that ripped right through me. I wanted everything inside my skeleton to be alive again to have my wedding day. 'It's me, Arden!' I beckoned to him. When I saw the terror on his face when he looked at me, the shame crumbled me to my bony knees. He had never seen me alive, never knew that my beauty once matched his own. In his efforts to escape the horror and run for help, he dropped a gold band and did not stop to pick it up. But I saw where it landed. So, I crawled to it, found it, and placed it on my left hand. It was just the band I would have worn on my wedding day, the day I died." The memory pricks my skin. I pause when I remember the next moment. Vesta, I can still see her standing there.

"Please, continue." Kyrie brings me back to the story.

"And that is when I saw her, the new bride-to-be, the living one. She was standing still as death, waiting to see what I would do next. It was at that moment that I realized Taryn was proposing to her with my ring and my song, and he was singing it to her when it called me from my grave."

"What happened next?" He asks, absorbed in my story, so I continue.

"She was lovely and alive, ethereal even, with golden-honey skin that matched her long golden-honey hair, and aqua blue eyes. I was a skeleton, a corpse-bride, already forgotten. In that moment, I was terrified of what the crowd, so quickly gathered by Taryn when he ran for help, would decide to do with me. But Vesta seemed so strong when she addressed the crowd, and she told them all to leave. They obeyed her, and then it was just she and I."

I swallow again, remembering the next part.

"She came and knelt in front of me, took my hands in hers, and tenderly said, 'I see you, and I am not afraid of you. My name is Vesta, and you are the Albatross, my good omen. You found me, and we are going to share this life.'"

Kyrie, immersed, nods for me to continue.

"I looked at her pleadingly and said, 'I...I just wanted a chance to be free, to get married, and have a family. But now it is all gone.' She looked at me with such utter compassion, it made me shiver, and she said, 'I know, and that is what I want to give you, but the only way I know how is to promise to live this part of the journey for both of us. I promise you will be free again one day. When the time arrives, you will be called to heal the present between the past and future. Then, it will be your turn to live that part of the journey for us."

"I wonder what that means?" Kyrie ponders aloud before asking, "What happened next? What did you do?"

"Well, I was dead, a corpse-bride, and of course he was choosing her, the living bride. I knew there was nothing I could do but surrender. Her beauty is unmatched. I nodded to her, knowing that I needed to receive her gift of peace and return to my death. But I also sensed in her a safety that I could trust. It was the first time I had ever felt that way."

I look at his face and realize that today, with him, is the second time I have felt that foreign kind of safety, a safety I can trust.

"So, I willed my heart and said to her, 'Take my life then…and…let it be yours.' Vesta picked me up and carried me like a small child all the way back to my grave. She gently set me down and tenderly straightened out my bones and my dress. She placed my hands above my waist, kissed my forehead, and compassionately slid the golden band from my finger and placed it on hers. Then she covered me back up with dirt."

My mind writes another silent poem in the air. My
shadow is a poet.

> The power of the living bride
> Is her compassion.
> Only she can bury
> The corpse-bride
> and grant her wishes.
> Only she can avenge
> Her death and live her life.
> The living bride holds
> The power of gold
> And speaks with the wise voice
> Of the corpse.
> You are right to feel afraid.

Three

{One hundred and five years before the present}

Dear Florin

I see you. You have not been forgotten. It is now time for your rescue. I am sending a fisherman with a pure heart to pull your bones from your watery grave. Trust him. I will need his help to fulfill the prophecy.

~the Powers Above

Arden

Finally, Kyrie says, wide-eyed. "I am sorry it took me so long to find you. When I first went to your province six months ago to look for you, I was too late, you were already gone. No one was willing to answer any of my questions because your father had made a decree that forbid anyone to speak of you."

My brows furrow. I cannot imagine why my father ordered that I be forgotten.

He continues, "So, I returned home not sure how I would ever find you. Many months passed, and then I heard someone in my province tell the story of Arden Valray's corpse appearing at the proposal of the groom she was betrothed to marry before she disappeared. I asked for every detail that they knew and traveled back to your province seeking any answers I could find. It took some time, but finally, I found Vesta. As soon as I explained who I was and what my mission was, she pledged her help. She then explained to me that your body had never been seen again since the morning of your wedding, until your corpse appeared at her proposal. Everyone, especially Taryn, was so shocked to see you."

His words sting. Hot, prickly stinging, like a heat rash threatening to take over.

"Vesta said that when she picked you up into her arms, she had a strong knowing, like a sixth sense, that led her to where you were buried. But when she arrived, there was no coffin in the ground; it was unmarked, just a random place in the forest ground."

I blink. I know this means something important, but I cannot reach it fast enough.

He reads my face, "Arden, the person who buried you never wanted you found. This is why it took me so long to find you."

I choke on my breath, "What? Why would I have just been left for dead? I have no enemies," I hear myself say.

"Vesta realized the same thing and decided to keep the location a secret, to protect you from any more harm, while she tried to figure things out. So, she marked your grave with a rose plant from her garden. She took me there today; it was just outside the city walls of your province, not too deep into the forest lands beyond, but she was brave to have carried you out there by herself that day. She said she just knew what she was supposed to do."

I see the words trace across the air, even before I hear them in my mind, or know them in my heart.

When they buried the corpse-bride
They never thought she would

Come back from the dead
And rise to haunt them-
Never thought she would have an ally
Amongst the living.
No one expected the living-bride
To take pity and understand
And not fear.
No one saw the possibility of an alliance.
No one expected the living-bride
To embrace her like a child,
Tucking her back into death's bed,
Promising life will come again soon.

"Wait, was Vesta there when you pulled me up? She knows about...this?" as I use my hand to gesture to what is now this new version of me.

"She respectfully stood back and watched, but also with a protective dominion over you. She said that she would guard you with her life, you are that important to her. We agreed that if you decided to come with me, she would patch up the ground, leaving nothing behind us but the rose bush. I am glad to have her as an ally in the Lashga realm since I do not know who can be trusted."

It is a lot to digest all at once. I look up at Kyrie, and it finally strikes me like an arrow to my chest, "So, my death was not an accident? Someone wanted me dead and never found again. I was not brought home. I did not have a funeral. I was just tossed in the ground, never spoken of again?" My chest is rising and falling faster than my racing thoughts, and the rest of me just freezes. I cannot move my arms or legs even if I want to.

Kyrie comes over and kneels close beside me. He places one hand on my back; I can feel his warmth against my shocked body. I cannot even cry yet. I want to hear more of the horrible truth while I am numb, hoping it will hurt less this way.

"How did Taryn and Vesta even meet anyway?" I ask, bracing for the impact. The pain in my voice hits a fever pitch.

"You never arrived at the wedding, and there was never any sign of the bridal carriage again. Taryn's family was deeply offended and insulted that you did not show up for the wedding, thinking you called it off, so they traveled back home immediately. But Taryn stayed even after his family left; he was the only one who felt it was not true; he believed that something bad had happened. So, he asked everyone in the province who was willing to help look for you to form search parties. That is how he met Vesta in the days following, searching for you. That is how their bond began, trying to find you. He never went back home to Wincot because his family refused to meet her because she was not from a wealthy or royal line. He insisted that he would not marry any other, but it cost him his place as heir."

The heat starts rising to my face, my nose and brow wrinkle up, and when my chin finally quivers, the hot, painful tears start streaming. There is an ache wrapping around my heart. "If he were so intent on finding me during the search party, then how could he fall in love with her so quickly? He fought to have her, gave up everything for her, but not for me, he grieved me for only a fortnight!"

The soft, tear-catching cloth is in front of me, and I bury my whole face into it. It can have all my tears; I do not care; I do not want them. I was abandoned, left alone in the ground, forgotten. Unmarked. It is too much to process, even in small pieces. My sobs are no longer quiet; they become loud, guttural moans from the deepest place within me. Kyrie stays kneeling at my side. I sense that he is conflicted. He needs my tears, which requires me to keep crying, but the uncomfortable experience of it is something he wants to stop.

"Arden," he says so soft and gentle, "I believe his intentions and feelings for you were once true. The power of the song proves the love behind it. I can understand how seeing you appear as a corpse bride was frightening for him. I can also understand how he fell in love with Vesta soon after the tragedy. Her goodness is rare; we have both seen it, it must have been a balm to his grief. Her strength covers his weakness. I cannot explain it, but she loves you."

Is this agony what I chose to live for? To be butchered by the secrets of my life. What is the point again? I am not sure if I made the right choice to leave my grave. How can grief like this not send me back under the ground? I hate that I have no other option but to face the truth. I hate that I might not ever find the truth. I hate that my second chance at life is just grieving the unsolved mystery of my first life. I cannot stop sobbing now, it is guttural.

"I will stay with you here while you process this news," he says softly, and I curl my knees up to my chest and wring myself out. Why did I have to die? I was so close to finally touching happiness. I wanted to know if it truly existed. Obviously, it does not. My shadow mourns for me.

> I cut the flowers for my funeral and
> Put on the black dress and eyeshadow.
> I crawl into the casket
> But there is no one to carry me
> Out to the grave.
> I showed up to death
> With a bottle of wine
> And the oil and spices

To anoint all the pain,
But the tomb is silent
And empty.
There is no one here
To roll back the stone.

Four

Vesta

The Powers Above revealed to me that I had two gifts awaiting my arrival in Valray, prompting me to remain vigilant and attentive. My purpose was to find the Valray bride and safeguard her. Upon meeting Taryn, I instinctively recognized him as one of those gifts. Yet, during my engagement, I came to understand that Arden was my second gift; she embodied the essence of the Albatross.

When Kyrie arrived with inquiries about Arden, I leaned into my intuition and all I had learned throughout the years. I guided him to her grave that fateful day. I will never forget the moment I saw her come back to life, and how they left the realm together. I made him promise to return for my wedding, so I might ensure her well-being and that the prophecy would continue to unfold as foretold.

I often desire to share everything with Arden all at once, yet I understand that the truth will reveal itself to her in its own time, as she is prepared to accept it. This is the true nature of the power and how it works.

Arden

I do not know how much time has passed, but long enough for him to sense my impending descent into a darker spiral, so he asks, "Arden, may I take you down to the water?"

I nod, not really caring what happens next. I have never cried in front of a stranger before. I cannot decide if I am embarrassed or proud that I have given him what he wants. I want to hand him the soaking wet cloth and ask him if he is happy now. I also want to cling to it in case there is more to come. I want to be mad as hell, but he has been too kind and gentle to be the target.

Against my shock and dark grief, the view outside is breathtaking; it jars my senses for a moment, forcing me to breathe. I can see the aqua waters ahead. Built around the large pool is a beautiful white stone structure with steps leading down to the water. He helps me to the steps, and we walk down low enough to put our legs in without getting completely wet. I notice the water's coldness and wonder if he swims here.

Staring at the specks of light upon the water helps calm me. I am afraid to ask any more questions, knowing that every answer will get worse, but I need answers more than I need anything else. I fear there will never be enough hours to find all the answers to my two lifetimes of questions.

Then, he asks, "Arden, do you know why Vesta called you an Albatross?"

"No," I reply and shake my head.

"In the Pallayes realm, the Albatross is a sacred bird, and we revere them. The Albatross mate for life and are a sign of everlasting love. They are an incredibly good omen when they appear on a journey; they offer protection. But they become a terrible curse for anyone who ends the life of one. That guilty person wears the regret and burden of the Albatross's body around their neck. And to anyone who comes upon a dead Albatross, it is their responsibility to honor its life and give it a proper burial. They are chosen to carry on its journey symbolically."

I let the words reverberate. I am an Albatross. Vesta found me and marked my grave with roses. She offered to live life for both of us until it was my turn. I think of her. My shadow imagines her even better than I can.

> I lay awake in the night
> With my ear on the pillow,
> And I can hear your
> Corpse's heartbeat pulsing
> In the soil below.

Waiting,
Waiting,
Waiting,
For your turn with the living.

Then I look up at him. "What does it mean for the one who beckons a dead Albatross back to life?" I ask him, hoping that he knows the answer and that it is a good one.

"I hope it means freedom." He looks straight into my eyes and then beyond as if he can see another realm within me that he intends to travel one day. "Your choice to live again, despite facing the painful truth of your past and going through this process of grief, I just know, somehow leads to my freedom to fully live life again too."

Helping him to be free is going to be more complicated than I initially thought, especially since I've never experienced freedom myself. I felt like a prisoner my whole life, only to die and be held captive in dirt. My shadow taunts me.

I am sorry I had to stand
On your grave last night
To keep you from climbing out.
I could feel you banging
Against the dirt
Begging to be let up.
Your cry went through me

And I considered crawling
Down into your dark bed,
To let you have a turn
With the living.

I focus on our conversation, and then I think of one more question I need to ask him. "Kyrie, how were you able to give me my life back?"

"I did not. I do not have that power," he replies thoughtfully.

"Then, how?" I ask, struck with surprise.

"Honestly, I just had hope. I figured that someone listed in the Book of Unbinding as a cure for the spell of the Veiled Heart could not just die and stay dead. I gambled on the off chance that if I found you and asked you to live again for a greater purpose, that somehow, life would return to you. I desperately needed you to live again, it was worth trying anything. So, I just started with asking, and you saying yes was the power that gave you life."

I blink. I brought myself back to life? I do not understand. I am not sure if I believe it. Is that even possible?

"But why was I listed in a book to break spells?" I ask, feeling dubious that I could be mentioned anywhere in anything of importance.

"The line from the book says, 'a maiden born into the Valray line," he replies.

That is a relief, it is not specifically about me. I do not know how to tell him that I do not have much life experience, my father did not even want me and my sister to become educated. He said our job was to stay pretty, that we would never need to make important decisions. The only person who understood my thirst to know and understand the realm around me was Olsa, my favorite staff member. She took pity on me, and over the years, she would sneak books in for me to read each week. Everything I know comes from those books. I realize I need to ask Kyrie more questions, but the old childhood fears rise; I was silenced every time I asked a question. I need to break past this fear; I no longer belong to my parents. Who do I belong to now? Is it even possible to belong to yourself? Who am I beyond my conditioning? Who am I beyond my wounds? How do I become who I truly am?

"So, what now? Am I living here? With you?" I fire the questions all at once.

He smiles, "This is your new home now, if you would like to stay," as he raises his hand towards the villa and the province beyond. "I arranged the room upstairs for you so that you would not feel alone, so that I could take care of you. But there is a guest house near the pool that you are more than welcome to claim as your own at any time." He offers graciously.

"Thank you, I will think about it and let you know," I reply.

"You will be safe here. The people who wanted you dead do not know that you are alive and would not expect you to be in a different realm. We are two adults, trying to solve mysteries, both trying to reclaim something that was stolen from us. I hope we become close friends," he says gently but matter-of-factly.

No one has ever told me before that I am an adult. The new revelation charges through me. I guess my transition from child to adult happened underground, in death. I feel wild with rebellion, but terrified of this new, unknown feeling.

> I will wrap up
> This despair
> Into a treasure
> That I will unwrap
> Later for myself.

Five

{Seven months before the present}

Dear Mazek

The betrothal of the Valray bride has been announced and the wedding date is set. The prophecy will soon unfold, and you know what that entails.

It is time for you to travel to Vaxxa to find Earl Menstus.

Present yourself as the expert on the prophecy. He will want you to translate it for him to attain Dashel, but I need you to inconspicuously prepare him for what is to come.

Inspire him towards a curiosity that leads to the good of others instead of selfish gains. He will need your counsel; much has happened recently that cannot be undone, and much more will soon happen.

His time has almost come.

I put all my instructions for you, Florin, and Vesta, into the suitcase.

Thank you for your faithful friendship over the years. I am positive your family's bond of love is strong enough to hold this mission and see it through.

~the Powers Above

Arden

"I hope I get to show you the beautiful places of Kallos, and if we break this spell, I would love to show you the whole Pallayes realm," Kyrie says, drawing me back to the present moment.

I let that thought soak in. My new home. My new body. My new life. I feel like an imposter in his house, trying to help him break a spell. But I am too scared to be sent back to the hole in the ground when he finds out I am of no significance. I hold up my arms and look at my new hands; I touch my face and feel my hair. I am alive. I startle when I notice that even my dress is new, a fresh white gown I have never seen before, but love anyway.

Even though I have lost my old life, as I look at Kyrie's face, I sense that I still have this new life to live, and I demand everything in me to live it—to stay alive this time. A new chance at freedom and adventure feels worth living for. But I hate feeling like an imposter, so I must be honest and tell him the truth. He deserves to know.

"Kyrie, I want to help you, I really do. But I think you should know the truth." I begin.

"The truth about what?" He asks.

"I am afraid you have the wrong person. You are looking for someone who can help you break a spell, someone significant, important. I am just me, a girl who has been nowhere and has done nothing. I am unremarkably obscure. I think you have dug up the wrong Valray maiden." I nervously admit.

He looks at me intensely with those cosmic eyes, and I resist the urge to dive into them and fall into another galaxy far away. Then he says, very thoughtfully and methodically, "Arden, when someone cages or chains something, it is because they are afraid of that thing. When someone killed you and put you in an unmarked grave, they were trying to render you powerless. When your memory is ordered to be forgotten, it is not because you are insignificant. That is not logical. People only get rid of and silence those who have great power, that they themselves are afraid of for some reason. The only rational conclusion that I can come to, from knowing the details of your story, is that you are incredibly significant, very important, and extremely powerful. I have no doubt that you are exactly the right person needed to help me."

I blink twice. My eyelids are the only part of me that can move; I am blindsided. I want to believe him and never question it again, but that would require a blind faith that I do not have. I still need more answers to understand what happened to me. The person he just described is someone I have not met yet, even if she is me.

He sees that I am frozen in disbelief and says, "Let us head back up to the villa so that you can rest. It has been a long day. You have a lot to process, and we still have so much more to talk about tomorrow. I know time is precious, but I want to make sure you have enough time to adjust to all of this. I know it is a lot all at once."

We walk back in silence, both of us heavy with thoughts. Then I admit to him, "I have only heard of Pallayes in conversations. I was never sure if it was real."

He says, "Our cultures are so different. Many myths and legends have been created about the two realms over the centuries that it is hard to know fact from fiction. But Pallayes is south of the Lashga realm, and just as real."

"There is so much of Lashga that I have never experienced. My father traveled, but my mother and sister and I were not really allowed to leave the province, much less explore the rest of Lashga. I know so little about the realm I grew up in, only what I have gathered through books and conversations that no one knew I was listening to." I explain.

Kyrie asks if I want to join him for dinner, but I decline, as it might be a while before I can eat. He walks me upstairs to my new room and gives me a gentle hug before leaving. He turns back, "Are you sure you do not need anything? There is plenty of food."

"Thank you, I am not hungry, I just need to lay down and rest."

"Okay, goodnight. I am just downstairs if you need anything. Thank you again for coming here to help me."

"Goodnight," I say before closing the door.

I climb into the bed, and although the soft covers caress my new skin as I close my eyes, I cannot fall asleep. I toss and turn, aware that it is the first time my body has not slept underground in over six months. But it does not feel like half of a year; it feels like decades. I can hardly believe I am twenty-two; I feel like I must be forty-two. Will I ever feel normal again? Will I ever get my appetite back? How will I keep the grief from eating me alive? Nothing seems appetizing. I worry that he will send me back to Valray once the spell is broken, and I will be in exile again. I also fear that we cannot break the spell, and he dies, leaving me here abandoned in a strange new land.

Another poem dances across the silent darkness.

> Those with guilt on their hands
> Never expected the two brides
> To ever meet
> And patiently wait.
> Now, there are two brides
> On either side of time,
> On both sides of life,

And they speak to each other.
Their secret is patience.
It is right to fear their understanding
Of being both dead and alive.

It is now midnight, and I stare at the ceiling, trying to keep my face blank. But salt tears stream down, and I remember to catch them with the cloth. Who knew the truth could be an endless, horrible agony? I replay his words, trying to uncover the mystery of my death and why my father would want me forgotten. I cry for all that I lost, but more for all that I never had.

Six

{Twenty-six years before the present}

Juris Kallos

What have I done? I lost control, and my rage took over once again. No one can know the truth, especially Reown. I would lose her completely—if she were ever truly mine to lose. She must never find out that he came to see her. If I have learned anything, it is that there is nothing a good lie cannot cover or fix. I will think of something, some explanation, if he even survives. I will be ready to protect what is mine.

Arden

This morning, I wake up needing answers. The little sleep I had was filled with strange dreams. The one scene I remember best is of me climbing out of my grave to find Taryn holding a birthday cake with one hundred candles, singing to me, and Vesta saying she made the cake herself. I have dirt under my nails from clawing through it, and I wonder if they will still give me a piece. Someone then smashes my cake into the ground, puts me back in my grave, and fills it back up with dirt. I try to scream, but my mouth fills quickly with dirt instead of air. I woke myself up, trying to breathe.

> I remember how to die
> But I forgot how to rise.
> There is no one at my tomb,
> There were no witnesses.

I put on the softest clothes I can find in the wardrobe and head downstairs.

Kyrie is already at breakfast. "Would you like anything?" He asks.

"No but thank you though...I still do not have much of an appetite." I reply as I sit. I am not sure if I can chew on anything else but the answers I desperately need.

"So, why do you need my tears?" I finally ask the question I should have asked at first but could not reach it until now. I have layers of questions, and I finally understand they cannot all be answered at once.

Kyrie walks over to my chair and gently leads me to the morning terrace, where an enchanting view of the water awaits, along with the softest cushions This is my favorite place at the villa. After we are settled, he begins...

"The spell of the Veiled Heart was cast on my province twenty-two years ago. I was not yet four years old. It struck my mother the hardest. When she finally fell into an unconscious-like state last year, my father and I did not have much hope left, until we heard that the cure might be found in the Book of Unbinding. If we were brave enough to find it."

I need to hear his story. I need to understand how I am connected to him and this spell. "Did you ever find it, the book?"

"Yes, we did, but that is how my father died, and we never got his body back. I could not even bury him."

"Oh, Kyrie. I am so sorry." I grab his hands. "I am so sorry, that is terrible. When did that happen?"

"It happened eight months ago. My father and I traveled across the mountains to the city of Vaxxa, where the ancient library of Olstar is located. This is where all the sages and scholars gather to trade books and tales of ancient prophecies, translations, magic, and their knowledge of them. But the Book of Unbinding was never to leave the ancient library. My father had the idea to 'borrow it' so that we could learn how to break the spell and then planned to return it afterward. That plan did not work out. My father was a stubborn man who was convinced rules did not apply to him. I went to protect him…but I failed." He draws in a long, deep breath and then exhales loudly. "When I returned home over a month later, my mother was in an unconscious state. She still does not know that my father is dead."

"I am…I am so sorry for your loss, that is tragic. It must have been so lonely, and so incredibly sad for you," I offer.

"I still remember standing there next to him, looking at the page in the book [How to Break the Spell of the Veiled Heart] when the door bolted open, and the next thing I knew, my father pushed me out of sight before he was taken. He hoped that I could at least make it back with enough knowledge to save my mother. I managed to stay hidden and out of sight the rest of the time I was in Vaxxa. I have the power of invisibility, but my father did not. Even so, I was never able to read the whole page. The book became locked and guarded very quickly when they realized it had been damaged."

With this, he pulls a folded piece of old paper from his pocket and lays it on the cushion between us. "It happened so fast, but when my father pushed me aside, I instinctively tried to take the cure with me. The page is torn, and the only part I have is this…"

'The tears of grief must be cried…

maiden born into the Valray line. Her…

required to break the spell of the veil…

It is a slow death until she brings ba…'

"I am confident the rest of the page is needed to understand what to do and exactly how to break the spell. I have just been so desperate to make it all right again," he says humbly, if not a little defeated. "But I am just not sure how to do it exactly."

I study the lines and can see that some important words are missing.

"But why are the tears from a Valray maiden needed to break the spell anyway?"

"I think it has to do with Earl Menstus' back story."

"Who is Earl Menstus? Although I do not want to know, do I?" I ask, shaking off the fear.

"He is the one who put this spell over our province. My father told me that the spell is meant to cause the province to crumble from within, so that Earl Menstus would easily be able to take it over. Kallos would be defenseless without its Sovran seat. My father said that Earl Menstus has been patiently biding his time, waiting for our downfall to claim the seat for himself."

"Where did he come from?" I ask.

"I do not know much about him, but I did some research while I was in Vaxxa, and I found the legend about his ancestor who first cast the spell of the Veiled Heart a century ago." He takes a slow breath and begins the story he remembers…

"When the last maiden from the Valray line became pregnant for Earl Dashel, heir of Dashel, she sought refuge in her lover's province. She hoped it would give her security from her family's scorn, because they had already arranged her betrothal to the heir of the Zenif province. But after the baby was born, Lord Dashel refused her claim that the baby boy belonged to his son, Earl Dashel, heir to his seat. When Lord Dashel forbade his son from ever seeing Vera again, or else Earl would lose his right to the province seat, she threatened to cast a spell on the province if they were kept apart. But Lord Dashel did not relent, instead he banished her from the province.

"The maiden took the baby and left, hoping that for sure her lover would come to retrieve her and claim his son. She grieved and cried until she wrung herself dry. Afterwards, she cast the spell and declared that the only way to break it was from the tears of grief of a Valray maiden. She was the only maiden left in her line at the time.

"But Earl never went to her because he feared his father and losing his right to the seat. Even after Lord Dashel died, Earl still did not go to find the maiden and his son. Instead, he claimed his seat and ruled, but he then watched in horror as the whole province quickly perished.

"That is why the Lashga realm has only three remaining provinces; the Dashel province passed away under the spell of the Veiled Heart, cast by Earl Menstus' great-grandmother. It was the first province to end without any heir to claim the seat.

"But that little boy, the first Earl Menstus (that is what she named him), grew up to be the perfect likeness to Earl Dashel, the last ruler of the Dashel province. It was the young maiden's only proof and vindication that her story was true. But it was too late by then; the Dashel province had fallen. The Valray maiden lived in exile, never belonging anywhere again, and raised her son alone without any family or province. She was cast out of her family for her disgrace, written out of the Valray bloodline, and her name erased. She became known as *Baba Yaga,* and stories were told of her collecting the bones of the fallen Dashel province, always seeking the bones of Earl Dashel. Some say she found him and brought him back to life. Others say she haunts the province, keeping watch over all the bones from Dashel."

My mind suddenly paints a picture of her. But I know how stories are created and elaborated as they are passed on, just like my infamous corpse-bride tale. However true mine is, I am sure exaggerated versions are being told. I shake off the images and focus back on the story.

"The little boy grew up and eventually had a family of his own, passing down his name. They lived in obscurity, but the family story was passed down through the generations. Earl Menstus grew up hearing stories about his old grandfather, who was said to be the true son of the last ruler of the Dashel province. He declares that he is the rightful heir to reclaim the seat of the Dashel province and rebuild the province. But in the meantime, he lives on the outskirts of Vaxxa and has been plotting something for over two decades."

"I cannot believe I have never heard of him before." I say quietly, thinking about the Valray maiden and her tragic heartache. "And I cannot believe I never heard of her." My shadow conjures its own thoughts.

The human heart
is complex
And when you must
Play to win,
Sometimes, you plot revenge.
Especially when
The sheets are cold.

Seven

{Eighty-five years before the present}

Vera Valray

They call me Baba Yaga, a name that sends shivers down spines and curls the toes of the bravest souls. If only they had known me before when I was called *my darling, my tender love,* even *my starlight.*

Yes, it was I that caused the fall of Dashel, but I have been conveniently blamed for every unsavory event in the whole realm ever since that day. They say I go and collect the bones of my victims, but I have only returned to Dashel once, after the spell was cast. After the complete fall of the province. And I did find what I was looking for, but it was not bones. It was my necklace. The one he wore around his neck and was still wearing after his death. It was all that I had left of my lineage, my family, my identity before I was cast out. The Valray Oak pendant. Proof that I once belonged to the Sovran seat of Valray. Proof that I was a destined ruler, but I gave it all up for him.

I went back to at least find it and reclaim this part of myself. Why should he get to still take from me in death? No. This necklace and the letter I found next to his rotting bones are what I will pass down to my son, Earl Menstus, should he ever need them. That pendant carries the final piece of the prophecy, a thread connecting us to the great tapestry of the Powers Above. We may have been discarded, but at least my descendants will be connected to fate. I will pass down my story, and one day it will be told. I will not be erased from history, or slip into obscurity, no matter how hard they try.

My grandmother, the great Corin Valray, always told me that the enchantment would protect me if I learned how to harness my power. I am not sure that I have. I only know that when I was rejected and abandoned by all those whom I thought loved me, my sacred grief and rage swept out from me, scattered those bones across the land, and then returned to me, where it nestled deep inside my soul. It is the dark magic within me now, and I am its mage.

Arden

"When do we even know if the tears work, if they can break the spell?" I ask Kyrie.

"I am trying to figure that part out. I have some trusted workers crafting different ideas. That is where the special cloth is from. They designed it to be able to hold the salt crystals until they can be extracted and experimented with. Soon I will need to bring them what we have collected so far and see what can be done with it."

"You have mentioned the spell cast over your province, but you have not said what it is. What did it do?"

"The spell of the Veiled Heart," he says solemnly, looking straight into my eyes, "causes every member of the Kallos family and province, to progressively lose all feeling, emotionally and then physically, eventually leading to death."

"You cannot feel?" I am not sure how to comprehend this. "How is that even possible?" I ask.

"It begins as a dulling and then a fading of all emotions, such as happiness, sadness, anger, fear, enjoyment, until there is nothing left to feel. It just becomes a perception of logic alone, and things like crying no longer happen. The next part is a progressive diminishing of the five senses. So, the person begins to lose taste, smell, hearing, sight, and then the worst, is to no longer feel any sensation against your skin. Not even pain. Even the memories of those feelings fade away, so there is no more context or story left to draw on. My mother is in this phase of it. It is what caused her to lose all hope, when she could no longer enjoy any aspect of her life. It is like she has resolved to fade away as well."

I stumble through thoughts that lead to words. "I am so sorry, I cannot even imagine what it has been like all these years. I understand now why you will not stop until the spell is broken; this is worth fighting for." I want him to feel again.

"I am not sure how much time I have before I begin to lose my senses completely, they have just begun to fade over the last two years. I miss the full taste and smell of everything; it has all become bland. I miss hearing and seeing clearly and accurately. I really miss laughing, it is a distant memory. But I am thankful I still have some memories of feelings that I am trying to keep alive in my head. It is frightening after watching what my mother went through, and my father did not talk much about his personal experience, he kept it private. So, I have just been trying to navigate my own experience based on what I observe from the other people in the province around me."

"I cannot even imagine what you've suffered." I am at a total loss of what to say. How do you live without feeling? I wonder to myself.

"I have just been trying to stay out of Earl Menstus' sight while I search for ways to break the spell. It is why I have such gratitude for you every time you feel so deeply and let your tears pour out, and all of it for the sake of people you do not even know. I am ashamed that I could not even cry over my father's death. I have a logical understanding that it is tragic, but it is as if my thoughts are not connected to the emotions of it, or to the part that makes tears."

I look far into his eyes, wondering if I will ever know the part of him that can feel again, and decide I am willing to find out. "If my tears help you to feel again, then I will know it was worth it. Thank you for telling me your story."

I go to bed tonight, trying to imagine what it is like not to feel, and I cannot really. My feelings have always guided me because they were the only things I could trust, even though I was told that I was too sensitive, emotional, or dramatic. All our tragedy seems endless. I am gazing into a dark void, and the only flickers of light are more questions that I do not want the answers to. But I must find the answers for my true freedom, my authentic voice, and I want Kyrie to find his, too.

Now that I know his story, I replay my time with him. It explains some of his responses and reactions, and yet he has always been so kind and gentle. I let tears fall into the cloth. I think about how these tears are needed to break the spell for someone who can no longer cry. I draft a poem for Kyrie in my mind.

> The richness of life
> Was taken from me,
> So now I collect it
> In the form of tears.
> I ache for things
> Unexpressed deep inside,
> Things not yet experienced
> Or distant memories forgotten.
> I ache for that which I
> Do not know that I ache for,
> The parts of life I may never know
> Or never have again.
> I am trapped in the walls
> That I haunt,
> A ghost hovering
> Above all the feelings
> I no longer feel.

At midnight, I wake up with a memory: sitting up gasping and sweat running down the back of my neck. It is not just a nightmare, it is a word, a name which breaks my sleep. Vaxxa, I have heard it before. My father traveled there before my wedding. My shadow fears for me.

> I kneel in the heavy rain
> Mixed with wet tears.
> Unseen
> Palms up
> Face down
> Screaming
> Why all this destruction?
> I am lost
> In the flash flood.
> Taken away
> By the current of loss.

Eight

{Eight months before the present}

My dear Canton,

I am afraid I cannot go on as before. I do not dare to speak of it in person, to you, or to anyone Please accept this letter as a formal request that you step into a more significant role as Regent; I hereby confer upon you all the daily responsibilities of the Sovran seat. I cannot trust Juris with this task; you know how unreasonable he can be. I will put things in place that will allow Kyrie to inherit the Sovran seat on his twenty-sixth birthday, or upon my death- whichever comes first. I trust you Canton, more than any other in this province. You have been my most faithful friend and confidant. Please keep in touch with Deirdras. I fear she will not return, but I am glad she is in a better place. She may have a chance for happiness now that she is in Clemen. I am taking to my bed now, and I do not know when I shall ever rise from it.

Always,

Reown

Arden

I am overwhelmed by how many questions I still have unanswered. I do not care how long it takes me; I need to find out how I died and why. My shadow agrees.

My innermost has caved in
And my voice falls silent
Under the rubble.
I swallow the silence.
It is my daily wage,
My compensation,
My unjust reward,
For paying the price
Of admission.

When I arrive downstairs and find Kyrie, I tell him, "One of the nightmares I had was about Vaxxa. I woke up remembering that my father traveled there a few months before my wedding."

"Do you want to sit out on the terrace?" He asks. I nod yes and follow him to where we sat yesterday.

"Arden, will you please tell me about your father? There is more to the story I began yesterday, I just did not want to overwhelm you," he admits.

My memories begin to swirl in a dark cloud. There are gaps. "My father? I am not sure what to say. He was more like a distant figure that I rarely caught glimpses of growing up. Except when something terrible happened, then he was in the middle of it. I was told never, under any circumstances, to bother him about anything. He surely did not bother himself with me for most of my life. He was always busy with his affairs- business and personal. I had even stopped trying to get his attention."

"What do you remember about his trip to Vaxxa?"

"Well, it was after he returned from Vaxxa that he became interested in me and was curious about my power. I did not know what he was talking about. It is like he discovered something about me that I did not even know about myself. He offered to give me anything I wanted if I agreed to call off the wedding and travel to a secret destination. I was terrified."

"What did you do?"

"I tried to tell my mother what was happening, but she told me to keep quiet and act as if everything was fine, to just keep the peace. I pleaded with my mother to hear me out, and she said that I would just make it worse for everyone if I made him angry. She told me to stay in my room and wait quietly for the wedding. For all of this and more, I could not wait to be married and escape all of it. I wanted to create a new life for myself, far away in Wincot, and never return."

I exhale the memory and continue.

"But she did not understand that staying in my room and waiting for the wedding was exactly what angered him, that is what made it worst. I finally refused his offer, and the strangest thing happened. My sister packed her bags and left. My mother refused to answer any of my questions, and my father never spoke to me again after that day. I spent those weeks alone. My life was always like a caged bird. Taryn's letters were the only good thing that happened to me while I waited to leave my parents' house. Olsa was the only person I saw. One day, she even brought me a piece of cake. Eating that cake alone was the last bitter-sweet thing I did before I died."

Kyrie slowly leans forward, takes my hand, and places it in his. "Arden, your father was in Vaxxa while my father and I were there. Even though I have not figured it all out yet, your father is somehow connected to your death, and it terrifies me that I cannot protect you from the pain of that truth. It was too much to tell you everything yesterday."

My weight falls into the pillow I am holding. All I can do is just stare down at the floor as my mind tries desperately to scan every memory and comb through every conversation I have had with my father in the last months of my life. My shadow beckons the truth.

> Why is tragedy
> Always
> At arm's length?
> I am about to give way,
> About to break even more.
> All I had to do was stay alive.

"Kyrie, I need to know the whole truth. Please tell me everything that you know and do not withhold anything. I know I have been in shock, but I am not too delicate to handle it. I will get through all this grief one day, but right now, I just need to know what happened to me and why. Please." My voice cracks, and my eyes plead for the truth.

"I understand. There is so much I still do not know. My father hated answering my questions too, and I always had a sense there were some important things he never told me. But I promise to tell you all that I know, and then to help you find every answer that I do not have. I promise I will see this all the way through with you, no matter what happens. For as long as I live, I will try to find the answers to the mysteries that remain unknown, for both of us."

An exhale of relief floods out of my chest. I did not realize I was holding my breath. Its force gives me the strength to continue listening, ready to collect more answers as Kyrie begins the next part of his story.

"After they took my father, I was trying to figure out what to do next. I did not want to leave Vaxxa without him, but I did not know where they took him. I spent days hiding and listening to conversations. On one of those days, I heard some of the men speaking secretly. One of them said, 'Did you hear that Nulfest Valray is here from the Valray Court in Lashga?' That name was my only clue to the cure from the book, so I knew that I needed to find out who he was. I watched and waited, and then I finally saw him. I followed him closely, remaining hidden, and that is when I saw Earl Menstus approach your father. I tried to listen, but they spoke mostly in secret. Earl Menstus was seeking to broker a deal, and I am worried he offered a price your father did not refuse."

My blood runs cold—the hairs on my neck rise. My jaw opens.

> Why always the sensation
> That something is wrong?
> That something is innately
> Flawed and broken?

"What did Menstus want with my father?"

"All I know is that you were born right before the spell was cast twenty-two years ago. I can only assume that he needed you because as the first Valray maiden in the current line, you have the power to break the spell or keep it from being broken."

My eyes go wide. "This is what my father found out about me in Vaxxa. He was trying to take me to Earl Menstus, but I cannot imagine what he would have traded my life for?"

He gently takes my hand. "I have told you everything I know so far. Everything else, we will need to discover together."

No one has ever told me that they have told me everything they know. I grew up knowing that I was intentionally not being told what everyone else knew, much less being invited to discover the unknown answers. I want to ask him what it is like for him when he sees me experiencing an emotion. How does he know how to respond with such gentleness? Each interaction must take a lot of effort to make me feel as safe as he does. I grew up with my emotions being manipulated and used against me. If his perceptions and reactions are logical, even if they are mechanical at times, they would be more honest than what I experienced growing up. I want to ask him if he can still feel my skin each time he takes my hand in his. I do not know him, but I want to.

Where is the possibility
That all is well with me?
Why always the feeling
That I am missing?
Struggling through,
Surviving.
Why the long nights of pain,
Sweat, confusion, ache?
Where are the what-ifs?
Is there anything left to be
When I grow up?
Nothing beyond my hand ever
Felt possible,
Just bound.
I always feel bound.
I have looked through to the other side.
Is there anything left for me
To dream anymore?
Is it all still withheld
From my grasp?

Nine

{Ninety-five years before our present story begins}

Florin

"Vesta, it is time for your bedtime story," Florin says to her young daughter as she folds back the bedcovers.

"Can you tell me the one about the prophecy?" The little girl asks in her sweet voice as she climbs in and covers up. "It is my favorite."

Florin smiles at Vesta's request and slowly begins as she always does...

"Once upon a time, in the united realm of Olstar, there ruled a wise and gifted man named Claudegus. With the power of longevity bestowed upon him, he rose to be Olstar's sole leader for two hundred years and was beloved by all. He only used his marvelous powers for good because he had a heart of gold, and his land and people prospered beyond imagination under his blessing. A blend of races and a wealth of diverse cultures thrived there. Olstar was indeed a magical realm under Claudegus' rule.

"One day, an enchanted woman arrived in Olstar. When Claudegus met her, he soon fell in love. He traded his power of longevity to marry and grow old with her, and his dark hair became a dazzling pearl-white."

"Yes, because his body had not yet aged beyond twenty-four years." Vesta chimes in.

"You are right my love. They made an ancient vow, called the Redamancy. Do you remember what it means?" Florin asks.

"It means a love returned in full." Vesta smiles proudly at her mother as Florin bends over to kiss her forehead.

Arden

I do not have the energy to cry anymore. I need a break from the heavy truth that is still mostly a mystery. Before I can say anything, though, Kyrie asks, "Would you like to take a drive through the province and see the fields?"

"Yes, please. I could use some fresh air to clear my mind."

Parked outside the villa, his dark blue glider has a sleek design. It has just enough room for the two of us to sit next to each other. It has a transparent shield that wraps around from my side to his, but the top is open to the air. When it is in motion, it hovers above the ground in mid-air, but when it is parked, it has support rims that slide down for stability. It is as if an innovator imagined what it would be like if a small boat could fly. It must have been made in Wincot and sent through the bypass.

The landscape is like an artist's palette of greens with pops of red, orange, and magenta. I have never seen fields like this before. It is extraordinary. I let the view, the scent, and the fresh air embrace me. This is precisely what I need to help me metabolize the mix of emotions trapped in my body.

"What crops are those in the fields?" I ask.

"Coffee and cacao," he replies. "And also, many spices."

"Coffee and chocolate come from here? In Kallos?" I ask, amazed, then admit, "I have only tasted chocolate once. I still treasure that stolen moment. Coffee and chocolate were such rare commodities that if any arrived at our house, my sister and I were not allowed to have any, my father said it was just for the adults. But one time, my favorite staff member, Olsa, snuck a piece from the kitchen and brought some up to our rooms for us to try." I tell him, still remembering that moment. "But I have never had coffee before."

"Well, whenever you are ready, you will be able to indulge in them here whenever you want," he replies with a smile.

I can hardly believe the thought of it. I have been taken from my grave to a realm of coffee, chocolate, and spice. He just needs my tears to be free. I want us both to be free, here in this decadent paradise.

> Because you woke me
> From my grave,
> You cannot escape
> The breaking of chains
> That binds you.

I turn my attention back to what he is saying.

"But yes, the Kallos people are growers of numerous spices, our climate here allows for many different ones to thrive. My favorite is cardamom," he smiles. I smile back, silently deciding that he wears it very well. "Most of the spices you have had in your life have come from here."

"I guess sending spices through the bypass is a lot easier than large pieces of furniture." I muse on the Valray furniture industry since we are the only province with master wood craftsmen.

"Actually, I remember my mother having a dresser with exquisite carvings and details sent here from Valray many years ago, but it was so difficult to get it through the bypass that the staff said they would never do it again." His eyes dance with the long-ago memory. I wonder if the dresser looks like the ones I grew up with.

We spend the afternoon riding along the provincial fields, with him pointing out various spices to me. When we return to the villa before dusk, I curl up on the terrace cushions while Kyrie makes his dinner. I am still not ready to eat. My hunger has not yet returned to me. He brings his plate and sits next to me.

"What about the other provinces here in this realm?" I just want to lie here and listen to the sound of his voice.

"Well, we have a trade agreement with the Clemen province. Their apothecary industry produces oils, wine, teas, and tinctures. They grow the assorted fruits from which natural oils and wines are produced, like olives, avocados, and grapes, so we trade our precious spices for their pure oils and premium fruits. They use our spices to make their wines and medicinal teas, and we use their oils and fruits to make our gourmet chocolates and coffees. The trade relationship between our provinces grew stronger when the spell was cast, and my parents had the Clemen healers create everything they could think of to help break the spell. Even though nothing was successful, a better trade agreement was formed, and then a more permanent alliance was made when my sister married into the Clemen line," he explains.

His last sentence strikes a personal chord. I had never considered that an alliance might have kept me bound tighter to Valray when I was thinking that marriage would be an escape.

"My parents assumed the alliance would keep them in regular contact with my sister, but she never returned after the wedding. She was afraid to come back." He trails off in his thoughts. His words feel so relatable.

I wonder if I would have ever returned to Valray if I had married Taryn. I cannot say that I would have wanted to, although I would have obeyed any expectations. I have never rebelled before.

He smiles, and I feel safe here next to him. "Teahn is a province of scholars and teachers. They are writers, along with printing and publishing books. The books you have read have come from Teahn."

I raise my eyebrows as I remember the books I used to hold and read and imagine their journey across the bypass to get to me. I had no idea.

"Amara is a more exotic province that I do not know much about, it is the furthest away from Kallos. But I do know that they have an abundance of precious stones and rocks that they create into magnificent pieces of jewelry and art sculptures. Most of the provinces' Sovran crowns and ceremonial pieces are handcrafted in Amara. My mother has a few pieces that were made for the future rulers of Kallos to wear and pass down to their heirs. By the time the commissioned order was completed and delivered, she was already fading away and was no longer interested in them. They are still in a box that has never been opened."

My imagination tries to guess what these pieces of Kallos jewels look like. It does not take long before I begin drifting off to sleep, with images of bracelets, rings, brooches, and necklaces dancing through my mind.

When I wake up, I turn over and notice the extra blankets Kyrie must have brought out here to cover me with. What time is it? I sit up and see a beautiful sunrise announcing a new day over the mountain ridge. I revel in the thought that I slept for so long, and I did not have any nightmares interrupting my sleep.

My mind feels clear and renewed as I lie here on the terrace, watching the early morning haze lighten into a lavender sky. I think about the day ahead. Kyrie must still be asleep, so I head upstairs to get dressed.

Ten

{Ninety-five years before our present story begins}

Florin

"This enchanted couple soon had two daughters, Lashga and Pallayes. Sadly though, when these girls reached adulthood, their mother received the inevitable call to return to where she came from. Claudegus' heartache was so palpable that the land cracked, and a fault line ran right through the middle.

"Even after her body was gone, she always was present though. Her handwritten notes appeared with stories, legends, maps, and plans—a future that she could somehow foretell. Claudegus kept all these handwritten plans, maps, and family portraits inside his brown leather suitcase."

Florin hands Vesta the canvas paintings from the suitcase to look at as she continues the story.

"In time, Lashga and Pallayes both married and began having children of their own. Every time a new baby was born, a handwritten note appeared with the baby's name and instructions for Claudegus to share one of his powers with the child. There were eight grandchildren in all, each daughter having four babies."

Arden

I pick out the golden yellow dress from the wardrobe and put it on. I like this color. I turn away from the mirror before I can look at my image; I am not ready to see myself. I brush my hair before I head down the stairs.

Kyrie looks up and smiles. "You look so beautiful."

I blush with his eyes on me. No one has ever told me this before. My insides squirm, not knowing how to receive it. I almost want to hand back the words; I feel greedy for keeping them.

"We need to leave soon," he says.

"Where are we going?" I ask.

"To Taryn and Vesta's wedding."

I stifle a silent scream. "What? I already wrecked their proposal. Now I am going to crash their wedding?" My cheeks flood with heat.

"Vesta made me promise that if you left the grave to come with me, that I would bring you back for the wedding," he says, pleading his case.

"But I do not want to be seen at their wedding. I still do not know how I died. I do not think I should show up alive in a place where I was obviously wanted dead, never to be spoken of again. I do not want my second life to be shorter than my first one." I plead back.

"You are right, and I have a plan. I will wrap us in my invisibility cloak, and we will watch from the loft. You will be invisible. If you decide at any point that you want to be seen, it can easily be removed and then put back on."

"Why did you not tell me about this before today?" I ask emphatically.

"When I woke up this morning and saw the date, Vesta's words came back to me, and I remembered it was the day of their wedding. I promise I was not keeping it from you; I have just had everything that we have been talking about the last few days in front of my mind. I am so sorry for catching you off guard," he says apologetically.

I want to believe him. I am not used to people telling me the truth. Since my parents lied to me my whole life on big and small matters, I struggle to know if everyone else is lying to me, too. I am not sure if his inability to feel would make it easier or harder for him to lie to me. He needs my tears, and this is one way to get more of them.

"On one condition. After the wedding, you take me to my parents' home while we are in Valray. I need to look for answers. With the invisibility cloak."

His eyes widen. "I do not love this idea, but okay, deal." So, I shuffle behind and follow him into his sleek, dark blue glider.

"Tell me about Taryn. What made you fall in love with him?" he asks sincerely, but I know he is trying to distract me from my wedding guest anxiety. I decide to play along, hoping it will help.

"Well, since I had never met him, I see now I must have fallen in love with the idea of him, and a future that took me away from my family. I can see now it was an escape plan, not a relationship. I remember putting on the dress my mother chose for me and the white flower crown woven into my hair that morning." I pause when I remember sitting in front of the mirror, waiting for someone to say I look beautiful, but no one ever did. My mother seemed unable to give me that small gift. I have not looked in a mirror since.

> I stand waiting
> In the silence,
> And eternity extends
> Through the mirror.
> Deep into the dark stone in my soul,
> Where grief and sadness

Hide like prisoners of war,
Waiting for something like
Joy to release them.

I shake off the thought.

"I remember stepping into the bridal carriage and climbing in. I was nervous. The coachman handed me a 'cup of blessing, to settle my nerves.' And then…nothing. I do not remember anything else." I surprise myself with how quickly I came to the end of the story even though I thought there would be more to tell. He studies the confusion on my face and gently takes my hand in his.

We travel easily through the bypass, the space between the two realms. I can tell by the difference in the air. When we arrive at the church, he hands me a new cloth to catch my tears and then wraps us in invisibility. We enter the church and climb up to the choir loft. That is when I see it all, the wedding I was supposed to have: the candles, the flowers, the music, the guests. I struggle to keep all the emotions contained; I am not sure how long I can hold it all in. When everyone stands for the bride's entrance, I hold my breath and peer down. Vesta is the most beautiful bride I have ever seen, even more breathtaking than my reflection on my wedding day.

In the meantime,
The living bride

Is fortified
By the haunting words
Of the corpse bride.
Sometimes, when she imagines
The unfolding of their plan,
A satisfied smile greets
A faraway glimmer in her eyes.
It is fleeting,
But you can catch it if you've seen
Her long-held gaze with the invisible.
Like she can see or hear
What no one else can.
In the meantime,
She lives the life of the bride
That sleeps beneath her feet.

A hot tear escapes and rolls down my cheek, curves under my jaw, and down to my chest. I focus on breathing and distract myself with the beauty of the church and its decorations. But when she reaches Taryn, and I see him smile at her, the dam holding back my tears cracks open, and I am helpless to the sorrowful agony that may be considered somewhere between envy and heartbreak. It was all supposed to be mine, and I cover my face with the cloth, knowing it is too small to contain all this liquid grief. Kyrie's warm hand is on my back, trying to soothe me, but this loss cannot be soothed. I must surrender to it.

I lift my face to watch them exchange vows. I have never seen it done before. I want to know what it would have been like to face him and hear him say those words. My body shakes from crying as I listen to his voice, cracking beneath the weight of his own tears, his honest love for her cracking him open right there in front of everyone.

When it is Vesta's turn, my cries pause as I take in the same wonder as everyone else in the church as we watch her long, golden, honey hair become pearl-white. She glows with an incandescent light radiating from within. Her vows have somehow changed her. Then, Taryn begins singing my song, but like at the engagement, he sings it to her.

Come to me

I've made a place

Come to me

So, stay a while

I'll sing to you

For your love

This melody

I'd go the miles

Come to me

Come to me

Come to me

Come to me

My Love

My Love

There's a door

Here I am

Here's the key

Faithfully

I see you smiling

Don't leave me

Back at me

Just a memory

Come to me

Come to me

Come to me

Come to me

My Love

Come to me

To my horror, my feet lift slowly from the ground, spellbound, and the song calls me again. My invisibility trades itself with a milky haze that makes me appear to be as authentic as any ghost anyone here has ever seen. I shake my head 'no' to Kyrie, trying to tell him that I am not choosing this. As I begin to float up and over the loft wall and then down towards the song, the crowd starts a wave of gasps as they slowly look up and see me levitate towards the altar. I look back towards Kyrie's face, and his expression tells me he is as shocked as everyone else. The last time this happened, I was dead and appeared as a corpse-bride. Now that I am alive again, it has transformed me into a ghost.

I land between Vesta and Taryn, feeling nothing but horrid embarrassment. I am only conscious of my awkward movements; I do not know where to put my arms or my eyes. When Taryn sees me, his singing stops, and his jaw slowly lowers and remains open. Vesta steps forward, pulls me into an embrace, and whispers into my ear, "You are here! Now I know how to call you; the song has the power to call you."

> All fear the corpse-bride,
> But the living-bride knows
> How to speak her language.

I feel the lace fabric of her dress under my fingers, "I am so sorry…it did, it just pulled me down here…and made me ghostly again. I did not want to come, but Kyrie said he promised to bring me."

She is regal, this woman, whom I have only known after death, still holding me. She says, "I know, but I am so glad you are here today. You are an Albatross, remember, my good omen." I step back and look at Taryn, and my heart catches in my throat; he is so handsome in his navy suit. Any last flickers of hope that he still wants me too, fade away. As he stands there, the loss of my life, he cannot even look at my ghostly face. I do not feel like a good omen. I swallow a silent cry.

> You put a chainsaw
> To my well-fortified dam,
> I am defenseless.
> My tears cause erosion
> And a deep crater
> Is revealed.
> The hole within me
> Is now the biggest part of me,
> My ever-wondrous void.

Eleven

{Two days before the present}

My Dearest Rex,

Something terrible has happened to me and Nella is away, so I cannot send for you. You were right, we should have left sooner, but I could not bear to leave behind our girl. And now, all is lost. I am a fool. I should have known better than to trust his doctor. There is no one here to help. Will you ever forgive me?

Maren

Arden

I look back at Vesta and say goodbye. Then my feet lift from the floor, and I float back up to Kyrie's side. Kyrie takes my hand and leads me down the stairs and out of the church to his glider. After we sit, he breaks the silence, "I am so sorry! I had no idea that would happen! I did not know the song could remove the invisibility cloak; I never imagined that happening. I thought it would be safe, and I let you down," he says repentantly.

I lift my tear-stained eyes to him, and my words drip with self-deprecation, "Well, now you know what the horror in his eyes looked like on the day he tried to propose to her. It is how he will remember me for the rest of his life. A jealous corpse-bride sent to haunt all his attempts at a new life." I am numb. I put my head back against the head rest and close my eyes, stifling the rage that begs to be released.

"Take me to my parent's home. I might as well haunt them too, while I am a ghost."

I put the wet, tear-filled cloth to my face.

Taryn's sad, beautiful face haunts me. He will never be mine. I cannot blame him. I can finally see it from his perspective; he was the one left waiting at the altar, waiting for a bride that never showed. I was his hoax, and Vesta was his cure.

> The corpse bride
> Crawled up out of the earth,
> She was ready for her turn
> With the living.
> She disappeared with sole intent
> To return to haunt you.

I think about Vesta's words today, and my body shivers. Is it even possible to hear the song's call across the bypass? Will it drag me through the realm shift alone as it pulled me from the dirt and the choir loft? I hope not. I draw another poem to myself, to give myself the closure and goodbye he could not give me, to provide myself with the reason he chose another bride. I imagine him singing these words to me, and I silently howl inside my heartache.

> I was there,
> I was there waiting for you.
> I was there waiting alone.
> You didn't come,
> And you didn't write.
> You didn't show up at my side.
> I was there,
> I was waiting all night.

And I waited alone
Until she arrived.

We arrive at the Valray estate. Nothing has changed since I last saw this view. Its beauty is hidden by neglect.

Kyrie gently takes my arm before I get out and says, "I will protect you in there. I will not let him hurt you."

We quietly enter through the back door, but it does not seem like anyone is here. Is anyone still on staff? It looks as if nothing has been tended to in a long time.

> Take your time
> And I'll take mine.
> Patience will be my secret.
> As I wait for
> The moment
> To avenge my death.

We stalk up the back stairs, reach the second floor, turn the corner, and enter the first doorway. The air is thick with sickness. There is my mother, once beautiful, sitting hunched over a cane, aged and unkempt. Her breathing is labored. She is unrecognizable. Something terrible has happened.

"Mother," I go towards her and kneel by her feet. "Mother, it is me, Arden." I need her to see me. I need to see in her eyes if there is any flicker of love left for me. If she remembers me at all.

She slowly lifts her head and turns it in my direction. She squints, trying to focus her gaze on me. I can see the confusion on her face. I reach out and touch her hand so that she knows that I am real. I watch her look towards my hand and then slowly back to my face. Her now yellowed eyes are haunting, and I dare to let them stay fixed on me. I even search them, trying to find any answers.

"Find…Aster." She labors through her last breath to get these two words out. "Tell her…" is all that escapes next before there is no more breath within her. Her spirit has left her vacant. I can feel it as it brushes by me on its way out. I can see it in her hollowed, now empty eyes. She is gone. How did it come to this?

"Mother!" I cry out as I collapse over her lap. Kyrie comes over to me.

"I am so sorry Arden." He gently picks me up and puts my head to his chest and wraps his arms around my grief.

There is so much I will never know or understand about this woman I call 'Mother.' The hungry place within me that craves her will never be satisfied. Can a mother's love be fed without her hand on the spoon? Or is this a food that every child must learn to one day feed herself? I have layers of confusion and numbness, and an anger I cannot yet reach.

Twelve

Taryn

Deep down, I sensed something terrible had happened to Arden, but there was no proof, no evidence, no trail to follow. As the days turned into weeks, I questioned how long I should continue the search. Vesta, however, kept my spirit alive. She was relentless, refusing to give up, even when I was ready to let go.

By then, I had fallen completely in love with Vesta and began planning to propose. Even if Arden had returned, I knew in my heart I would call off that engagement, I was meant to be with Vesta. I felt unspeakable guilt for these thoughts, though, as I was looking for my missing fiancé. I did not know how to reconcile these two experiences. The search for Arden, the finding of Vesta.

I remember the moment I surprised Vesta in the rose garden with a ring and everything spiraled when Arden appeared as a corpse-bride. Panic gripped me as I ran for help, terrified that I would lose my future with Vesta over some old law binding me to Arden.

That day marked a turning point; Vesta finally called off the search with Arden's return. I did not fully grasp what was happening at first. After Vesta put Arden back to rest, she unpacked a suitcase and began revealing secrets I had not anticipated. It took months to sift through everything, and even then, uncertainty lingered. Despite it all, I trusted Vesta completely.

When Arden showed up again at our wedding, I was rattled, scared our union could be threatened again. I had no idea that a simple song had the power to summon her. But when I saw Arden and Vesta embrace during the ceremony, something shifted within me. An understanding washed over me—a glimpse into what I can only describe as an ancient magic. In that moment, my destiny crystallized, and for the first time in my life, I felt whole. The dread of losing my future melted away, leaving only a profound sense of elation and peace.

Arden

After I catch my breath and refocus, I realize I need to question my father; haunt him. I need to know what happened to my mother, to Aster, to me.

"Kyrie, follow me, we need to find my father. He is probably in his private study. It is on the first floor, near the side entrance. Keep your invisibility cloak on and look around his desk for anything that looks important while I interrogate him. I will try to draw him away to the other side of the room. If you see that he is becoming petulant, on my cue, start throwing his books and make a mess. He might need motivation to cooperate."

We stalk discreetly downstairs. Just as I thought, my father is there, at his desk. We both take a nervous breath and quietly enter.

"Father." I conjure up in a slow, deep, ghost-drawl as I levitate into his den.

He looks up, and in that split second, I see his surprise.

"You...I heard about your awful ghost showing up to haunt Taryn. You should be ashamed of yourself. Your mother and I were so embarrassed to hear about it. You were always so dramatic. Your mother hated that you ruined someone else's proposal."

I do not know how my haze can still be white; all I feel is hot red anger.

"Why is Mother dead? I watched her take her last breath. What happened to her?"

"Dead?" He asks with curiosity, not panic. "You and your sister abandoned her, that is what happened. It is both of your faults she is in the state she is in."

I refuse to die today of heartbreak. I try to focus.

"I know about your exchange with Earl Menstus. I just want to hear about it from you directly. I have learned things in the afterlife."

His face goes still and pale.

He looks at me, pointing, and says, "You! You have ruined my life! I am no longer allowed into Vaxxa because of your stubbornness!"

I cannot keep a scoff from escaping my bones. I try hard to keep it from turning into a hideous laugh, hysteria daring to creep in. I swallow it down, resolving to save it for later.

Right on cue, Kyrie begins hurling books and paperweights across the room. Two books shatter through the glass window, a paperweight lodges into the wall, and a crack ripples up.

> I have learned the
> Necessity of having an ally
> And the danger of not.

My father stomps his foot on the floor like an angry child.

"What deal did you broker, father?"

"He said that if I succeeded in bringing you to him before the wedding, while you were still a Valray maiden, he would give me the ancient books that held the secrets to immortality. And if I failed, I would never be allowed in Vaxxa again. He agreed to give me until the day of your wedding to show up."

My father agreed to send me to a dark magician in exchange for secret powers. My shadow pours out its pain.

> You are a master at the loom,
> Creating a weave of hurt
> To wrap around my heart,
> Tying that final knot just so.
> Landing your mark
> Right upon your aim,
> Your eye on my heart
> Telling me, I am to blame.
> I marvel at your work,

At your skill,
To take a fragile love
And use it for the kill.
When you speak the wounding blow
And crush me with the weight,
I ran with my heart in the bag,
Trying to escape my fate.
Loving you,
Is a gas-lit trip through hell,
Keeping me wounded and small.
I know how to nurse my pain
Till all the words pour out,
And that is my corpse reviver
Truths you will never hear about.
While your ego comforts you,
I will let my words comfort me
They take me back inside myself,
Where I enter the void
And cross the sea.

"Start from the beginning, father. I am not leaving until I hear everything you know about Earl Menstus, and you still have a lot of things left here to destroy."

I make eye contact with Kyrie. He manages to light a fire in the fireplace and feeds it with papers and books. A partner in crime, a friend to defend me. Whether it is planned or accidental, he throws something extra flammable into the fire right at this moment, and a small explosion erupts. I use the distraction to gather my wits and focus.

My father looks up, "You are destroying everything! You are hysterical!"

"Am I?"

"Damn you, Arden." His loud sigh of defeat pairs with a stomp, and his hand smacks down onto the armrest of the chair.

He finally sits and then begrudgingly answers. "Earl Menstus learned that Reown's husband, Juris, from the Kallos province, had turned up in Vaxxa trying to steal the Book of Unbinding, and that the page that had the cure to break his spell was torn out. Menstus was furious. Then, someone told him that I was in Vaxxa as well, and he sought me out. I did not know anything about the book or that the spell could be broken from a maiden in my bloodline. Menstus asked how many daughters were in the Valray bloodline. I admitted that only one was indeed in the bloodline, because when your mother promised me a son, she gave me an illegitimate daughter. It is just as my father told me; women cannot be trusted. My father warned me to never give the Sovran seat to a woman. Menstus told me that I had a choice. I could either willingly bring you to him, or he would make my life difficult. I told him that it was absurd. But then he made me watch the torture of Juris Kallos. I knew I could not deny him anything. So, I agreed to bring you willingly to him."

Kyrie pulls down the entire bookshelf, and it crashes on top of the desk. My heart aches for him, hearing about his father's death, and not being able to fully feel the rage, and my heart aches for me that my father could so easily gamble my life to protect his own.

"Who is my sister's father?" It is the first question that flies out unexpectedly.

"I do not know him; he is of no consequence to me. A useless bastard, I am sure."

I refocus. "What did you do with my sister?"

"I did not know you could be more infuriating dead than when you were alive. When will this useless interrogation be over? I have business to tend to, and now I have your mess to clean up," motioning to the room around him.

"I am sorry to inconvenience you, Father," I roll out sarcastically, as Kyrie swipes everything off the desk with one stroke of his arm.

He rolls his eyes and huffs with exasperation, stomping his foot and fist again.

"Your sister wanted to go."

"Where?" I ask, confused.

"To Earl Menstus." He says, as if it is the obvious answer.

"You sent Aster to Earl Menstus?" I implore with disbelief.

"I had to since you refused. I did you a favor by sending Aster in your place, a nice substitute, so you could have your wedding. I wagered that Menstus could be fooled into thinking that she was you, the daughter who could break the spell, and he would be satisfied, and leave the rest of us in peace. Your sister jumped at the chance to be chosen for something special. She was more than happy to go and prove her worth and not have to stay and watch you have all the attention. Her desperation became useful, so easy to manipulate."

I knew my father was selfish, but I did not anticipate this level of darkness.

"And you did nothing to try to save either of us? Is she still there?" I ask in disbelief.

"There was nothing I could do against Menstus. I do not know where your sister is or if she is still alive.

"Were you ever going to try to find out?" I am mortified.

"Your sister sealed her fate the day she left, just like you, when you refused to obey me in the first place. You might still be alive if you had not been so stubborn."

This is brutal news. Kyrie throws the desk chair, and it shatters the large mirror across from the fireplace. My father ducks his head.

"When you did not arrive at the church, I assumed that either you tricked us all and ran away, or that Menstus realized the truth and came to get you himself. It was not until we heard about your corpse-bride ghost appearing at Taryn's proposal that I knew you were dead. But I never knew how you died."

When you self-protected,
You broke me.
All my words left me,
And none of them
Came back.
I am broken,
I have no more words.
You ripped it all away
To prove you are right.
I want to evaporate
All of me,
I have nothing left to say.
I lurch back into my box
In the corner,

The ultimate revenge
Is not what I thought it would be.

"Father, what you've done is unforgivable…" But I cannot finish my sentence because he interrupts me, as he stands and begins to creep slowly towards me.

"Now, let us stop all these questions and join forces. Let us put our powers together. I see that you have acquired even more in the afterlife, and that can be quite useful to me. We will be more powerful than Earl Menstus, and all the men in Vaxxa."

I am triggered back to the past. My heart begins racing in my chest, and I hear it drumming in my ears. I cannot breathe. My panic is about to consume me and swallow me whole. The memories flood in faster than I can stop them. I am paralyzed in fear, and my mind goes blank. Everything vanishes except the drum of my heartbeat, which is pounding too fast. I watch him smile as if he smells my fear. I am a fool for coming back here.

Even though Kyrie cannot feel my terror, he must be able to see it, and his logic has chosen to defend and protect me. I watch the dagger rise from the desk and move towards my father, guided by Kyrie's hand, and, as he raises it, he must be taking his aim. I cannot move. I just watch.

I jump aside in reflex when I feel something race past from behind me and graze the air against my skin. An arrow makes its kill shot through my father's heart, pinning him back into the chair. His eyes are unable to widen any larger than they are, his mouth gaping, releasing a stifled roar, and his hand instinctively draws up to his chest. I watch him suck for the air that he can no longer consume. His head slumps forward, and the room falls silent. He is dead.

I turn around to see a brown hooded figure reload his bow with another arrow. He aims it at my ghostly image and yells, "Leave here at once!"

I feel Kyrie brush by me, quickly taking my hand and arm and leading me out of the side of the house, and then everything goes black.

Thirteen

{Two months before the present}

Nulfest,

So, you are hoping to travel beyond the realms? We received your drawings and believe we can build what you have in mind, but it might take some time. However, we were surprised to receive a request for another investment proposal from Valray after the last one did not go as planned. We are sorry for your loss. We, too, are mourning the loss of our Taryn, who has become bewitched by a villager in your province and has renounced his place to the Sovran seat to marry her. We will not be at the wedding, of course. When we have drawn up the final contract, we will send our son, Barrow, to receive payment and signatures.

The Wincots

Arden

The sadness plunges
Into my body,
And is left desolate
In my throat.
I cannot speak of it.
How do I throw it up
And give it back to you?
I fall under the weight
Of it all.
I can no longer hold this for you,
I am too small,
I am too small.
Trapped within the walls,
Maybe this is where
The psyche breaks,
And the chest pulls tight
On the left, not the right.
Yesterday, I thought I won,
But I see now
Who holds the gun.

I need the dark. I need only the darkness of my
room and the bedcovers over and around me. Nothing
else. I cannot eat. Sleep only comes in waves, in and out. I

am sinking. Drowning in grief. I am wet with sweat and tears.

> The grief swallows me whole
> And I am lost in the darkness of it.
> I cannot find my way out.
> The weight of it has crushed my bones
> And the marrow is sucked dry.
> Death comes in waves
> In and out, like the tide.
> Sometimes, I go out
> To meet it.
> Sometimes, I let it
> Take me under.

Life, death, and the after, what part is not marked by loss and betrayal? It is as if a finely sharpened blade has skillfully chiseled out my existence. I do not know what parts are true. Everything I know might all be lies. I have no way to tell the difference. I come back up for air just before drowning in it.

I comb through memories, searching for clues. Nothing makes sense. Was my father part of the plot to kill me? Did Menstus do it to prevent the spell from being broken?

> I fall into the riptide.
> The weight and strength

Grab my ankle
And pull me under.
I am overcome and seized,
I try to fight it.
The anger, the rage,
The ultimate defeat.
I must let it take me,
I have to surrender.
There is nothing to numb
The power of its force upon me.
It is black now,
I let it take me on its course.
As I float and stroke the water
In its current, moving with it.
I do not want to unite with it.
I do not want to go
Where it is taking me,
But it has the strength
To swallow me whole.

My father is dead. My mother is dead. And where is my sister? My bones ache and feel too weak to hold the weight of my flesh. It was easier being dead. Ache has a sound, and I have it on repeat.

Floating,
Then overcome
By the weight

Of the waves,
The grief mounts
On my chest.
Deep heaviness,
I want to breathe,
But the air is too heavy.
The dreams shake me,
They show up and mock me.
Betrayed,
Abandoned,
I carry this heavy heart
In a bag over my shoulder.
I want to set it down,
Run, and not look back.
But all the questions find me.
They all find me holding the bag.
Every one of them wants a piece.
I lay my heart on the table
And cut it up like a pie.
I am a distributor of questions
I cannot answer for myself
Or anyone else.

I drown in my ocean of grief and try to come up for air, only to choke on streams of tears. I throw the covers off me as a new wave of heat crawls over my skin, and I sweat again. I am so angry, so horridly angry, and I do not know what to do with this hot red emotion that is ready to burn me alive. I want to smash the furniture through the walls, and the belief that I have the strength within me to do it scares me more than anything. I am sustaining the sorrow. The sickness in my soul has been exposed. It oozes its way out of my body onto the floor.

> I need a map and compass
> To navigate,
> I am lost.
> Unfound.
> Missing.
> Without clues,
> I made do.
> I survived
> A cover-up,
> A destruction,
> A deep, heavy longing.
> I ran as fast as I could.
> All I could hear was the
> Sound of my breathing.
> My heart beating
> And my feet hitting
> The ground.
> It was dark and wide,
> I was alone,
> And I ran to escape them all.
> I went invisible to survive.

> I gave up everything,
> Even my voice.

I see light crawling up the wall. I can sense Kyrie's silhouette walking towards me.

"Arden, please let me help you. It has been three days, and I am so worried," he pleads. "You have been in a fevered dream since you passed out. I have been so afraid to lose you."

I roll over to see his worried face, but it just makes me cry more. My head hurts so badly from crying. I hate that he sees me like this. I feel repulsive. I ache. He gently kneels at my bedside. He wipes the hair back from my face to see my eyes. He gently wipes away the tears on my cheek with his thumb.

> And now I must make the perilous
> Swim back to the place where I started.
> To collect my things on the shore
> Of where it all began.
> I am so far from that place now.

"I hate myself…for all of it…for going back there, for thinking that getting answers from him would help me understand, help me feel better. I hate myself for not being able to save my mother, and for losing Aster. I hate myself that I am so relieved that he is dead, and I hate that I wanted to watch you stab him in the heart with his own dagger. I hate that I do not even understand what happened and I hate that you will have the memory of me like this." I admit all my horrid darkness.

"Arden, it all makes sense with what you went through. You are so brave. Please, trust me, and look around deep inside for any tiny flicker of light. It has the power to cover all the darkness. This light is the love you create for yourself, and it is your most precious treasure," he says, each word very slowly and gently so as not to overwhelm me.

> I come to the edge of my psyche,
> My breath catches in my throat,
> As I see the jagged cliff
> That beckons me to jump off
> Into the realm of obliteration.
> My body feels the lack of gravity,
> As I begin to float towards it,
> Losing control of my goodwill.
> The weight lands on my chest.
> The air is thinner and disappearing.
> Help me, I am so scared.
> I am lost,
> I am lost in all of it.

As he speaks, I close my eyes and hold onto his words like a lifeline. I am looking for it. I search in the darkness of myself until I see a small flame. It is mostly blue, but there is just enough yellow-orange at the tip to tell me that there is hope. I squeeze his hand, trying to communicate that I have found what he is talking about.

"That flame is your self-love, and it has the power to heal you. But you must find it...tend it...and protect it above all things. It needs to burn brighter than all your doubts, fear, and anger. It is the only thing that can carry you through the grief." His words roll into me like medicine. I feel the longing for death leaving me as he continues to soothe me.

I grab hold of the small flame I see inside of myself. I know I need to follow it, not let it out of my sight. I need to let it grow into a fire within, one that provides light but does not destroy.

I find the strength to ask him, "How do you know this?"

"One of the elder women in the province taught me this when I was younger. I had not lost my ability to feel yet, but I knew it was coming soon and wanted to find ways to keep myself alive for as long as I could in hopes of saving the province. She told me that there is no such thing as bad feelings, especially when you are clinging on to the ability to feel anything at all. My parents did not know how to give me the answers I was looking for, but many of the elders were willing to share what they knew before they passed on. I check my inner flame every day to make sure it is still lit. It is how I have made it this far. It is from them that I learned how to honor my essence and protect my self-love."

"I just want to be free of all this confusion and pain. I am in so much pain. I was never taught how to love myself. I do not know how to be free. I was just taught to make sure everyone else was pleased. I learned that abandoning myself was the favor that I could give them to ensure their happiness and comfort. My needs were an inconvenience; my presence was an unwanted burden unless it needed to be used for something. I did not learn how to protect myself or that I was even worth protecting. I only learned of my unworthiness. I do not understand why my father was so selfish. I do not understand why my mother left me starving for her love. I do not understand why I could not be loved and cared for. And who am I if that is who I come from?" I admit it all. The words come loose and pour out with my searing, hot tears. Each word pounds against the top of my skull and bangs my teeth on its way out.

"I think your ability to face the truth and grieve it is what will set you free. I look forward to the day when I can fully feel life with you. I believe in it. The elder farmers would tell me that the best prayer does not begin with please, it begins with thank you and the confidence that it has been answered."

When I look at his face, his words feel true. I want to have confidence in my future, too. I begin to feel some of the darkness lift.

He continues, "Some of the elders also told me about the dark night of the soul. It seems similar to what you are going through. They told me to never abandon myself if I ever got to that place of darkness within. Through their love for me, they warned me to never let go of my inner flame. They made sure I understood that even in the darkest night, any amount of flame would bring light. I know you must feel so abandoned, but I want to help you so that you do not abandon yourself. They told me that kind of abandonment risks the flame disappearing. Arden, even in your death, I do not believe that your inner flame ever went out, so I do not want it to happen now that you are alive again." He gently wipes the tears from my cheeks.

A soothing warmth begins to flow inside of me. I am grateful for his friendship. I reclaim the land within myself. I tend the fire and set up camp. I am here, I am my own, I am the fire. I will not jump off the cliff; I am the cliff. I will not drown beneath the water; I am the water. The air will not leave my lungs; I am the air. I am the tree whose roots go down deep beyond the soil and find the water far below the surface. I am the ever flame within. I am wild with color, and I dance with words across my mind. I reclaim my power and hold it tight. No one is to take it from me. It is mine only to give. I begin to feel my strength returning slowly. My resolve is my medicine.

> I have lain here long enough
> To find the edge pieces
> Of my broken mind.

Then I hear it, and I grab Kyrie's arm, "Please do not let it take me away! Please come with me! I do not have the energy yet to face it alone."

"What is it? Arden, what are you talking about?"

"The song...I hear Vesta calling me with the song. Will you please come with me."

Kyrie picks me up into his arms like the day he pulled me from the ground and holds me tight in his lap. I rest my head on his chest and relax into his strong arms.

And then, the song pulls us through the realm shift.

Fourteen

{Presently}

Nela

I tried not to get too attached, to stay neutral, to just do my job. But, like Olsa, I could not. We raised those girls as if they were our own. And then all at once, they both went missing. We tried to stay busy, hoping they would soon return.

The doctor gave Maren concoctions to settle her nerves, to ease her anxiety. Nulfest called it "hysteria." How did I not notice the signs, though? The poisoning. I must have been blinded and distracted by my own grief and worry. Nulfest must have increased the dosage while I was away visiting family last week. I even had a terrible feeling that something dreadful had fallen upon that house. I decided to get back a day early, just to be safe.

I will never forget the eerie silence when I crossed the threshold. Nulfest shot with an arrow, his study sacked. Maren, dead upstairs. My brother, weeping over her body. The undelivered letter in his hands.

We spent the next few days cleaning up the study and burying the bodies. That is when Aster arrived. She collapsed in grief when she found out about her mother's death. I fell to my knees to embrace her, and she clung to me with the weight of an orphan left alone in this world. I knew then that it was time for her to know the truth.

Arden

We arrive at Vesta's cottage doorstep. It is surreal being here again, this time alive, this time noticing the beautiful garden. The song turned me into a ghost again, but I let the ghostly haze lift. I want her to finally see me alive, even though I feel half-dead inside and look even worse.

She opens the door before we get to it and welcomes us in. "Thank you for coming," she says.

When I see her warm smile, I immediately want to fall into her arms and cry. Her female presence is the closest thing I have to a mother, and it buries my defenses. All I am aware of is my inner ache to be known and loved by a mother.

> The longing trails behind me.
> The lost, abandoned longing
> Follows me home,
> Hoping for some comfort
> And a glance of hope
> That it may crawl in and stay for the night.
> I cannot lose it,
> I cannot get rid of it.
> The deep longing inside of me,
> It keeps showing up at my back door,

Waiting for the bowl of milk
To quench its deep hunger.

She embraces me with the gentlest rock, wiping the hair out of my wet face. She feels steady as she walks us inside, still holding onto me and steering me to the sofa. She sets me gently next to Kyrie. They are like two strong towers beside me.

"I called you here because I need to tell you something very important." Her words fall out.

But Kyrie cuts in to explain, "Vesta, Arden has not been well for the past few days; she has been in shock. Her mother died, and Nulfest Valray is dead."

Vesta's face drains of all colors. "What? How?"

"It is a long story, but if we skip to skip to the end, I nearly put a dagger in his heart, but someone else beat me to it and struck him with an arrow."

I feel her body tense and pause as she reacts to the news. She pulls me into a warm embrace and says, "Oh, my bird, my sweet bird, you are so brave. I have you; you are safe." I melt into her compassion.

Then she says, "I think this confirms what I need to tell you, but I need to start at the beginning, for it to all make sense."

I reposition myself on the sofa to lean against Kyrie's side, not sure that I can hold myself up. After we get comfortable, I nod for her to begin.

"My father, Mazek, is from Teahn." She begins.

Kyrie replies, "My father was also from Teahn, third in line to the seat before he married my mother and moved to Kallos."

"Yes," Vesta continues, "When I met you the day you arrived looking for Arden, I immediately recognized your name and knew who you were. I knew I could trust you with Arden and wanted to help you."

Kyrie nods for her to continue.

"I called you here because I need to talk to you both about the prophecy."

"The prophecy?" I ask, confused.

"Yes. It is a beautiful poem, but it is also a riddle written in a mysterious language. Many have studied it over the centuries, but it is wrapped in a magic that allows only someone with a pure heart to understand its meaning in the context of real events. This is why Earl Menstus is so frustrated. Since his heart has turned stone cold, he needs someone else to solve it for him. He believes that somehow, it is about him, and once it is solved, he can claim the Dashel seat."

Kyrie and I both try to keep up.

"My father is a famous scholar who specializes in the ancient writings and translations, including the genealogies of the original bloodlines all the way to the current ones. However, his main work is deciphering the Claudegus prophecy. He is the first and only scholar to complete the whole translation."

She pauses so we can all take a breath and brace for the next part.

"After your betrothal was announced, the Powers Above sent my father a message that it was time for him to travel to Vaxxa to find Earl Menstus. It was time to begin the plan that had been set out for us many years ago. My father was tasked with finding Earl Menstus in Vaxxa to prepare him for what is coming. He was to remain there until someone helped him leave Vaxxa without Menstus's knowledge. My mother and I were to travel secretly to Valray and await the signs that were to begin here. We never gave up hope that my father would return to us."

"But what happened to your father?" I ask.

"Your sister was his rescue. She helped cover for him while he traveled here."

"What?" Our eyes are wide, and Kyrie and I are both gripped by the story. "That means my sister is still alive. Is she still in Vaxxa? Where is your father?"

"Yes, your sister is alive, and my father said he is indebted to her for helping him. He said she is well and will return to Valray soon. She is not in any danger. With Aster's plan, he left Vaxxa unnoticed and arrived here this morning."

"Your father is here?" I ask, still stunned.

"I called you here with the song just after he and my mother, Florin, left together. They have a long journey ahead of them and wanted to leave as soon as possible. They have a secret place on the coast of the Amara province where they made their Redamancy Vow a long time ago, and its location is only known to them. They will be safe there, and it will give them a chance to recover the time they lost together while they were apart. But today, while he was here, I told him about all that has happened here in Valray. I told him about you, Arden."

"Me?" I ask, puzzled.

"Yes. My father had already heard about the stories of the corpse-bride, the rumors made it all the way to Vaxxa about your ghost appearing at our proposal and then recently at our wedding. That is how he knew it was time to plan his departure and get to Valray quickly."

I want to understand, but the room feels like it is slowly spinning around me. I hold onto Kyrie's arm to try to steady myself.

She lifts a paper and says, "This is the only remaining copy of the translation of the prophecy. It is only missing the last piece, but you will be there when it is found and read. My father has confirmed that it is all unfolding right now, your death has marked the beginning. Arden, the prophecy is written about you."

Her words jumble and the room picks up a little speed.

"What? How can the prophecy be about me? I do not understand..." I look to Kyrie for answers, but he seems just as surprised.

She holds up the old paper and reads it aloud to us.

"Marked by a rose,

Underground

The ghost is an

Albatross.

The uniting of both realms,

Comes only after

The bird follows

True love's power,

And crosses

The forbidden divide

To find the other.

An omen-

A sentinel for those

Beyond years.

A weight to those

Who stole its life.

So, collect its tears

To heal veiled hearts

And grieve

The betrothal broken.

Take off the gold band

For it will be replaced

With something new-

A vow around the wrist.

New life has been given

In retribution,

Protection, and then freedom.

Only the pure of heart

Will understand,

Why the grave

Is empty.

The foretold arrow

Through the heart,

Begins the unfolding

Of vindication to come.

When love returns

All feelings lost,

Death is finally brought

To his knees.

After the wall becomes

The bridge,

The Powers Above

Will welcome love home.

When the fabric is torn

And the hand writes the scroll,

The bird will be called

To heal the present

Between the past and future.

If the Albatross rises

And only love remains,

The legacy will be restored

And the people saved.

Fifteen

{Ninety-five years before our present story begins}

Florin

"When he was on his deathbed, Claudegus had a vision of what was to happen after his death. He saw the future loss of one of his provinces after the realm split into two lands and the near destruction of others. He vowed not to abandon his land in such a divided state. He pledged to hold it, even in death, until someone somehow united all the people again. He then had a vision of 'the one who would cross the forbidden divide to find the other' and of how those two descendants will create a union that pulses with a love more extraordinary than any before, a love that will unite the realms again. His heart was relieved by this vision of hope, and he passed away soon after.

"As news of Claudegus' death spread, the collective grief of the people of Olstar was so heavy, that the sadness of the people deepened the original fault line of his own grief. As he had foreseen, the land split into two separate realms. The only thing left connecting the two realms was a mysterious bypass, and few people had the courage or the ability to travel through it."

"Do you think we will ever cross that bypass together?" Vesta sleepily asks her mother.

Arden

My eyes cannot get any wider. "What? Me? What do you mean? It does not make any sense. May I see the paper?" I try hard to reread it, but the words are swimming around on the paper. I try to focus. I recognize the line she spoke to me before she buried me back up. I still do not understand what it means.

It is laughable to imagine this is about me.

"I know it is a lot to take in, but I think you will just know what to do when the time comes, or none of this would be written in the prophecy." Vesta adds with a confidence I do not possess. "And this is just the beginning, there are still many more parts of the poem left to unfold, but it will all make sense very soon. My father told me to call you here and give you all these instructions. It is important that you become aware of what is happening, so that you are ready for it when the time comes."

"Time comes for what?" I ask.

"The realms uniting," she says matter-of-factly.

I try to steady myself, and my thoughts are swirling along with the room. "To be part of the cure that breaks a spell is one thing, but to be part of a prophecy that unites realms is a whole other thing altogether! I do not understand why I am involved in either of them!"

"Look," Kyrie says, pointing to a line, "the prophecy even mentions the veiled hearts, even the spell was foreseen. Somehow it is all connected."

My expression is one of doubt, fear, and panic, and Vesta sees it.

"Arden, I see the great love inside of you. More than the father-wounds and the mother-hunger, I see your own beautiful love. I see the firelight shining within you. You are not just the corpse-bride made new; you have been resurrected for a purpose greater than yourself, and we believe in you."

Then, she gets up and brings over an old, worn leather suitcase.

"My father also told me to send you with his suitcase of papers for safekeeping, but most importantly, for you to start learning everything you can about the information it contains inside. You of all people will need to know all that you can about the secrets of the provinces."

I, of all people, need to learn the secrets of the provinces? I suddenly review my past life. It was a quiet, solitary life, not by choice. So, I read books to escape loneliness. It was my only sense of adventure. Everything

I know comes from books. But nothing I ever read has prepared me for this. I should have read more fantasy.

> I need to mend
> My broken wing
> So that I can
> One day, fly again.

Her words bring me back to the present.

"I am sure you both agree that for now it is best that no one knows that you are alive, Arden. Your best protection right now is everyone believing that you are dead," Vesta offers. "And that you two are not working together on breaking the spell."

My stomach turns. I cannot join in their conversation because my mind is stuck on one impossible thought: what if I must face off with Earl Menstus?

"Yes, we had decided on that before we went to interrogate her father, no one should believe that she is more than a ghost," Kyrie explains.

I startle when Taryn arrives outside the window, holding a rose bush. I look at Vesta in confusion.

"When I told my father that I had marked your grave with a rose, he asked Taryn to go dig up the rose today. He was worried Earl Menstus might look for your grave since he now understands part of the prophecy. He knows that you are the Albatross. I will be right back."

I shudder at the thought of being dug up by Menstus. I do not know what to say or think about everything else.

I turn to Kyrie. "Did you know about any of this? Had Vesta already told you about the prophecy when you first met her? Is this how you knew I needed to break the spell? I need to know the truth, are you all in this together?" I am desperate to understand.

"Arden," he looks into my eyes, "I promise I am finding out about all this right now with you, I had no idea about the prophecy. I would have told you if I knew, I could never have kept this from you. She did not tell me any of this when she helped me find you."

Sixteen

{Twenty-two years before the present}

Earl Menstus

When she chose him, she broke me. Still, I returned to ask for my Valray pendant, the only possession I had of worth. I did not think there could be any pain greater than being refused to speak to her one last time.

But he was the worst pain I ever felt. When he stole my manhood, my heart turned cold. When I returned and found my mother long dead, my heart turned to stone. But I decided to live in hopes of changing the narrative.

I cast the spell. But not like my great-grandmother did it. Not quickly, swiftly, in one fell swoop. This time, it is slower. Much slower. A longer, slower spell for the Kallos seat. For her, Reown. Frozen in time. To remember. To give her time. To remember.

And with a Valray maiden finally born into the line again, I will have tears to break the spell, for when Reown wakes up and remembers me.

Arden

Given all the shock and confusion, I do not know whether my gut feelings or rational thoughts work accurately anymore. I brace myself for the moment Taryn will first see this version of me, alive, although I look like I am dying. I have been in the dark, sweating and crying for days. It is so embarrassing. My hair is a mess, I am sure my eyes are swollen, my nose is red and runny, and I will use every ounce of strength inside of me to hope that he will not run away again in horror seeing me like this.

Just maybe one offering,
A small token,
A word,
Even a nod my way,
Anything
That lets me know
I am not invisible,
Forgotten,
Replaced,
And thought of no more.

They both walk back inside, and it feels like the oxygen leaves the room. I feel so undone, so...awkward, like the floor is coming out from under me. I do not know what to say.

"Hello," Taryn says first to Kyrie and shakes his hand. Then he turns to me.

I look at his face. I wish I could hear his thoughts. There are a million words I want to tell him, ask him.

"It is so good to finally meet you in person," he says. I am shattered. My knees will buckle if I do not concentrate on not collapsing. I instinctively hold onto Kyrie's arm for balance.

"You too," I hear myself say. I cannot stop the awkward words from leaving my mouth— "I am sorry that my ghost scared you. The song has the power to pull me towards it; I cannot stop it from happening."

"It is okay. Vesta explained everything to me after the wedding. I am sorry that I panicked and ran from you. But I am so grateful that my wife," he says as he pulls her to him, "was able to cover my fear with the dignity you deserve."

All I had to do was stay alive, and I would be the wife wrapped in his arms right now. A cold sweat forms down my back, along my hairline, and on my top lip.

Vesta cuts in, "Would you two like to stay for dinner?"

I cannot eat in front of Taryn. I just want to escape this embarrassment I feel standing in front of him. I want to turn back into a ghost and float away. I hate what is happening inside my stomach right now.

Kyrie looks at my face and says to them, "Thank you so much for the offer. I think we should get back and find a safe place for your father's suitcase. If it is okay with you, we can take a rain check and come back in a few days to discuss this new information after we have gone through some of the papers."

I look at Kyrie for a stolen second and love him. I do not know how he knows, but for this, I do not even need an explanation.

"Of course, you have a lot of news to process." Vesta says. "Come back in three days, we will know more then, and we can discuss everything."

She hands Kyrie the suitcase and gives me the warmest hug. The men shake hands, and Taryn and I meet eyes. My cheeks burn, and then, after we leave the cottage, we travel quickly back through the realm shift.

We end up back in my room, right where we were before the song called. We both stare at the suitcase for a moment and decide to keep it in my room for the night. I do not have all the words I want to say right now because I am still in shock from everything Vesta told us. I just do not understand how any prophecy can be about me. But I need to thank him; I need to find the words to tell him I noticed what he did.

"Thank you for declining the dinner invitation. I felt like I was dying of embarrassment, meeting Taryn for the first time looking like this," I said, motioning to my face and hair.

"I do not know how, but it is like I could feel your nervousness, and I just knew that I needed to bring you home and get you comfortable. But Arden, I need you to know that even when you are feeling your worst, you are the most beautiful woman in the room."

I blush from the wave of heat that travels across my face. He is the only man who has ever told me I am beautiful. I hope to feel that about myself one day, to be able to see what he sees. But more than that, I want to believe that I am beautiful, from a place deep within myself.

He continues, "I cannot explain it, but somehow, I had a flicker of what you must have been feeling tonight, and I just wanted to make you feel safe again. It was not just a logical guess, I felt it. I felt some of your pain in my heart. I do not know how, but something happened inside of me when Taryn walked into the room. I felt it as soon as I saw the look on your face. When I felt your knees buckle, something awakened in me. When you wrapped your hands around my arm for support, I felt an electric current surge to my heart."

I look at his eyes and search them for clues. What does it mean? I want to ask him. How do I ask him? Is he beginning to feel…something…for me? I do not know what words to say.

"Did it hurt?" I dare to ask.

"Yes, but it was the best pain I have ever felt," he says, shyly.

"I hope this is just the beginning of what we have been trying to do, even if we do not understand it." I tell him softly, debating in my mind if I should reach out and hug him.

He smiles softly and says, "Me too. I would love to go through this suitcase of papers with you over the next few days, if that is okay?"

"Of course. I cannot imagine doing it alone. Besides, you will have more context clues. My parents taught me nothing about the realms around me, much less the history of provinces and bloodlines. I never even knew there was a prophecy or a Lord Menstus."

"I will tell you everything that I know about what we find in there, I promise."

"I believe you." I tell him.

"How about we start in the morning?" He asks. "I will make us coffee," and gives me a hopeful smile.

"Yes. Good night, Kyrie." I offer my hand; he takes it and gently squeezes. I want to ask him if he feels the electricity, too.

"Good night, Arden," and he softly closes the door behind him.

I have trouble falling asleep. I replay every word that was spoken at Vesta's. What if fate was altered? What if Taryn was the one I was supposed to unite with, and Earl Menstus kept us apart to keep the prophecy from happening? What if Menstus succeeded in keeping me apart from Taryn? Or what if the prophecy is not about me at all? Or what if Vesta's father has interpreted it all wrong? The panic spirals inside of me. I follow it and let it take me under; it is too strong to fight this time. All I can do is just surrender to the terror, not afraid of it ending me, almost hoping it does. I do not know how to defeat dark lords and unite realms. But then I think of Kyrie being able to feel tonight, feel something for me, and it stops my free-fall because I feel something for him that I have never felt before in my life.

> I am clawing myself toward goodness
> With my mangled body
> Dragging along the ground beside me.
> Deficient in life force and rest,

And the reserves sucked dry,
My depleted soul crawls toward the light.
In tattered threads laid bare,
I used my body as a shield,
As the fence.
My broken body
pulled me through the years,
As it pulled me through the dirt,
And through the realm shift.
I no longer fear dirt under my nails.
I dance, begging for the rain,
I fall prostrate to the flame.
I gather every holy salt in my tears,
And put them on my lips.
I write poems in the air,
Waiting on the gaze of the Powers Above.
The floor still bears the marks
Where I crawl,
Scratching my way towards
My destiny.

Seventeen

{Ninety-five years before our present story begins}

Florin

Vesta yawns as Florin continues the rest of the bedtime story. "Holding to tradition, the eight original children each appointed their eldest child to become the next heir, keeping the original name, no matter if they were daughters or sons. Until eight generations passed, no one could marry outside of their province, and no one could form any unions across the realms. As time passed, the eight provinces maintained their own unique set of powers, blessings, and skills based on the personalities of their original namesake, including the traits of their potential downfall. And as foretold, one province ceased to exist."

"That part always makes me sad," says Vesta.

"Legend says that when it is time for the prophecy to unfold, someone chosen from each province will play an essential part in ensuring that the realms unite again and Claudegus will be freed at last. The power of true love will only cross the forbidden divide once it is time, and that is how we will know when the prophecy is unfolding."

"And now, that brown leather suitcase belongs to Daddy," Vesta says proudly. "I think he will be the first one to understand the prophecy because he's the smartest man in the entire realm."

"Yes, he was given a very special gift," says Florin, kissing Vesta goodnight. "Because he understands the power of true love."

Arden

I open my eyes to the sunlight and try to remember where I am. I am disoriented. I roll over and see the suitcase sitting there, and the memory of yesterday comes back to me, the prophecy. Then I remember that I have not eaten in days. I waste no time getting dressed and getting back downstairs to eat my first full breakfast.

Kyrie is already there. "Good morning, did you sleep well?"

I shudder at the memory of my dream. I was alone in the black sky, balancing on top of the outer realm dome, trying to get back to Kyrie, when Earl Menstus appeared as a giant. He grabbed me with one hand and swept me away into the darkness. I screamed for help, but no sound came from me.

"I am finally hungry. And I am ready for that sip of coffee." I say with a sheepish grin as I begin to serve my plate full of food.

He smiles with satisfaction and wastes no time preparing the first brew. I let myself indulge in the smell and anticipate my first sip. When he brings the cup to me, it feels like a lifeline in my hands, just like his tender care. I can see that he has made it an art. A beautiful leaf pattern is imprinted on the creamy white top. I close my eyes as the hot liquid passes my lips, and I let my whole body enjoy the pleasure of this first experience. I can taste the subtle notes of the different spices, and I am impressed. He does not take his eyes off me that whole time, as if he can clearly see that he has initiated me into the realm of coffee lovers. Our eyes meet with a knowing that this is the first of many cups to come.

"Thank you," I tell him, in between sips and bites of lemon poppyseed muffin. "I will always remember this first sip. I am glad I waited until now." I try to slow down when I notice how fast I am stuffing the food into my mouth. It just feels good to finally feed my starvation.

He smiles, "You're welcome, it was my pleasure."

"Would it be ok if I go get the suitcase and bring it down?" he asks.

I nod yes to him as I serve seconds onto my plate, and he disappears for a few minutes.

"I will set it up on the terrace…we can sit out there and go through it together after you eat."

When I finish eating, I head to the terrace cushions with my hot cup and get comfortable. He unlocks the leather straps and lets the suitcase open completely. I have a sense that magic lives inside that brown suitcase, and I am slightly terrified that I need to understand its contents.

On top of all the papers are rolled-up canvas oil paintings. We unroll them and look at two family portraits before us. It takes a moment before we see the names in beautiful handwriting across the bottom of the canvas fabric and realize who the people are. The first painting is of Lashga, her husband, and their four children. She has long, straight black hair and teal-green eyes, and creamy skin the color of poplar. Her husband has dark mahogany skin, golden topaz eyes, and rich brown hair braided into a crown. He looks noble. Valray looks like her mother with dark hair and teal eyes, but her skin is warmer, like the maple. Wincot also has dark hair and emerald-green eyes, and his skin is like smooth teak. Dashel has dark brown hair, with his father's topaz eyes, and skin the shade of an oak. Zenif has his mother's ebony hair with dark walnut skin, even darker than his father's, but his eyes are different from everyone's; his are silvery gray. The six of them are an exquisite mix to behold.

Kyrie looks up from the canvas and says what I am thinking as well, "You look a lot like Lashga and Valray." I nod, still trying to understand how I can look more like very distant ancestors than my own mother.

The second painting is of Pallayes, her husband, and their four children. These two sisters could not look more different. Pallayes has warm cinnamon skin with nutmeg freckles, curly golden-streaked copper hair, and bright turquoise eyes. Her husband has golden hair, amethyst-colored eyes, and olive skin. Kallos has his mother's copper skin, freckles, and hair, but he has eyes that I have never seen before. One is turquoise, and the other is purple. I look at Kyrie and wonder if that is how those galaxies were passed down and formed in his eyes. Teahn looks just like his father, with golden hair, purple eyes, and olive skin. Clemen has his mother's cinnamon-copper skin, but without the freckles, and his father's golden hair, but his eyes are darker, like sapphires. Amara's long, wavy hair and smooth skin are all one of the same color, the perfect blending of cinnamon and ginger, and golden-brown honey, and she has much lighter eyes, the color of aquamarine.

"Wow, you really have the Kallos genes," I say with a smile, and he blushes.

"Oh look, there's one more canvas in here," he says, reaching in and pulling out another painting. He unrolls it, and we gasp. "How did Vesta's father get a painting of Claudegus? I have always imagined what he looked like," Kyrie says, amazed.

I realize that I did not grow up hearing stories about the man whose image is in front of me, so I never imagined him. He also has two different eye colors: emerald green and aqua blue. He has long, pearl-white hair, pulled back behind his head in braids like Kyrie's, and dark skin the color of cloves. He looks majestic but also entirely down to earth, as if he would have a fantastic laugh and might slap his knee if he thought the joke was funny. He is clearly a big man, with a large neck and chest, and I notice his large, dark forearms and hands under his rolled-up white sleeves. He is sitting with Lashga and Pallayes on either side, their hands resting on his shoulders, and a woman stands behind him between the daughters. She is regal. Her long hair is a shiny silver woven with teal braids, and her opal-moonstone skin is lit from within and freckled with glimmering copper shimmers. Her eyes look like a glorious sunset. They are a mixture of purple, pink, orange, and magenta, with a little bit of light blue. She looks like she knows everything. She is ancient yet incandescent. She seems enchanted.

"I wonder what happened to her?" Kyrie asks aloud. "The legends do not mention her name."

I frown, thinking how sad that is. She looks like the most powerful one in the family. Certainly, there must be a mention of her somewhere. It is hard to pull my eyes away. I want to keep looking at her, as if she might have something important to tell me.

"It is amazing how all these genes pooled together and made all these beautiful combinations," I say aloud, lost in my thoughts. This whole family looks like a regal collection of beautiful woods, spices, and precious stones.

"Yes, it really is incredible too, how after all these years, the people in each province still have a strong resemblance to their original ruler. I think the striking difference that we see between Lashga and Pallayes in the paintings, remains between the realms today," Kyrie says.

I think about the people of Valray. There is a mix of skin tones, but everyone has dark hair. I have never seen someone with Kyrie's coloring until now.

"So, there are only two granddaughters, Valray and Amara. Two girls standing as bookends to all those boys," I say, smiling, looking at those two beautiful girls who look so different from one another.

Kyrie smiles and looks back at the work in front of us. "We can try to organize these papers and sort them into piles. One for the prophecy, one for the province genealogies and bloodlines, and one for the legends."

I nod in agreement, not really having any better ideas of my own. We begin sorting the piles we are each holding. A lot of it is in symbols, and some in another language I do not recognize. Each page is covered with handwritten notes. There is a different handwriting of scribbles around the edges. I am afraid it will take me many months just to begin learning what it all means. I reach in and pull out a large document folded in thirds. As we open it together, a chart detailing each province is laid out before us.

Lashga Realm

Valray
- woodworkers & carvers, master artisans, furniture makers, adventurers, travelers, food enthusiasts, lovers of life

Wincot
- innovators, inventors, clockmakers, instrument creators, musicians, singers, boatsmen

Dashel
- hospitality for travelers, creating places of refuge and enjoyment, naturalists, beekeepers & honey producers, animal lovers

Zenif
- textile artisans, fabric designers, tailors, artists, basket weavers, performing artists

Pallayes Realm

Kallos
- spice growers, coffee and cacao farmers, tastemakers, connoisseurs, collectors

Teahn
- scholars, teachers, writers, bookmakers, storytellers, dancers, fishermen

Clemen
- apothecaries, vintners, herbalists, healers. master gardeners, perfumers,

Amara
- master jewelers, miners of precious stones, explorers, sculptors, artisans of hats and shoes

"Kyrie, this is amazing. It is the list of the original industries and interests of the provinces. It is as if it was all planned."

"And it is all mostly still as it is today. Except for Dashel…it is tragic that it is all gone. Look, each province seems to pair up and match with another from the other realm. Look how amazing it would be if these provinces could easily travel and trade with one another."

As I read the words 'tastemakers,' I realize I have not yet asked him an important question. "How is your province of farmers and tastemakers still able to produce such high standards with the loss of taste and smell? Is Kallos suffering economically from the spell?" I ask, suddenly feeling compassion for all these farmers.

He looks into my eyes and lets me see the locked-up sadness in his own. "I am desperately trying to save our economy and industry along with the lives of the people. If Clemen cuts off our trade agreement, I am not sure we could recover the loss. I have told every grower and maker to trust the process, the recipes, the calculations, everything that is measurable and logical since most of them cannot trust their senses anymore."

"Can you still taste the coffee and chocolate and spices?"

"Barely. Everything has the same bland taste, but I force myself to remember, to use my memory with every bite. It is why I enjoyed watching you drink your first cup this morning. I long to taste it again the way I saw you experience it. I miss that pleasure."

I blush with heat when I remember the way he watched me. I look back down at the list, trying to hide my cheeks. Then I tell him, "I want to wait to have my first chocolate here with you when the spell is broken, and we can enjoy it together. I want us to both be able to taste it."

He smiles with an internal gratitude I have never seen in anyone else.

Eighteen

{Just over six months before the present}

To my trusted coachman,

For your final payment, bring me the pendant as proof that you have completed the job.

Sayszye

Arden

I pull out the portraits of both families and set them next to the list. "It is like you can almost see the personalities of these eight kids in both the paintings and the province descriptions together." I ponder it all, amazed that what was established at the beginning of the two realms has lasted this long.

"Take a look at this," Kyrie says as he unfolds a large folded-up document. "It is the genealogy of the Valray bloodline."

I gasp at the sight of family names and ancestors I never knew I had.

He points to a place on the paper, "This name is circled in red. Vera Valray. The note here says Earl Menstus' great grandmother."

"She is the sister of my great-great-grandfather. Are Menstus and I from the same bloodline? I do not know why it did not click before when you told me the legend of the spell." I take a deep breath and stretch out, trying to breathe. The oxygen in the room feels heavier.

"There is more." Kyrie adds, still reading the paper. "It looks like Menstus was Vera's father's name, Menstus Valray, your great-great-great-grandfather. And If I remember correctly, Vesta said the name Earl can be found in the Dashel genealogy. It should be in here somewhere."

I wait for him to find it, gladly taking the time to get air into my lungs. All this ancestry stuff makes me nervous.

"Yes, here it is. The name Earl Dashel is the last ruler of the province before its demise almost one hundred years ago, just like the story said. Well, at least the dark lord's name is not random. Vera Valray strung together the names of the two men who sent her into exile and left her there."

"Do you think Menstus knows all of this? I mean, do you think he is as cunning as he pretends to be?"

"No. He is more desperate than clever. Besides, we have the translated prophecy, and all of this," as he motions to the suitcase of papers.

I think of all eight provinces. Dashel is gone. Kallos is already under the spell, its downfall looming, and the Valray province is currently a sitting duck. It finally dawns on me.

"Kyrie, if I had married Taryn, I would be in the Wincot province now. Who would even be next in line for the Valray seat? My parents never talked about these things. I have learned more in this short life with you about how all this works than in all the years combined of my last life."

"That is a good question, and I do not think they were planning on it being either you or your sister," he says somberly.

"How could my parents have given me to another province if I was the heir to the seat?" Hearing these words cracks open a blind spot. I was not groomed to be the next ruler. That was never discussed. 'He was never going to crown a daughter.' You heard him. He was waiting for a male heir."

"That is odd. The seat always goes to the eldest, even if it is a daughter. Her husband, who would not be the eldest from his own province, takes on her province's name. Like my father, he took my mother's name and became Juris Kallos. It is unheard of for the eldest daughter of one province to marry the eldest son of another because of the heirship problem it would create in one of the provinces. Co-rulers have never existed before."

I am thinking about this for the first time. "Taryn is the eldest son. He has a younger brother, the next heir now that Taryn was cut out. But I was supposed to move to his province and take his name after we married. That would have left the Valray seat wide open after my father's death."

"Arden, you said the betrothal was formed because of an alliance between the two provinces. What was the agreement? The only reason your parents would have sent you to another province would have been for some greater gain, but even that still does not make sense."

"I feel so foolish...I am just now realizing how ignorant I was, how much I was kept in the dark. I did not even know there was so much more for me to know and be aware of. I was trained to not ask questions or be burdensome in any way, so I just stopped asking. I have asked more questions since you have found me than before I died. It is like I came out of my grave made of questions. I have no idea what the alliance was, or what was exchanged. I just wanted to escape and be free. The strange part is that it was my mother who made the agreement; my father seemed to have cared less."

"It is strange that he was not concerned about the future of his province or the next heir to the seat. It is like he did not think he would need one, like he would live forever or something."

Strange, distant memories begin crashing in like waves, getting closer to the shoreline of my memory. "Kyrie, that is it. That is the power he was always trying to harness. He believed he was going to escape death and outlive everyone, live forever. That is what he went to Vaxxa for. To learn how to master the power of immortality. That is why he easily traded my life for access to those books."

We sit for a moment in silence, looking at each other, trying to understand what I just said.

"It sounds like he was subtly grooming you to believe it too and to not question or worry about your claim to the province seat. It is as if you were brainwashed into seceding over your birthright," he says in a way that I can finally see it and believe it.

"I may not ever know why my mother made this agreement with the Wincot province. What was her motive to keep me out of claiming my rightful place?"

"I am not sure. She was just as much under your father's control as you were."

"Do you think Taryn knew about this? That I was just a pawn, and that his province stood to gain from me giving up my seat to the Valray province?"

"I do not know. But I also would not be surprised if Taryn found out that he was also being used as a pawn. It may be part of the reason he gave up his seat to marry Vesta."

"I wonder if I should ask him when we return for dinner."

"I think it is worth a try," he says with tenderness.

Nineteen

{Seven months before the present}

Elspeth

When I got Florin's message that she and Vesta were leaving Pallayes, I thought my heart might stop in my chest. My darling beloved girls. More precious to me than all the jewels of this land. She did not tell me where they were going, not wanting to risk her letter falling into the wrong hands, but that they had a new mission in the Lashga realm.

If even a single hair on either of them is harmed, I will send out my guards to hunt down and find the culprit. Even if they must cross the bypass. Fools be damned. I have lost my Florin once; I will not lose her again.

What are these realms coming to? I remember before the fall of Dashel, when everything was just as it should be. A time of peace, before tragedy and heartache at every turn.

Arden

A new question appears in my mind. "Do you think Earl Menstus uses the same dark energy that my father was trying to master? Because I became paralyzed with fear trying to face my father. I am worried that I will not be able to face Menstus if it is the same darkness and that I will fail the prophecy."

"I do not understand it all, but I think the difference between a void of love and the intentional conjuring of dark magic to use against others, lies within that soul's ability to be transformed and restored by the power of love. Love is the most powerful force that exists in any realm. It is a law, an energy source, a power so incredible that it restores life. Any dark power is a void, an actual lack of love itself. So, when love is no longer present, the void appears, and some draw power from this void. It can feel powerful when it gathers strength between people who all draw from the lack. But it only takes one person full of love, knowing the power love has over the darkness, therefore, without fear, even fear of death, to shatter the power of the lack. That is how life after death is possible. The power and weight of something is always more than nothing; it is just natural law and physics, really. No amount of the lack of love can ever be enough to completely extinguish even the smallest bit of the power of love itself." He smiles and adds, "More wisdom I learned years ago from the province elders before they passed. It is just a matter of what happens when the darkness in a soul is faced with light. Whether the darkness between your father and Menstus is the same or not, what matters most is their reaction to the light."

I believe what he says is true, and for that, I love him. It somehow gives me hope.

"So, all you have to do is have a greater amount of love than Menstus's amount of lack, and you will defeat him," he says, as if it is perfect logic.

"You make it sound easy," I say with a sheepish grin.

"Well, you will not have to do it alone," he says, taking my hands in his. "I solemnly pledge my life to help you, always, spell or no spell, and we seem to have been chosen for this time in history." We both look down to where our hands are clasped when a flash of electricity lightly glazes across them. He looks up at me, and I can see the question on his face before he even asks it.

"Yes, I felt it too." I smile, gazing at his gorgeous face, soaking in his genuine bond of friendship, pondering his words. I realize that on the day he first found me, when I agreed to go with him, I had pledged my new life to help him, too. An incredible sensation of balance flows through me that I have never felt before.

He looks at me, and I see new thoughts behind his gorgeous eyes, careening across his mind like shooting stars. I nestle back into the cushions and try to let myself relax. I push away the anxious thoughts, the worry of what will happen if we break the spell, and I am not needed here anymore. Would I still live here? I do not want to be a burden or overstay my welcome. Would I stay in this realm, or go back to mine? Would I become a nomad, wandering around for a new purpose? That is it, I will be free to create my own adventure and travel the realms. But I need to know, I need to ask him.

"Kyrie, have you ever been in love? I mean, is there someone you had feelings for, but the spell has kept you apart? Is there someone waiting for you as soon as the spell is broken?" I ask nervously, quickly, before I lose my nerve.

He tilts his head at the same time his brows gather, like he is caught off guard, but also like he is not sure where these questions came from or what they mean.

"Sadly, no. I have never experienced those feelings before. I have friends from school, and I have a lot of acquaintances around the province, the farmers, the business owners, the elders. It is like a whole community helped raise me since my parents were not emotionally available. There were people less affected than my parents by the spell, who were able to guide me and pass down their wisdom. They made space for the feelings I did have at the time, but there was never someone my age that I had a connection with or had formed an attachment to. I guess I have always been on my own in a sense. My whole life has been trying to navigate the effects of the spell, trying to break it, and save my family, the people, the province. A romantic relationship is something I have never had the luxury to experience." He pauses, and then, "Why do you ask?"

"I am trying to understand what will happen after the spell is broken. I will need to make plans of some sort...I just did not want to be a third wheel or offend anyone by my being here. I am just trying to sort through what my new life is going to be like, since I am not sure I can go back home." I say, fighting back any self-pity. "I did not want to assume that I would just stay here after the spell breaks, but I am not sure what else I would do."

A moment of silence passes as he tries to understand what I have said. Then he says, "I am glad we are talking about it. I honestly had not even thought beyond breaking the spell. I did not make any plans; I was not sure how long it would take. If we break this spell, you will be held in the highest honor by this province, and I promise that you will always be provided for. I promise that you will never be abandoned, discarded, or homeless.

When I asked you to come with me, and you said yes, I saw you as someone who would always be in my care, someone who would be in my future, not just a temporary part of it. Of course, you have the freedom to choose what you want to do. You are not ever bound to stay here, but it is my honor to make sure you never feel alone, lost, or unwanted ever again."

I do not even try to hide the warm tears that are slowly running down my cheeks. I have never experienced this before, this assurance of being taken care of. I did not even know it was possible. I have never known anyone to take pleasure in caring for me; I always felt like a burden growing up. I thought I would be doing him a favor by removing myself from his life. I want to stretch my imagination to understand his perspective on me. He sees something in me that I do not yet see in myself, and it is not lost on me that he feels this way about me without being able to feel anything for me.

"And," he adds, "if we cannot figure out how to break the spell with your tears, and things take a turn for the worse in Kallos, or with my health, I promise I will secure a future for you before I do anything else. You will not be abandoned here."

I hear a deep sigh of relief break through my chest, and everything inside of me relaxes with a sensation that is still very new. I believe him, I can rest now. I offer him a smile and a nod, letting him know I understand and appreciate his words as I wipe my tears.

We sit in comfortable silence for a few minutes, letting this new understanding between us settle in.

"Would you like to take a small break, grab some food and walk down to the water?" He asks.

"Sure, that sounds nice." I reply, happy to take a break from sorting through all these mysteries.

Twenty

{Yesterday}

Kyrie

Kyrie opens his desk drawer and is looking for his old journal. The one he has not pulled out in months. It has his favorite recipes, memories, and ideas on how to survive this spell. His hand finds the leather, and he pulls it out upon the desk.

As he flips through the old pages, he cannot help but remember, even though it is much fainter now, the whiffs of spice and coffee trapped in the paper. He grabs his pen and writes:

So much has happened in the last few days. Arden is here. The bravest person I have ever met. Someone I can trust.

Arden. Her very name is as beautiful as she is. I wish I could feel her touch. She has inspired me to hope again.

Even though I cannot feel it, I know it. Somehow, she is the one.

The invisibility cloak did not require as much effort as it used to. Yesterday, putting it over us was an easier action; I did not have to focus so hard to make it happen. I did not need to recover because I did not experience the weakness afterward as I had before.

It is like some strength is returning to me. It is like the fog in my mind is lifting, and I can think more clearly. I sensed it while I was driving through the province this morning; it was like I was seeing things again that had faded from my view long ago. Some memories of feelings came back to me as well.

I do not know what this all means. I feel parts of myself returning, instead of slipping further away. I am not sure how, but it is like I am waking up from a long sleep.

Also, it is strange, I can travel instantly through the realm shift since Arden has been here.

Arden

We pack up some food, walk down to the pool house, and sit on the steps near the water. I dip my feet into the cold water. When he takes a bite of fruit, his eyes widen, and he gasps, looking at me with surprise. "Arden! I taste it! I really taste it," he exclaims.

"What do you mean?" I ask him.

"I can just really taste this fruit for the first time in years! I had gotten so used to it being so bland, this intense flavor surprised me." He takes another big bite, and his eyes are wild with delight. "This is even more delicious than I remember! Arden, I can taste it!"

He looks around, and I see his next idea as he rolls up his loose pants and dips his foot into the water. I know it before he says anything. He can really feel the temperature of the icy water. I smile at him, at his expression, his exuberant surprise. His grin is suddenly intoxicating.

"Arden, how do you think this is happening? The inventors have not had any luck with the experiments so far, but I am starting to feel things again. I had no idea I had been swimming in such cold water! I could not feel the temperature or the sensation of it anymore."

I try to gather some words, but before I can form sentences, he pulls off his shirt and dives into the pool. When he comes back up for air, he throws his head back and laughs. It is the first time I have heard it, and I know I want to hear more. He has a fantastic laugh, and it has finally been unlocked.

Then my eyes take him in, and his chiseled shoulders slay me. I stifle the hum in my throat. I am having new feelings as well. Something comes alive inside me; I wonder if that small blue flame has just ignited into something bold and fiery.

"I really feel the water against my skin! I cannot believe this is happening! And I just laughed for the first time in years! Did you hear that? Tell me something funny, I can laugh now!"

His excitement is contagious. I cannot think of anything funny to say, so I just get up and cannonball into the pool with him, creating the biggest splash I can manage. I can hear his laughter above the water while I am still under, and when I come up for air, my breath catches...he is breath-taking. I see him, his inner beauty becoming unveiled, the shackles coming undone. I am mesmerized. I can feel his exhilaration inside of me. He puts his hand to his chest, where his heart is, "Arden, something is happening...I can feel something happening around my heart. It is so painful, but I will gladly endure this pain if it means the spell is breaking." He slowly moves to the edge of the pool to hold on for support.

I watch him work through the agony. His eyes are clenched tightly closed, and his brow is furrowed. He looks up at me and catches his breath. "Can you feel this? Do you hear it too?" He reaches out for me to come to him.

As I move closer to him, an electrical current dances between us. As he welcomes me into his arms, I put my hand on his heart and my ear to his chest. I can feel movement under his warm skin. I can hear it too, the sound of threads unbinding, unraveling…like the swift whooshing looping sounds of ropes on a sailboat. Then he wraps both arms around me, holding onto me in his painful undoing, with something like elation breaking through his holy agony, and I know, for the first time on either side of death, I do not want to be anywhere else. My insides turn into a warm liquid. I have never felt this way before, and I know now that life will never be the same. It feels so pure it stings.

How did I not understand it before? I was so worried about who the prophecy would have me united with, and he was right in front of me all along. I become acutely aware of how intensely I feel about Kyrie as if I have seen something I can never unsee. I no longer care about tears and spells, prophecies and dark lords, provinces, and bloodlines. If my future does not have me in his arms, then I do not want it. The realms will need to save themselves.

"Is this possible?" He asks. "Is this really happening, or am I dreaming?"

I look up at his face, and his eyes are filled with tears. His chin is quivering, and his questions are desperate for a true answer. The spell has broken, and his feelings are unleashed. I have never kissed anyone before, but I know that it is the only answer I have for him. My heels lift, I cup his neck into my hands, and I pull his lips slowly to mine. I kiss the man who dared to pull me from death, who asked if I would be willing to live again, who believed in me and trusted me with his future. I kiss the man who protects me and vows to tell me everything he knows and helps me find every answer I need. I kiss the man who teaches me how to find the flame within myself, who sees the beauty in me even when I cannot, and who finds pleasure in caring for me. He holds me tight when I whisper, "This is real."

Time stands still for us. I swear I hear the Powers Above sigh in relief.

> I know why the clock
> Has a face,
> And arms and hands.
> I know why the sky
> Has a sun,

And planets and stars.
I know what it is like
To be held in time
And cradled by the moon.

Kyrie gathers me up off my feet, my body pressed against him, and he carries me back to the steps. He gently sets me down and kneels on the lower steps in front of me to face me. We are in the warm orange glow of the sun, and I see a new future in his eyes.

"Arden, I am so overcome. I am feeling emotions that I forgot existed. It has been so long since I felt them. But there are other things I am feeling right now that I have never felt before in my whole life. I just need you near me or I am afraid my heart will explode. It is like it has just been untethered and the freedom to love you is taking my breath away. The words fail to fully explain it, but I am overcome." Everything about him is raw and pure, and he is desperate to feel it all at once.

"I am here. I am not leaving." I wrap my arms around his neck, sliding down the step to get closer to him, where he can wrap his arms back around me to hold onto what is true.

"I did not expect this to happen today," he says. "I do not know what caused the spell to break so unexpectedly."

"I know, it caught me by surprise…but now, it just feels…right, like I am finally home."

"Yes, I want to be your home," he says, his arms holding me with a security I have never known.

"Kyrie," I begin, "I was thinking about your words before we came to the pool…you pledged your life to help me. I wonder if that was the piece needed to complete the bond to break the spell?"

"What do you mean, to complete the bond?" He asks sincerely. Both of us release our tight hold and sit back so that we can see each other's faces.

I focus, hoping for the right words to explain what finally seems so clear now. "Well, when I left my grave, I pledged my new life to help you break the spell…and we have been spending these days trying to help one another solve the mysteries of our pasts, and future, and you have been saying that things have been changing inside of you, like the spell was starting to break…and maybe when you just pledged your life to help me, it made a complete bond between us. It is the power of love you were just telling me about. It is not about the literal tears, but the sacrifice that happens when two people pledge their lives to help one another heal and overcome the adversity together."

I look at his eyes, and his expression shows how much my words resonate with a truth in him. "Arden, you are so right, it makes so much sense now. A true love for one another broke the spell. I was so focused on the tears that I could not see what I can see now; it is the love for the maiden crying the tears, and her love in return, that has the power to break this spell. It is the one thing Vera Valray wanted, to be chosen and loved."

"Wow, the spell was her desperate cry for love. In her heartbreak, Vera Valray tried to create a bridge that only Earl Dashel could cross. It is so tragic, but I can imagine how valiantly the story could have ended if he would have been brave enough to go against his father's pride instead of repeating the cycle," I say, soaking in our discovery. "If Earl Dashel would have loved her beyond his fear of his father, or fear of losing the seat, the spell would have been broken and the province saved."

"It reminds me of Taryn giving up the Wincot seat for Vesta. Can you imagine if Earl Dashel would have had that much courage?" He adds.

I cannot help but think about how devastating it is when someone gives up their authentic self and the pursuit of their destiny to maintain a connection to family, because their worth has become dependent on that attachment. I juxtapose the memory of my past unlived life, waiting to be rescued and accepted, with this rebirth and resurrection, awakening to this new unfolding of my authenticity. I can now decide on my own self-worth; I no longer need or depend on my parents' estimate of my worth or their plan for my life. I am now free to give myself what I needed from them, but they were incapable of ever giving me. What if I am worthy beyond my wildest imagination? I am finally tasting the glorious sweetness of my own appraisal. I can follow the signposts of my sacred journey. My shadow bows in agreement as it conjures a prayer for me.

I petition myself
For favor and supplication.
I say the invocation,
Lead the benediction,
And give the sanctification.
I do my own intercession
Grant my own blessing.
I authorize my freedom
Give it sanction.
I consent to my own endorsement,
With an embrace of provocation,
As I espouse myself to me.

Twenty-One

{Four months before the present}

My love, Mazek. My fisherman.

Without you here, I feel as if my soul is outside of my body. I am writing again as a form of consolation. Even though you cannot read these words now, they are somehow something passing between us. They hold me steady, keeping my memories alive. I have been dreaming of the night by your fireside when you so gently untangled my cold bones from your fishing line and refashioned them into place. A mysterious skeleton woman. If you had not found my bones upon your fishing line, I would still be at the bottom of the sea. Oh, I remember how thirsty I was, and how delicious your tears appeared upon your cheek as you slept that night. I licked them up, greedily drank them as you wept in your sleep. They rehydrated my soul, and I, too, fell into a deep slumber next to your warm body, as my heart began to beat again, as my body came back to me. I will never forget waking together the next day, the shock you had when you saw a woman lying beside you! You screamed, "But where are the bones? Who are you? How did you get here?" I lifted my head, and, in my own surprise at seeing my body, I laughed until I cried. I said, "I am the bones you fool; your tears brought me back to life." And then you began to laugh, and cry, and you held me, and traced every inch of my body with your careful hands. Those gentle, tender hands. We did not leave your quiet fishing hut for days. It is where we made our vow. That sweet Redamancy. I still feel it after all these years, even with this distance. I still feel you.

Love, Florin, your skeleton woman.

Arden

"Do you want to head back up to the house? We can change into dry clothes and meet back on the terrace—the water is a bit cold, " he says with a laugh.

"Okay." I smile with a new awareness of myself. I do not need anyone to give me what I can give myself. I died and rebirthed myself. I am free, and I can choose who I want to share my life with.

We walk back up to the house, our fingers intertwining. It is painful to part, and we both feel it. I can see it in his eyes.

"I will be right back." I reassure him with a kiss. When I enter my bedroom, I am grateful for the dry, comfortable clothes in the wardrobe.

I sit and look at myself in the mirror for the first time since my wedding day, and I finally see a woman, not a girl, staring back at me. My cheeks are pink. I feel beautiful for the first time in my life. I wonder if there were any signs of love in my life before death. Did I ever know or see love? How is it that only after death am I so free to love and be loved?

I crawl on my good knees
Gathering all the broken pieces,

Undaunted,
Because I know how to put back together
What is rightfully mine
Before the taking and breaking
The scattering and shaming.
Patience is my secret,
Because I have learned to love
Broken things,
And the art of restoration.

I go back downstairs to the terrace. The suitcase is just as we left it. The late afternoon sun is low, and the birds are happy. I feel it, too—true happiness. No longer in a cage, I am free.

When Kyrie walks in and sees me here, he pauses, his hand moves to his heart, and I watch him catch his breath. He is overcome. He walks straight to where I am sitting and kneels before me.

He lifts the two intricate golden bracelets that he is holding. "In Pallayes, we do not have large wedding ceremonies, as you call them in Lashga. We have what is known here as the Redamancy Vow. This means a love returned in full. It happens privately between two people who vow to partner together for life, equally giving and returning in full measure all the love they can exchange in their lifetime. Matching golden bracelets are worn by each of them as a sign of the vow. It has become very rare in the Kallos province over the last decade because of the Veiled Heart spell. With the inability to feel joy and desire, most people are no longer falling in love and making the vow."

I smile while a calm excitement thrums inside of me. This moment is perfect; I could not have even imagined it. I listen with my whole heart as he continues.

"My love for you began the moment I found you, even though I could not feel it yet, it was there. I loved watching you come back to life, and helping you search for your answers, as you freely gave me your tears, not withholding or hiding your pain from me. You trusted me with your whole life, and you have let me help you and care for you through your darkest days. You have allowed me to love you completely as you are, and you are the first person to love and accept me so completely as I am. You ached with empathy and compassion for me when I could not feel, you shared in my newfound joy of healing, and I know I can trust you with all my grief. There has always been complete honesty between us, trust, and security, which has allowed a deep love to grow from our friendship. I want to give you a lifetime of the love I have first received from you, a return of love in full measure. If you are willing, Arden Valray, I would like to make the Redamancy Vow with you."

I watch fresh tears roll down his cheeks, and his chin quivers with vulnerability. His heart has awakened after years of fading away under a veil. But he never gave up hope, never lost sight of his inner flame, followed it like a compass. I realize at this moment that I would follow him anywhere, even back into death.

"Since you have brought me here, I have slowly awakened to myself. Through your friendship, you have given me the opportunity to experience true love. When I am with you, I feel completely safe and at peace because you honor the essence within both of us. You have given me so much hope that healing is possible. Even when there has been such heartbreak, you have shown me that life is worth fully living." My holy tears escape faster than the blush that fills my cheeks and my arms that wrap around his neck. I bury my face into the corner of his neck and shoulder, my new home, and I am the safest I have ever felt.

He buries his head down into the matching spot on my neck and weeps softly. His body is trying to remember how to release emotions. I want to be the place where he is safe to feel everything again. He sits back and opens the clasp of my bracelet, slides it over my wrist, and seals it. "I vow to you a lifelong partnership of love and fidelity, even into death." He kisses the bracelet on my wrist.

I open his bracelet and slide it over his wrist, sealing the clasp, and say, "I vow to you a lifelong partnership, a sacred devotion, even back into death." I kiss the bracelet on his wrist and smile. This is what it feels like, a love returned in full, as gorgeous as his eyes, as strong as his shoulders, as tender as his tears, as hopeful as his heart, and as gentle as he has always been.

At this moment, a beautiful, delicate rain falls from above amidst an orange glow and a lavender-pink sky. I remember the line from the prophecy, ' A vow around the wrist.' It is unfolding, telling the story of my new life. We embrace each other with a newfound awareness that this is our future, and we are like pioneers in awe of what we are discovering. A shimmering radiance begins to glow off both of us. I do not know what it means, but it feels like a sign.

"There are legends that speak of this — the power of love creating such beauty," he says as specks of copper glimmer appear across his skin. "This is all so incredible."

"Yes, it is," I tell him. I did not know he could be any more gorgeous, but the new dusting of copper sparkling on his skin…well, it is just mesmerizing.

"You are exquisite!" He says with reverence, his hand delicately touching my new strands of hair. "And your eyes!"

But I cannot yet see what he is seeing. "What is it?" I ask.

"Your teal green eyes now have new flecks of gold set in a beautiful pattern. And brilliant colors of teal are shimmering through your hair, matching the color of your eyes. You look, enchanted," he says with awe.

"Arden, I have never loved a woman before I met you. I need you to know, you are my first everything. Because of the spell, I did not fall in love or experience desire until now. I am new at this."

"It is okay, so am I. You are the first man to ever hold me or kiss me. But I want to figure it out with you. I want to start at the beginning with you and learn everything together," I say with a smile, which is an invitation.

Then, I feel his graceful strength as he, in one fluid movement, scoops me up into his arms and carries me up the stairs.

Twenty-Two

{Presently}

My light and sky. My powers above.

The air ever around me and within me.

When you passed from this realm, my world broke in two. As did my heart.

My only thoughts are of you.

I long for the prophecy to be fulfilled. I long to be returned to your arms.

I am sorry I held onto this land and these people too tightly. I did not know how to let go. It was all I had left of you. Of us.

But now I am ready. I am ready to let go.

With one word from your lips, one stroke of your hand, and I am unbound, Free to return to you.

Claudegus

Arden

This morning, I wake up knowing about the luminous power of love and how it can transform a longing ache to love and be loved into a vulnerable satisfaction of inner peace. I let myself be fully known, and I enjoyed every moment of discovering a whole new landscape that is now my homeland. I unapologetically claimed my desires with a primal independence I never knew lived inside of me. Love and desire were both unleashed and set free to intertwine with an innocence that soon gave way to understanding.

> My bones have released
> The fears
> That have
> Rattled,
> Rattled
> My core.
> Like two doves
> Released
> On a wedding day.
> My bones rattle
> No more.

I open my eyes to a tray of breakfast and Kyrie's bright smile, and then I look at my wrist wrapped in gold.

"Good morning," he says. "I made us breakfast and this coffee is from a special reserve—I was saving it for when the spell was broken. I have spent years holding onto gratitude for this very moment—even though I could not feel it. I have imagined it every day for as long as I can remember. This moment is what kept me from giving up, and now I get to share it with you."

I savor every bite, letting myself experience the pleasure of eating like I never have before. I let every sip of that decadent coffee seep into every part of me. No part of me wants to be quiet or hidden, remaining dormant or unknown. I want to let every new experience fill my cells and pores as I make new memories that belong to a new lifetime. There is nothing like feeling like I am finally home. I look at him, take in his beauty, and notice his closed eyes and deep thoughts.

"What are you thinking about?" I ask.

"I do not know if I even have the words to explain how good it feels to be able to taste coffee again. I have missed this so much. I am so grateful for this experience with you. I have never been happier than I am right now here with you."

"And we have not even eaten the chocolate yet," I say teasingly.

His smile cannot get any bigger, so it breaks into a laugh, for the joy that demands expression. He hands me a piece and watches me ardently as I eat chocolate for the first time in this new life. I let it sit on my tongue and melt, and my eyes instinctively close as I experience pleasure throughout my whole body. There is nothing like it.

"Is that cardamom I am tasting?" I ask, savoring the fresh spice inside this sweet decadence.

"Yes, this is my favorite bar. I helped create the recipe. I have been waiting so long to taste it again."

My body has experienced more pleasure in the last twelve hours than in all my years combined. I love my new life. I watch him taste his favorite indulgence for the first time in years. I can see that he is wholly and completely back home in his body, and he is grateful for every second that his new sensations grant him this homecoming. I love hearing his moans of pleasure when his taste buds awaken to his new reality. I love our new reality. We eat the whole bar of chocolate together like it is a ritual, and we are here to worship.

"I was thinking that after we get up, we can figure out a plan to tackle that suitcase over the next two days, before we go back to Vesta's for dinner. I sense an urgency that only a purpose like uniting the realms can stir up," he says.

"Oh, right, I had already forgotten about that dinner." I say with a sheepish smile. I had forgotten about everything that was not him.

We lazily finish our breakfast, not leaving any pleasure untouched, untasted, or undone, and go downstairs to sit on the terrace floor with the suitcase between us so that we can spread out the documents.

"Do you mind if we begin with reading the prophecy this morning? It all happened so fast at Vesta's, I could not absorb all of it, and yesterday we were focused on diving right into the secrets of the suitcase. But I dreamed about the prophecy last night, it was calling to me with a song and a golden light. I was searching for it, trying to find it. When I finally found it, and opened it to read it, a bird flew out of the paper, and the paper vanished into thin air."

What does his dream mean?

He opens the prophecy, lays it before us, and reads it slowly. As he continues to read, I watch him blink twice. He looks at me with a new revelation. He looks down at our wrists and then back up at my face. He pauses and repeats the line aloud to himself, "replaced with something new, a vow around the wrist." He looks at me with awe, the same realization I had last night. "Do you think it is possible that we vowed a union that the prophecy is written about? Because I love you as deep as my hope and as wide as my faith. Do you believe this is about us? That our story was foreseen all those years ago?"

"I believe the power between us is a love that can defeat darkness and unite people. I think I have felt it since the first time I saw you, there were just so many questions about death and life to sort through, you know? I have always felt safe with you, even when I barely knew you, I felt as if I had always known you. When I made my vow yesterday, I pledged it with unwavering clarity and devotion, like it was the only next right thing I could ever choose to do."

He puts his hands around my cheeks and gently kisses me, and the wind uses every tree branch and leaf as a personal instrument, playing a song only the birds of the waters and sky know how to sing. I have never been this happy in all my life. He whispers earnestly through his kisses, "I love you beyond feelings and logic, I love you beyond space and time. I love you with a measure that I cannot even comprehend how to contain within my body. I love you beyond the realms and beyond death itself."

My breath catches with veneration, "Kyrie, I do not need the prophecy to know the power of our love, and of what enchantment began the day you found me. I want this no matter what happens in the realms, or what laws we have or have not broken, or what prophecies we fulfill. I want this love more than I want to be a ruler of anything.

If I am called by a prophecy, I will never do any of it without you by my side, my life-partner." And I kiss the top of his hands and hold them tight.

His eyes tell me everything as they let liquid love reply in agreement. I will never get over the way his lips and chin quiver when he is feeling so intensely from his heart. A heart that is released and set free, connected only to my own. We both smile with delight at what we know must be true: that somehow, this union resurrected both of us for a purpose greater than ourselves. This is the motivation that leads us to continue learning from the suitcase, so we are ready for whatever is ahead.

He pulls out the following paper and unfolds it in front of us. It is filled with lists of words in neat, cursive handwriting. We both look at it and gasp when we realize what it is.

Lashga Realm

Ruler's Power

Valray ~ instant travel

Wincot ~ power of song

Dashel ~ alchemy

Zenif ~ visionary seer

Traits of Downfall

Valray ~ delusion, negligence

Wincot ~ prejudiced,
    manipulative

Dashel ~ pride, foolishness

Zenif ~ greed, envy

Province Blessings

V ~ enchantment & legacy

W ~ luck & innovation

D ~ fair trade & hospitality

Z ~ abundance & rich in culture

Needed Antidotes

V ~ clarity & devotion

W ~ open-minded & trustworthy

D ~ humility, justice & mercy

Z ~ generosity & honor

Pallayes Realm

Ruler's Power

Kallos ~ invisibility cloak

Teahn ~ photographic
    memory

Clemen ~ instant healing

Amara ~ longevity

Province Blessings

K ~ hope & freedom to expand

T ~ intelligence & secure borders

C ~ resilience & peaceful unity

A ~ wealth & natural resources

Traits of Downfall

Kallos ~ resignation, apathy

Teahn ~ fear, aggression

Clemen ~ arrogant,
    controlling

Amara ~ impulsive, paranoid

Needed Antidotes

K ~ faith, fidelity

T ~ fortitude, kindness

C ~ meekness, joy

A ~ prudence, wisdom

Twenty-Three

{One hundred and one years before the present}

Corin Valray

I have been having visions of the future. It is the Zenif blood that courses within me, inherited from my mother's line. And being so close to death's door.

Vera Valray, my granddaughter, will be the last maiden in our Valray line for many generations. So, I have tried to teach her everything I know. The very enchantment that has defined our family for generations seems threatened by an arrogance that I cannot comprehend. These men, blinded by pride, refuse to acknowledge the sacred powers bestowed upon us. I am afraid that our magic, our enchantment, will be lost. These men see no need for it. What arrogance! What pride! To reject the powers given to this line from the beginning.

My grandmother taught me everything she knew when it became clear that I was next in line to inherit the seat. And I have tried tirelessly to teach Vera, but she is often distracted. Her gaze is beyond the horizon. She is natural, though. I call her my little mage. I hope that what she has learned will be used for good. I fear that all the deep feelings and emotions she embodies could easily erupt if not harnessed.

To Vera, I will pass down my Valray Oak necklace. I have hidden the last words of the prophecy that the Powers Above gave to me last night inside the pendant. I was to put them there for safekeeping. Vera will have them if she ever needs them. Her father has already arranged her betrothal to a man in line from Zenif, although I am afraid, she will not go willingly along with the plan. She is not one to let someone else write her fate. I sense a heavy secret veiled over her heart. A veil so tightly held that not even I can peer through. I do not know how she will cope with my death. I fear I will no longer be here when she needs me most. May the strength of our lineage flow through her, for the future seems ominous for Valray.

Arden

"We could study this for days," he says, amazed. I nod in agreement. It is a lot to take in; it feels like we just discovered the secrets of the realms. "Arden, we have these personal powers. This answers so many of my questions, but it also gives me more questions. I need to ask Vesta about this," he tells me.

"It is a good thing Vesta has a pure heart because who knows what someone like my father would have done with this information," I add. "Let me find the chart we found yesterday. I think they will make so much sense next to each other." I say as I look through the folded papers. I find the province chart and unfold it. We scan both side by side, and it is impressive how the industries, powers, and blessings all seem to fit together like someone created a master plan.

I cannot believe I really have power. I wish I had known about instant travel when I felt like a bird trapped in a cage in my previous life. But I wonder if I even had this power in my first life. Maybe I only have it now…maybe my destiny to be a ruler only began in this second life. It is a lot to sort out in my head.

"Look at this," Kyrie says, "Taryn is from the Wincot province. That must be why the song has the power to pull you towards it. It literally says, 'Come to Me.'"

I quietly wonder why it always turns me into a ghost, though. Kyrie's right: some questions get answered, but more questions form.

"Amara has the power of longevity, which sounds intriguing, and Zenith has seers. I wonder what that is like?" I ponder aloud.

"Look here," he points, "the Dashel line has the power of alchemy. Now that is one I would love to see."

"Look, my father's downfall of delusion and neglect is easy to see here…" I sadly admit, thinking about the Valray people, left orphaned.

"And somehow, I think your clarity and devotion is going to save Valray," he says.

"I do not know how I would even begin to save Valray. I do not understand how I would ever come to be its ruler."

"Arden, you have a source of immense power within you, more than just the power on this list. You have a power rooted deep into your core that brought you from death to life. This power has been entrusted to you for the sake of many, including mine. I think when you saw your father again, you became afraid that he could take that power away from you, because he conditioned you to give your power over to him. But yours is a power so deeply rooted in love, it cannot be taken from you. You would have to give it away, and you do not have to give it away anymore. I know the thought of facing Earl Menstus is terrifying, but I have a sense that if you stand in your power without the fear of it being taken from you and have the resolve to not hand it over or submit, you will understand how to fulfil the prophecy. When I saw the terror come over you that day, I trusted it. I trusted that you knew something that I could only imagine, and I concluded that if I did not do something to protect you, I might lose you. I was prepared to end him with that dagger, and that was even before I could feel- before our vow. You are too strong to need to be rescued or saved, but I will always defend and protect you with my life."

My eyes fill up. I remember it all, especially the terror, but more than anything, I remember feeling protected. I reach out and hold his shoulders, feeling his strength in my hands. I am safe here. I have the realization that I never had less power than my father; he just rendered me powerless as he conditioned me to hand my power over to him, which gave him double and left me with none. I need to learn to protect my power. I am my own bastion now, a fortress, a stronghold unto myself. The citadel within me will never be sacked again. I make this vow to myself.

I have broken out of
My prison cell
And they have sent out
The guards and the dogs
To find me.
But I will never be
In captivity again.
They will not bring me back,
I will outrun them.
My secret is patience.
I have been waiting all these years
For this moment.
I finally know my power
And how to use it.

"No one has ever believed in me the way that you do. You inspire me to believe in myself, thank you." I say in deepest earnest. After our long gaze into the knowing that resides behind our eyes, we both look back at the charts in front of us.

I smile at him and say, "Devotion and fidelity sound really nice together."

"They really do. It is a powerful combination." Smiling back at me, he adds, "Now I know that the way to keep Kallos from completely crumbling into downfall is to have faith that the province can be restored to something even greater than before."

"Kyrie, that is what you did, when you found me, you had faith that if I agreed to help, I would be given a new life. You believed that a corpse could somehow rise and help save many." I tell him.

"You are right, I never resigned to giving in to that spell. I always had faith, and it led me to you." He smiles and kisses me tenderly.

I look back at the paper and see the word *enchantment*, and I point to it. "Kyrie, look...this explains my hair and eyes changing. I never knew there to be any enchantment in Valray. I wonder what it would look like across the province. I can only imagine."

We both take in the list again.

"Did your sister experience any healing or relief from the spell after she married into the Clemen province?" I ask, thinking back on our conversation the day I arrived.

"Yes, the effects of the spell stopped progressing for her. She had not lost her feelings at the time she was married, so her condition never got to the extent of everyone else's here. So, it is fair to say that marrying into the Clemen line saved her. I guess I can understand why she was scared to return, and risk the spell affecting her again," he says.

I wonder if I will ever meet her. Will we be friends?

"I really hope one day that we get to travel and meet the rulers and heirs of the other provinces and see some of these powers and blessings in action," Kyrie says, with a faraway look in his eyes. "I can just imagine what it would be like if we could trade more easily across the realms, what it would be like to enjoy all of these blessings and products from each province."

"Do you know anyone else from the other provinces, besides Taryn and Vesta? I lived such a sheltered life, the three of you are the only people I know outside of Valray."

"I have family members in some of the other provinces, like my sister and her husband in Clemens, but we have never been close. I have only met him twice, but he is a good person. Everyone self-protected and kept to themselves after the spell was cast here, not wanting to provoke Menstus. Even my father's extended family in Teahn was too scared to reach out and offer help. My cousin has recently taken the seat there, but I have not seen him in years. Everyone I have ever been close to is in this province, but a lot of them have already died. My life has also been limited, the spell made everything so complicated, it kept us in a bubble."

"I am so sorry for all of the losses," I offer. I think about the two of us surviving childhood, me in a cage and him in a bubble. Both of us long for freedom.

Then, a vital question finally strikes me, "Do you think the spell being broken off of you now means that it is broken off of the whole province?"

Twenty-Four

{Presently}

Elspeth

Sometimes in life, there are moments when the perfect becomes flawed, like when the freshly laid wood floor becomes gouged by the pull of heavy furniture, when a delicate new garment's thread is pulled, and an unrepairable hole appears, when the treasured porcelain platter becomes chipped, and the polished metal gets its first unforgiving dent. Then one is forced to live with the memory of the once perfect, now marred with the unwelcome imperfection. For me, that moment was my wedding day. My once-perfect life was irrevocably tainted by the man I was forced to take out of duty.

When he groveled in on his knees with his hideous, drunken confession, a chilling certainty seized me. I extinguished his pathetic existence with intense purpose and intention, and then I grieved my daughter for the next thirty years. Those decades were the black hole inside my history. They still make me shudder.

I have had plenty of time to think about my life since I have been lying here facing my last days. And what a long life I have had. Longevity. A blessing and a curse. I never did find my true love; never had a need or desire to trade that longevity in for the tender comfort to age alongside a beloved partner. I have always been on my own, doing it all by myself. Sure, I have indulged in the company of lovers, but for my own pleasure. Florin was the only soul I ever allowed behind this mask of Sovran ruler, beyond the shadows of my guarded heart.

Arden

The surprise of this new thought catches him off guard. "I have been so caught up and overcome in the excitement of feeling again and falling madly in love, I did not stop to think if it had a wider effect. Would you come with me to my mother's estate to see what might be happening in the province? I cannot believe I did not think of it sooner!"

"Yes, of course. Let us pack this all back up before we go." I neatly fold and gather the documents and hand them to Kyrie. He locks the straps into place and finds a place to hide the suitcase.

"My mother's estate is in the center of the province. It will not take long to get there," he explains as we get into the glider and take off.

"How long have you been in your own villa? I was surprised that you did not share the same residence with her," I ask.

"I moved out here three years ago. I needed my own space. After my sister married, it left me under a microscope at my mother's estate. My father and I did not always see eye to eye on how things should be handled, with the province or my mother's health. I needed the freedom to come and go while I was seeking answers without having to debate with my father each time. And since my mother's health has declined even further, they wanted it very quiet there. I was afraid to fade away in silence; I still wanted a chance to live my life and not lose a second more of what had already been stolen."

I can tell it is still hard for him to talk about it. "Who is running the province now?" I ask.

"My mother's Regent, he has an office inside her estate, and everything passes through him. The updated legal contract of succession states that the province seat goes to me if my mother is still unconscious from the spell when I turn twenty-six, which is in six months, and Canton will step down as Regent. It also states that I will succeed to the seat immediately upon her time of death. Either way, you will be my partner in ruling the Kallos province, whenever the time comes."

"Wow…that's soon," I say, realizing his role more clearly.

He continues, "Canton will notice the bracelets and know about the vow as soon as he sees us. It is the power of Redamancy; the vow is made in private, but afterwards it becomes obvious to all who see the couple. It is the opposite to the large wedding ceremonies in Lashga, where the vow begins publicly, and then becomes private. The Redamancy begins in private and grows more obvious in public afterwards. We will never be able to hide or deny that we are partnered."

When we arrive, I take in the beauty of this estate against the scenic backdrop. I did not know any location could rival the beauty of Kyrie's villa—it is magnificent. We enter the front entrance, and a slight man approaches. When he notices the bracelets, I see the awareness travel across his mind, and then he bows with respect.

"Congratulations, Kyrie. This is big news." He turns to me with an extended hand and says, "I am Canton, Reown's Regent. It is a pleasure to meet the woman who is Kyrie's chosen life partner."

I extend my hand and reply, "Thank you." As I watch my hand raise to his lips, he says, "It is nice to meet you as well."

Kyrie cuts in before Canton can ask any more questions. "Canton, have there been any changes in the province, regarding the spell? Have you heard of any news?"

"Well, that is just the thing, I was on my way to your villa to speak to you privately and discuss the new developments. I was shocked, but relieved, when I saw you arrive."

"Let us go in and you can tell me everything." Kyrie motions for us to head to the nearest set of chairs in the front den, which is used for official meetings.

"Yesterday evening, your mother opened her eyes, sat up, and called for help. I rushed in, and her hand was holding her heart, and she said she was feeling immense pain. She feared the new and unexpected sensations."

I squeeze Kyrie's hand, and he holds tightly to mine. I can almost feel his pulse as it matches the sound of my own in my ears. Kyrie tells Canton to continue.

"I tried to calm her. We could both hear this faint whooshing and looping sound coming from her chest, and we both knew this was the moment everyone had been waiting twenty-two years for. She said that you must have found a way to break the spell."

Tears gather at the edges of my eyes. I will never forget the look on Kyrie's face at this moment.

"There is one thing, though, that I was not sure how to manage, and it's why I am so relieved you are here." Canton begins. "She has been asking for your father, and I did not know how to tell her the truth. I wanted you to be able to tell her yourself."

"Of course, thank you, I understand," Kyrie replies. "This is going to be an incredibly difficult conversation."

"If you do not mind me asking, how did you break the spell?" Canton boldly asks.

"Love," Kyrie replies. "We broke it with love. And it sounds like my mother awakened while we made the Redamancy Vow."

Canton lets out a sigh as his hand goes to his heart, adding, "I have always believed in the vow's power, although I have never experienced it myself."

I appreciate this softer side of Canton and offer a sincere, "Thank you."

"Oh! And Sir," Canton begins again, "Now that we are discussing everything, I am just realizing the gravity of word getting back to Earl Menstus about your mother. Do you agree that we should not make any announcements until we have a solid plan in place? I am just not sure what that lunatic will do when he finds out the curse has been broken."

"Most definitely. On that point, I agree with you." Kyrie states firmly and squeezes my hand again.

We stand up and begin our slow walk to the east wing, where his mother's room is. As we pass a large mirror, I no longer recognize myself as the young, naive, caged, forsaken corpse-bride that I was. I see a brave, strong woman, fiercely loved and protected, who will one day help rule a province, and I know this is only the beginning.

Twenty-Five

My Lady,

How patiently I wait each day for the spell to be broken, and for your return to us. I have lost count now of the months, forgive me. I am terrified that you will never wake, and my letters will remain unread.

The province is struggling. The people are scared. Kyrie is trying to hold it all together, but I see the fear in his eyes.

When he returned from Vaxxa without Juris, I knew we were reaching the end. My only consolation is that you do not know yet what has happened.

I still have not had any word from Deirdras. You were right. She has not returned. I cannot say that I blame her.

Your loyal Regent,

Canton

Arden

I can sense Kyrie's anxiousness about speaking with his mother for the first time in many years. We turn the corner, and he knocks gently on the first door on the right. Canton tells us to go ahead and enter. Kyrie walks in first, and I know the minute his mother recognizes him, her loud wail is unmistakable. It is gutting how painful it sounds. I stifle my small cry within. It is not lost on me, the memory of my own mother and the last time I saw her. I stay a bit behind and watch; the emotions are so intense.

"Hello, mother. It is me, Kyrie. I am here." He walks over to the side of the bed where she is propped up and sits next to her, then leans over to hold her in his arms. They both begin weeping, and I am afraid of being swallowed up in the sorrow that pulses through the dark room. Her sadness is palpable, hanging low and heavy in the air. It matches the heavy brocade fabrics and wallpaper, all colored in maroon and umber.

"It is okay, mother, I am here. I love you," he says a few times over. He gently rocks her, and she sobs.

"Oh, I have been gone for too long. My life has been robbed from me. I do not think I can do this," she says.

"I know mother," Kyrie tells her. "But I am so thankful that we all have a second chance to live again now with the spell broken. I am grateful."

"Well, I do not! I am angry, and I do not want to feel this pain! This is no way to live after all these years!" Her emotions quickly heightened.

"I know it hurts right now, but it will get better as you let the grief wash over you like waves. You just need to work through the pain. It will take time to get used to all these new feelings," he offers gently.

"No! I do not want to work through my feelings; this pain is too great. I do not have any more time to waste on pain. I have already lost too much time! I do not want to live like this! I want the life I had before the spell was cast. Where is your father? Why has he not come yet?" She demands.

The air in the room changes as if it were vacuumed out. I brace myself against the dresser for when the news hits her. When my fingers grip the wood and sink into a carved swirl design, I realize that I am holding onto the wooden dresser handcrafted in Valray. Just like me, it crossed the forbidden divide and traveled through the bypass to be here in Kallos.

"Mother, I need to tell you something, and it is going to be very difficult to hear." Kyrie takes a deep breath and then continues. "Father and I traveled to Vaxxa last year to look for the Book of Unbinding to find the cure that breaks the spell. We were caught, and father was taken away. I did not get his body back to bury him. I am so sorry." His chin is quivering as the tears of sorrow trail down his cheekbones.

She reaches up to grab the necklace around her neck and holds onto the pendant tightly. Her screams echo throughout the room and the hallway. It is more than any of us expected.

"I have lost everything! I have nothing left!" She wails. "Everything has been taken from me! It is all gone! It was all for nothing!"

I see the wave of surprise across Kyrie's face as those words strike hard. And then her screams of pain intensify. Her hands are over her chest, and her eyes are wild. I feel panic about what she might do next. She climbs out of bed and starts frantically pacing in a figure-eight pattern, still holding her chest, shouting, "I want my life back! I cannot live with this pain! Make it stop! Make the pain stop! I do not want to feel this pain! I did not lose twenty-two years only to wake up to more pain and loss!"

Kyrie slowly drops his head and closes his eyes. I am not sure he expected her to revolt against this new reality. I can imagine that he thought she would be as happy and grateful as he is. I watch him process the fact that she does not see him as part of a life worth living.

> Some parts of the heart
> Are icy cold
> Barren lands
> With fences closed in.

On one of her frantic loops, she spots me standing there and screams. It makes me jump, and my heartbeat is thrumming in my ears. I try to push down the panic that is creeping up my body.

"Who is she?" Reown asks accusingly, her dark purple eyes upon me, and I take in her terrible beauty.

"Mother, this is Arden, the woman I have made the Redamancy Vow with. It is what broke the spell yesterday."

"Where is she from?" She asks slowly as she takes another step towards me. "She clearly does not look like anyone from Kallos. No one here has black hair."

I do not think my heart can beat any faster. It is like I am back in my father's study, like a prey courageously dangling in front of its predator. It will take a long time to recover from the terror that I feel at this moment.

"Arden is from the Valray province, in Lashga." Kyrie admits.

It is at this moment that she stops in her tracks, turns to him, and pauses long enough to say, "How dare you! You know it is forbidden!" Her gaze towards him is piercing. I have the sudden realization that if there were no spell, and she were healthy, she would have hand-picked his partner for him. He would never have been given the freedom to choose for himself.

> It is hard to love
> When you are carrying
> Around within you
> A great war.

"How dare you choose someone outside of Kallos! Who arranged this?" she yells at him.

"No one mother, I chose it for myself. I made the Vow with the woman that I love. I did what I hope you would have done as well!" he says in defense.

Her eyes go wild, and her hand grabs her chest as she lets out a morbid cry of pain and then collapses to the floor. Kyrie jumps up and goes down to where she is, bending over her, calling for her, gently shaking her. He puts his ear to her chest and does not move or take a breath. He waits, listening, hoping for a sound. Then his eyes close, and he crumbles into tears as he starts the compressions on her chest, begging for her to come to. I watch his desperation. Canton comes to kneel next to her and places his mouth on hers and breaths in rhythm with the compressions. After many minutes, he places his fingers on her neck, checking for a pulse. A single tear rolls down Canton's face. He looks at Kyrie and slowly shakes his head I watch this whole scene play out as if I were not in the room with them, but as if I were a bird watching from above. It is surreal, and I grieve that it is a scene burned into my memory, one that may never fade.

It is quiet and still. They are both in shock. I can imagine that they are both realizing the shift in power, from Canton to Kyrie, and the air is humming with a thousand unspoken questions.

Canton breaks the silence first, "I am sorry for your loss, my lord," with a respectful head bow.

Kyrie nods his head once in earnest and says, "And I am sorry for yours; you've been a faithful Regent and friend to my mother for many years."

Canton nods, acknowledging the sentiment. "I can help you lift her back into the bed, my lord, where she can lay in wait until the proper arrangements have been made."

"Thank you, Canton." And with that, they place her body back on the bed and cover her up.

"What would you have me do next sir?" Canton asks.

"I need a moment to come up with a plan that protects everyone in Kallo, for everyone's safety. We are not prepared to battle Menstus while the seat is empty," Kyrie replies.

"I understand, my lord. I will be ready for your next instructions," Canton offers, bows, and then slips out of the room.

Kyrie is standing at the bedside, just staring down at her in disbelief. I walk over to where he is and reach for his hand. We both stand there in silence. I can feel the sorrow pulsing through him. He turns and pulls me into his arms and lets his cry pour out, his cheek resting on the top of my head. There is nothing to do but let this wave of pain crash over us.

"I am just so sad that she could not see the new life she had been given, the opportunity to finally know me," he says as he begins to choke on some tears. "I was just a boy, and I watched her fade away for so long, but I always had hope that I would break the spell so that she could come back to me, and know me, and love me. I waited for this moment for so long, and it was like she did not even see me. I felt so invisible…like I could not compare to the size of her loss."

I just hold him; there is more that needs to flow out.

"I am scared. There is so much about ruling the province that I do not know yet. And I am terrified of facing Menstus when he finds out that my mother died. What will I do when he shows up here?"

I ask the realms above for clarity.

"Kyrie, if we had never found the other paper from the suitcase, I would tell you that I do not know. But since we do know the secrets of each province, I know that you must have faith. Your hope has been a special power, and has saved you this far, but your faith and fidelity are going to prevent the downfall. It is understandable that your mother suffered incredible pain, more than she could handle, but any more resignation sweeping through the province must be counteracted with faith. You will need to inspire your people to live, despite the grief they may begin to feel now that the spell is broken."

He squeezes me tighter and holds me steady for a moment longer. "You are right, I cannot lose faith, even in this incredible sadness. I need to invite my people to rise and let love conquer evil."

"It is a bold move, but it is your best option. And I will be by your side."

He kisses my forehead.

"I know we do not have the luxury of time, but I would still like to go to Vesta's tomorrow and even ask for their help. I know if we do not show up, they will worry since there is no other way to communicate with them."

"Okay," I agree.

Before we walk out of the room, Kyrie places a kiss on top of his mother's forehead. "I love you, mother. I hope you are at peace now, and free of all pain. I promise to rule with fidelity, hope and faith."

He lifts the pendant, resting visibly now on her neck, to look at it closely. "I have always wondered what it was. She was so private. She never let me touch or look at it when I was younger. She would just tuck it back under her dress when I asked to see it."

I bend down to look at it too. I instinctively react to my instant recognition of the image and I blurt it out before I even realize what I am saying. "It is the Valray Oak, the tree on our Sovran crest. Only the maidens in the Valray line receive them." We both look at each other, confused.

I draw my hand up to my collarbone and realize I no longer have mine.

"What is it?" He asks.

"Mine is missing. The last time I saw it was on my wedding day. Why would Reown, of all people, wear this necklace?"

"It does not make any sense." Kyrie lets out a sigh of defeat. "I am sad this is another mysterious thing I will never know about my mother. There is so much I will never know. I know this sounds crazy, but I do not think I should bury her with the Valray crest. Do you think it is okay if I remove it?"

"It is your call. I do not know if anyone would ever know the difference."

He carefully removes it and places it into his pocket. On our way out of the hall, Kyrie meets with Canton. He asks him to make the necessary arrangements to prepare his mother for burial. He also urges Canton to invite everyone in the province to gather at the center arena the morning after tomorrow. "We need to keep her death a secret until everyone is there, and then I will announce it to everyone at the same time, and we will bury her."

"I understand," Canton replies.

"We will hold the Ceremony of the Sovran Seat the day after we bury her." Kyrie adds.

"Yes, my lord," Canton says as he bows and exits.

We leave the estate and travel back home to our villa.

Twenty-Six

{Presently}

Aster

There is talk about a revolution. I almost hope for it. For my father's sake. I want his revenge just as much as he does.

And I am loyal to another "father" as well. Earl Menstus. I want him to have his compensation, because then maybe I will have mine.

I want them both to have what they want. Because in the end, I just want the freedom to create my own happiness. They are all that I have left. My mother and sister are both dead.

I miss my time in Vaxxa, it was the last time I knew happiness. What an incredible city. I was able to explore it each day, not wanting to leave. But I did not know my mother was waiting for my return. I blame myself for what has happened to her. I should have never left her. And now, I cannot believe she is gone. I never got to say good-bye.

Arden

It is late, and we are both weary. Kyrie brews us each a cup of hot tea, and we curl up on the terrace together to watch the end of the sunset transition into the night sky.

"Why do you think there was such a big difference between the spell breaking for you and for your mother?" I ask, still trying to comprehend what happened this afternoon.

"Honestly, even though I am shocked, I am not surprised."

"What do you mean?"

"I do not remember a day since this spell started where I was not mentally training in some way, even when I was young. I always had faith that I could beat it somehow, so I was always coaching myself through ways to hold onto memories of feelings for as long as I could. I practiced every day whatever advice the elders would give me. Especially the power of love, and the inner flame of self-love. I kept it alive. I kept my hope alive. I told myself that no matter how painful it would be, I would get through the spell breaking and thrive again one day. I tried to convince my parents to do the same, telling them often about my daily practices, but they were not interested. It is why I needed to move out on my own. I knew what I was doing was crucial, and I did not want to waste my energy each day trying to defend it to people who thought it was foolish. I think what we saw in my mother today was years of resignation being blasted awake by years of both repressed and suppressed emotions. She was completely unprepared for what hit her."

"I am truly inspired by your perseverance all these years. I saw you face the pain and agony of the spell breaking with such strength and grace. Thank you for never giving up. It is like your younger version had so much fidelity to your future self. I am grateful for the little boy inside of you that kept that flame burning, because he helped re-ignite my flame as well."

We watch the stars turn on, some even shooting across the sky, and then climb into bed. We both have trouble sleeping tonight. His waves of grief for all that was lost come in and out, and I try to work through the familiar feelings her accusations triggered in me. But we hold tight to each other, feeling grief together, and we do not let go.

I am relieved when I see the sunrise. I dreamed last night that I was approaching Reown on her deathbed. Her eyes opened, and she turned her head towards me. She then grabbed my arm, her nails digging into my skin, and suddenly, she turned into Menstus. This time when I screamed, though, my voice was loud and shrill. I turned into a giant bird and flew out the window.

Though her body
Is soft and small,
Her voice is strong
And sure,
Emboldened even.
Patience is her secret.
She will be paid
Her due,
She will be compensated,
And there will be justice,
Maybe even vengeance.
She will point
And they will nod.
She will whisper
And they will understand.
The wood of the wheel
Submits in her hands,
As she reads the horizon
And smells the storm.
She speaks the language of the water
And holds the secrets of the air
Behind her smile.

Kyrie is up before me, with fresh, hot coffee ready. I awaken to its smell and smile, and I can experience a small delight amid this grief.

"Are you up for the suitcase today?" I ask tentatively.

"I think so. It might be a nice way to pass the time. It is like we are in the in-between of something passing away, and something not yet born. It is the kind of transition that makes time feel restless."

We sit on the terrace with our hot coffee, and I open the suitcase and say, "This might be the last time we get to sit and do this for a while. We will have a lot of new responsibilities to tend to soon."

I pull out a large, folded map. Kyrie helps me gently lay out the old paper. It is thick but still feels fragile.

"It is the map of Olstar," Kyrie tells me, recognizing it at once. "There is a large one hanging in Vaxxa's library. I looked at it while I was there." He points to the middle, where the bypass between Lashga and Pallayes is currently located. "This is where Claudegus lived, right here in the middle of Olstar. His estate is no longer there; they said it just disappeared when he died."

I notice the notes written around the edge of the map and read them aloud.

"Legend says that after the realm split apart, his estate evaporated into the bypass. When his daughters crossed through the bypass for the first time to see each other again, they said that the spirit of Claudegus was still there, holding the two realms together. Legend says that one day, when the realms unite, his original estate will be released from the bypass wall to become the new land bridge connecting everyone together again, and then his spirit will be free to join the Powers Above."

"Wow, that is so beautifully tragic, almost poetic," Kyrie says, still captivated by the vision. "Do you really think we have been passing through Claudegus' spirit each time we cross through the bypass?"

"I cannot decide if it is comforting or if I want to shudder," I reply, trying to conceive of the idea. "I can see now why he would be longing for the time of the prophecy to unfold and the realms uniting if it means he will finally be free. That is incredible. We are less alone in all this somehow, like we truly have help there, guiding us along," I say, captured by the thought of his presence.

"Look at this envelope. It is addressed to the Albatross," Kyrie says, handing me a small, sealed envelope. I open it and pull out a note with a uniquely beautiful handwriting. I read it aloud,

"Love is always the best-case scenario; it is the most powerful alchemy. It is an energy source as well as the map. Pure love provides benefit and pleasure. When the

clarity of love is at work, it creates treasures from within. It cannot be contained, and it is always a risk. Love is a stretching that is always begging to extend more for both the sake of self and the other. When the call to love is answered, the scales are reset and brought into balance. Love is a light that breaks any darkness."

I look up at Kyrie, and I can see that he is as struck by its profound beauty as I am. "Kyrie, I have the instinct that this is more than just poetry. It is instructions on how to proceed with everything that is about to happen. I do not understand it all, but it is somehow connected to the prophecy, since it is addressed to the Albatross. And I still do not understand how or why it is me, but I will receive any guidance I can find," I say, still in awe of this discovery.

"I believe in you, I believe in us., and I believe in the power of love," he says, grabbing my hands and looking into my eyes. "We have so much ahead of us, and all of it is a great unknown. It might be difficult, but we will navigate it together, using these instructions."

"I want to do that with you," I reply, "and somehow, this note tells me we are not alone. This new love that I have experienced with you tells me that there is truth in these words, and even though I do not understand it all, it is possible."

We spend the morning talking over what we find in the suitcase and the afternoon by the pool. Later, we pack up our things before leaving for dinner, knowing it is our last night here. We decide to leave the suitcase at the villa, but Kyrie wraps it in his invisibility cloak. I choose to keep the prophecy, and this new love note in my pocket, to always have them with me from now on.

Twenty-Seven

{Three months before the present}

Taryn,

We regret to inform you that your right to the Sovran seat of Wincot has been revoked and given over to your brother Barrow. You have lost all rights and privileges in this province until you forsake your engagement to that woman.

Your parents,

Berel and Mavis Wincot

Arden

When we arrive at Vesta's, the first thing she notices is my hair and eyes, and then our bracelets. For the first time since I have met her, she is speechless. Her expression is so priceless I can hardly read it, but I am fairly sure it is excitement mixed with…relief? When her voice finally forms words, she says, "The Redamancy Vow! That is amazing…I still remember my parents' bracelets and their story. May I look at them?"

We both put our wrists out for her to behold the golden bands. Then she says, "The vow around the wrist," and looks at us. "This is another part of the prophecy unfolding." I nod my head yes to let her know we have realized it, too.

The most significant relief I feel is when Taryn walks up, and it does not stir up butterflies. I finally feel at home in my body and steady next to Kyrie. I am finally secure and confident.

"Thank you," I say. "It happened very unexpectedly for both of us, but this love…" as I motion to the space between Kyrie and me, "broke the spell off of the Kallos province."

Vesta sits down in the chair near us to take it all in. "Wow, the tears of the Valray maiden really did break the spell."

"Well," Kyrie says, "we learned that it is not the actual tears themselves…it is the love for the brokenhearted Valray maiden, and her love in return."

"Wow…you two are the only ones who know the cure of how this spell is truly broken, and you discovered it together. I cannot wait for my parents to hear this story. All the legends used to be my bedtime stories, and I know them all by heart."

"We also found the paper that lists the powers and downfalls of each province. I cannot believe we have been able to learn this valuable information. I will never be able to thank your father enough for giving us the privilege to know these secrets," I say.

"It is truly what makes our two realms magical. Claudegus divided up all his powers and bestowed equal portions of his unique magic and province blessings upon each of his eight grandchildren, who all became crowned Sovran rulers. The catch is that the ruler's personal power only works when the heart of the destined ruler is genuinely good, like Claudegus's. And the province's blessings are only possible if the heart of the ruler is good. A ruler must possess the antidotes needed to unlock the blessings for the land and its people. He wanted them to always be motivated towards goodness." I blink, trying to absorb this new information; it is everything. I know I need to memorize the list and keep it forever.

"This is a lot to process…because I have the power of invisibility, and no one else in my family does, or has ever talked about it in stories from the past. And Arden has the power of instant travel. Vesta, are you saying these powers are signs that we are destined rulers?" Kyrie asks sincerely.

"Yes, and not just that, but with a goodness in your hearts that Claudegus decided is worth entrusting the powers to."

Our eyes widen.

"I am not surprised you are from Valray, and you are from Kallos," as she looks at each of us. "Valray was the first born of Lashga, and the first granddaughter. Kallos was the first born of Pallayes, and the first grandson. He had a special anointing for those two provinces to work together and create an expanded legacy that Claudegus himself would be proud of. My father told me that the exquisite Valray industry of hand carved furniture represents the legacy, it is supposed to be substantial and solid, lasting through time, and passed down with the generations. As for Kallos, the industry of spices, coffee, chocolate, well those are products that are meant to travel far and wide, like the blessing of expansion. The unique skilled industry of each province is a physical representation of the anointed blessings of the province."

Kyrie and I look at each other. Both wood and spice come in many colors and varieties, like the people in each of our provinces, and both are ingredients used to create beautiful things. Solid wood furniture is meant to endure time like a legacy, and spices are meant to be shared and enjoyed as lasting memories.

We have so much to talk about regarding what Vesta just taught us. I am always amazed at how much she knows. This is just the beginning of understanding something significant if we are going to be Sovran rulers.

Before I forget, I ask her, "What is the name of the woman in the family portrait standing behind Claudegus and his daughters?"

She replies, "Her name has not been written in the legends, but she is the great love that Claudegus traded his longevity to be with. His grief from her passing caused the original fault line across Olstar, the line where the bypass is today."

But I sense she knows more. She always knows more.

"Thank you for sharing this with us. It is a lot to suddenly realize, but we are so grateful that you have been willing to teach us what you have learned from your father," Kyrie says.

She smiles and returns the gratitude with a knowing nod.

"The other reason we wanted to come tonight is to tell you that my mother has died, and things are about to quickly change for us."

"What?" Vesta asks, surprised. "What happened?"

Kyrie answers, "When the spell was broken, the sudden painful feelings of loss and grief were too intense for her, it attacked her heart. It happened very suddenly, within moments of being able to speak with her for the first time in years. She was so consumed with her loss; it is like it just swallowed her whole. But it was when she heard that I broke the forbidden rule and made the vow with someone from the Lashga realm, that she collapsed. It is as if she could not live with the fact that I chose love over protocol, or that I made the decision myself for that matter."

Twenty-Eight

Dear Solange Menstus,

I hope this message finds you well. I am reaching out to you from the Healing Clinic in Clemen about your son, Earl Menstus, who was delivered to our care a week ago. I want to express my deep concern for his condition, which is currently critical. Unfortunately, he will require an extended stay with us as we focus on his recovery.

I encourage you to visit him if you feel it is appropriate, but please understand that he may not be aware of your presence. If you have any questions or need support during this difficult time, please don't hesitate to reach out.

Take care,

Dr. Mercer

Arden

I still feel a strange guilt for crossing the forbidden divide and falling in love with her son, the news that ended her life. I do not know if this peculiar feeling will ever pass, but it is so familiar to how I felt growing up. The irony is that this love broke the spell for her, but it was too much for her to bear. Our truth was too heavy for her to grasp and hold. I somehow feel responsible for her death, even though I know it is not true. I am also angry that she could not receive the gift of a new life that Kyrie had worked so hard to give her.

"Oh, Kyrie, I am so sorry. That is terrible," as she stands and hugs him. Then, to my surprise, Taryn does too.

"We have a lot to sort out very quickly, I am to be crowned the new ruler very soon, and we are trying not to garner Menstus's attention. My father said Menstus would show up to take over Kallos as soon as my mother died."

"I understand," Vesta says with concern.

"At least we were given this note," I say as I pull it out of my pocket and hand it to her to read.

"Was this in the suitcase?" she asks, and I nod yes. She continues, "I have never seen it before. You do realize that it must have been put there after we gave the suitcase to you." Even she is surprised. I do not try to understand how a new paper got into the suitcase. It is not that I do not want to know; I have just come to accept that my new life is now part of the beautiful, fantastic.

"I am not really sure what to think, but it feels important," I reply as I look around, finally noticing the suitcases. "Are you guys planning to leave?" I ask.

Vesta answers, "We have decided to head back to the Pallayes realm. The announcement of your father's death has not been announced publicly to the province yet, but somehow the people know, and there is fear in the air. There are also rumors of revolution. Some of the neighbors have said that Menstus and Aster have been seen together around the main parts of the province center, and at the main house. No one is sure what is going to happen. Our plan is to leave early in the morning, so we do not get trapped here."

This catches me off guard. I close my eyes and take a deep breath of relief. My sister is alive and back in Valray.

"Well, if you would like to come to the Ceremony of the Sovran Seat, it will be the morning after tomorrow.

You're always welcome in Kallos. We would be happy to have trusted friends there with us," Kyrie offers.

Vesta and Taryn glance at each other as if they are interested in something. "Thank you. We are open to a lot of new opportunities right now," Taryn replies.

Vesta asks, "How does this work with the Redamancy Vow since it cannot be hidden? Are you about to announce that Arden Valray is alive?"

"Yes." Kyrie replies with no hesitation. "I want everyone to know that this love has broken the spell, and that she is my equal, even on the seat at Kallos. I realize the risk that I am taking."

I look at him and see my home. I will never tire of trying to return love in full measure.

"Wait, you're going to announce Arden as your co-ruler?" Taryn asks.

"Yes," he says proudly.

"You two are about to make history…there has never been a ruler in either realm who has made such a bold declaration, much less to have a co-ruler from a different realm. That would have been forbidden. I do not want to miss this," she says as she turns and looks at Taryn, an invitation along with a plea in her expression.

"I agree," Taryn replies.

I look at Taryn, and for the first time, I can see him becoming a dear friend. Without the distraction of forsaken longing, I can truly appreciate him. I am suddenly thankful that Taryn has found love with Vesta. I know it has transformed him.

"Thank you," I say with all sincerity. "It will be comforting to know that you two are there." Kyrie smiles and agrees. I look over to Vesta. She is still the loveliest woman I have ever seen, and I am so grateful that she claimed me from the beginning, even in death. She never feared me, but she never needed to. I always felt safe with her. Her pure heart lights her from within, and anyone in her presence can feel it. I understand more each time I am near her why Taryn easily gave up the Wincot seat for her and how he fell in love so quickly after my death. I would have fallen in love with her, too.

Then I remember the question I want to ask Taryn. I look over at him, straight into his green eyes, "Taryn…were you ever told what the alliance agreement was between our parents when they made our betrothal?"

He pauses and looks at me as if he knows this will hurt. "I do not know the specifics, but your mother paid a large investment sum into one of our newest innovations in exchange for taking you out of Valray and ensuring that you never returned."

It takes tremendous effort not to let this news crush me from every side. "I just do not understand, and I am afraid I will never know…did she hate me? Or was she trying to protect me?"

"I am sorry, I do not have more of an explanation of why she did, but Arden…" This is the first time I have heard him say my name. "I just need you to know that I was genuinely happy to marry you, because of you, not because of your mother's investment. After my parents cut me out because I chose to marry Vesta, instead of being a dutiful son available to make another alliance, I understood how much they were willing to use me for their own gain. So, I can empathize a little bit with how you are feeling."

I look at him and nod with gratitude for his honesty and compassion. It is so intense to hear him talk about his original desire to marry me before I died. At least I know the feeling was once mutual, and I understand why his song had so much power over me. I want to ask him if he ever wonders about the 'what if?' What if I had not died? Does he ever wonder? But I need to change the subject, or I will crumble to pieces from the mixed cocktail of emotions I just swallowed down hard.

"Vesta, have you heard anything from your parents?" I ask, with sincere concern for these mythical people I have only imagined meeting, trying to keep my voice steady, but I know Kyrie has noticed my shakiness.

"No, there is no way to communicate with them where they are, but I know in my heart they are safe and well. I can feel it. It is the first time I have had this peace since the day before he was taken."

What would it feel like to have that kind of connection with my parents? I cannot grasp it. It is too far beyond the reach of even my sizable imagination.

We finish the meal and I am relieved that I was able to eat in front of them this time and enjoy it. We make our final arrangements for the day after tomorrow, say our goodbyes, and wish them luck for their upcoming trip. When we return home, we lie in bed, realizing this is our last night at the villa. Tomorrow, the Kallos estate will become our new home.

Kyrie asks me, "Are you ok? I imagine it was hard to hear about it for the first time."

"What part?" I ask.

"The part when Taryn shared about how he felt about marrying you. I know you have never had a chance to talk about it. I know it must still hurt, that loss."

I roll over and face him, recognizing his vulnerability. I can hear in his voice that he is worried about me. I can also sense that he is asking for assurance. I want to tell him the truth and secure him.

"It was bittersweet to hear it. Sometimes, for a fleeting moment, when I see them together, I wonder what it would have been like if I had not died. But in the next moment, I look at you, and I see my whole world. You are the only one I ever want to be with for the rest of my life." The tears well up just at the thought of how those intense feelings are still as true now as they were the day we made our vow. "Taryn may have been the loss of my old life, but you, Kyrie, are the great love of my new life, and I am so grateful you found me and believed in me. Your hope brought me back to life, and your love has completely changed me. It gives me the courage to keep choosing to live each day as fully as I can."

"I love you, " he says, wrapping me up in his arms and taking me to a place where grief cannot reach me. Tonight, I surrender all the what-ifs of the past. I never want to live in a moment where I cannot have this with him.

Twenty-Nine

{Four years before the present}

Deirdras,

I continue thinking about our time together during your family's last visit to Clemen. Although you have left the province, you have not left my thoughts. I would love nothing more than your return here, for more time together, to continue the meaningful conversations we had on our walks. If you feel the same as I do, please only say the word, and I shall happily arrange it all. You can stay here as long as you like, though I hope you never leave.

Yours truly,

Ellis Clemen

Arden

We wake up early to arrive at the estate before sunrise and before the crowds gather at the provincial center. Canton greets us at the door and says everything is in order. I have never been to a funeral rite, much less one for a ruler in a different realm. I do not know what I will witness today. We are all dressed in gray, the color of mourning in Kallos. Reown is dressed in her formal Sovran gown, made of a beautiful orange fabric that looks as if it could burn you if you touch it. She looks peacefully asleep, lying inside the glass casket. Elegant, even. I watch Kyrie's face closely as he approaches and looks at her. By his expression, I can see that he agrees.

"Thank you, Canton, she looks beautiful," Kyrie offers.

"Of course, my lord, her staff took the utmost care of her arrangements," Canton replies. "The carriage will be arriving shortly to transport her to the province center. Her Sovran tree has been burned, and the ashes are ready to be transported as well for her funeral rite."

Kyrie turns to me and explains that a Sovran tree is planted when an heir is born. It is tagged and cared for. If that heir becomes a Sovran ruler, it is marked again. When that ruler dies, the tree is cut down and burned, and the ashes are used in the burial.

"Do you have a tree?" I ask.

"Yes, although I have never seen it," he replies. "It is a bad omen to go look for your tree."

"I see. Is this a tradition done just in Kallos, or in all Pallayes?" I wonder if the Valray province has any traditions like this one. I am assuming I did not have a tree.

Kyrie looks over at Canton with an expression that asks if he knows the answer to this question. Canton understands and replies, "I believe, my lord, this is just done in Kallos."

"Thank you." I tell him sincerely.

"Is there anything else, my lord, before I arrange the transport?" Canton asks.

"That is all for now, thank you Canton," Kyrie replies.

"Are you ready for this?" I ask.

"Honestly, it is a bit overwhelming. I was wondering though, how do we handle the curiosity about your presence there today? People will have questions about the woman wearing the matching gold bracelet. But I do not want the announcement to happen on the day of my mother's burial. I want our own special moment to be unveiled to the province tomorrow at the Sovran ceremony."

"I agree. So, after your speech today, invite them all to return tomorrow morning to your Sovran ceremony, and tell them you will introduce me then. I think it will draw a crowd." I say with a wink.

"You're better at this than I am," he says, kissing my forehead before he pulls me into his arms. He lingers there, not ready to face the events of today.

It is a moment of peace before we both turn our heads towards a voice screaming his name in blame. "Kyrie! What have you done! First father, now this!" A beautiful young woman with long blonde hair and amethyst eyes is heading straight for us.

I look up at him for an explanation. "That is my sister," he says as I sense all the muscles in his body tense, like he has put up armor.

"Hello, Deirdras." I can almost hear the words he is holding back.

"What have you done to our mother! You were supposed to save her! I got a message to come home immediately, and now I am told we are burying her today!" Her panicked grief is palpable. It reminds me of his mother's frantic last minutes.

"Come sit for a moment and I will tell you what happened." Kyrie inhales and replies patiently, but I notice he forgets to exhale.

She does not really reply with words; she takes a step towards the chairs, expecting us to follow. So, we do. We all sit, and the air between us is awkward.

"Deirdras, this is Arden. She helped me break the spell off Kallos. She was with me when Canton took us to see mother. She witnessed all that happened. Canton was also there as well." He offers simply.

She only briefly looks at me but does not say anything. It is enough time for me to notice her mother's eyes; she has the same intense beauty. Now seeing her and Kyrie next to each other, I can almost see the resemblance, but the distance I sense between them is striking.

"Go on," she says to Kyrie impatiently.

"When the spell was broken, mother's first feelings were that of pain, anger, regret, loss, and grief. It overwhelmed her and she became very panicked. She said there was nothing left to live for, and then she jumped out of bed and started pacing. After she found out about father's death, it was not long before the pain attacked her heart, and she collapsed and died."

I notice that he left out the part about our vow being the final blow to send her over the edge.

"I did not get much time with her at all. We did not have much of a conversation because she was so frantic. I was just trying to calm and comfort her, but she woke up as angry as the day father told her about Menstus casting the spell. It is all she could feel."

"Why did you not help her? Why could you not stop her from panicking? I thought you were going to save her. That is what you said before I left."

"I have spent my whole life trying to save all of Kallos, especially mother. You have no idea what that has been like, putting my life on hold to try to break a spell, a spell that also affected me in case you have forgotten. You left and got married. No one expected you to save the province and bring mother back to life. I have done absolutely everything I said I would. But it was impossible to manage or control her feelings. Only she alone could do that. You cannot blame me for her death."

"Well, it's just not fair that I did not get to say goodbye." She replies with some anger towards everyone and no one at the same time.

"Deirdras, I am sorry for the pain of your loss, I really am. I feel it too." Then, Kyrie stands up, "If you will excuse us, I need to prepare to face the Kallos province with the news. You are welcome to stay for as long as you need." He takes my hand and gently leads me up and out of the room. I can see how tight his jaw is, the words he held back for her sake. I watch the air he tries to put back into his lungs as we enter a different room. He closes the door behind us and leans back against it.

"That was really difficult," he says after a moment of silence.

"I am so sorry, I know that was hard. And I can see that she is hurting too," I offer soothingly.

"I will be okay. I just needed to regroup before it escalated. I need to keep my focus on the burial ahead. Thank you for being my partner in this." He hugs me tightly and then leads us to his glider.

We travel a short distance to the provincial center. A crowd is beginning to gather. The hearse is also arriving, and Reown's body will be available for viewing soon, but for now, the casket is covered in a dark blue velvet fabric. Her death is still a secret.

Thirty

Deirdras

In seven months, I will be holding my own daughter. Even though I have no firm understanding of what it is to be a mother or any real memories of being mothered. I dream of her often, that is how I know it is a girl. No one knows this yet but Ellis.

After these years of struggling to conceive, I was beginning to fear the spell had caused infertility. Ellis was so patient and kind. He reminds me of Kyrie in that way. I carry the sadness that I do not have the big, vibrant, close-knit family that Ellis has here in Clemen. But they have embraced me as their own and I am happy there.

I wonder if Kyrie and I will ever grow close now that both of our parents are gone and the spell has broken. I know I do not make it easy for him to get close. Going to Clemen gave me a fresh start. It gave me a chance to become someone I could have never been in Kallos. My mother and father would have never allowed it. Such freedom to be myself. I regress each time I am in Kallos. It is why I do not come back home. My family has never known the better version of me. The version that only the Clemen family knows and loves.

Arden

The provincial center is where all major events take place. It is a large outdoor arena constructed out of a variety of beautiful stone slabs and columns, surrounded by magnificent ancient trees. Stadium seating is built around a stage area at the base. The air feels cool inside, with the breeze blowing through the trees and bouncing off the cool stone. I can imagine that everyone will hear Kyrie's voice. A place like this is sure to have perfect acoustics. We head towards the elegant chairs placed on the stage area for us. The covered casket is in the center, and Reown's staff have begun to arrange flowers and candles around it. I wonder whether the staff changes with each ruler or stays on through the transition.

Kyrie and I sit in two of the chairs. Canton takes one of the seats, and from a distance, I watch Deirdras arrive and walk toward the last empty chair. She does not look at either of us. We wait a bit longer for the crowd to fill in and take their seats. I notice all the heads with mostly shades of copper and gold hair, like spices of paprika, cinnamon, ginger, nutmeg, and saffron. I can see why Reown knew immediately that I was not from here.

The curiosity is pulsing throughout the arena. Finally, Kyrie stands and walks up to address the crowd. "Thank you all for gathering here this morning, especially on short notice, and without a full explanation. As you all know, I am Kyrie, son of Reown, and it is with deepest sadness and regret that I tell you that my mother, Reown Kallos, has passed from this life."

With his last word, two staff members remove the velvet cover to reveal her identity, and the crowd shakes with a broad mix of reactions. He gives them a moment to process before he continues. There are whispers, gasps, and murmurs throughout.

"When the spell was broken, my mother's heart, which was weakened over the many years of being in her unconscious state, could not handle the intense onset of painful emotions that surfaced very suddenly for her. When she found out that my father was no longer alive, she collapsed soon after and died."

The crowd's empathy and sorrow can be felt as loud as it is heard. "It was important to me that I announce her passing to you in person, and to also address the state of the Kallos province because of the recent events. As many of you know the story from my father, Earl Menstus promised to show up after her death to try to claim the seat…" The crowd gasps and murmurs at this, "So I think you will agree with me that it is in everyone's best interest that we all follow the plan I propose to you now."

The crowd hushes in anticipation, not wanting to miss a word. "I would like to give you all a chance to join me today in mourning the loss of my mother and giving her the burial she deserves without drawing Menstus' attention to her death today. Tomorrow morning, I invite you to rise with the dawn and join me here again for the ceremony of the Sovran seat, where I will become your faithful ruler. It is then that I would love to introduce you to my chosen life-partner..." the crowd takes a collective breath in, "and tell you how we broke the spell of The Veiled Heart."

It is too much for these people who have just recently begun to feel again. Their emotions are all over the place. There is crying, there is clapping, there is lament, and there is electric anticipation. He held space for all of it.

Then he adds, "In the meantime, I ask that we keep the news of our recent events inside of Kallos, so that we have the chance to complete the prepared ceremonies over the next two days without interference."

I have never seen a whole crowd of people bow in a show of honor. I am in awe of their devotion and faith, and it inspires hope within me. Canton rises from his chair and walks over to Kyrie, and Kyrie nods to him to proceed with his announcement.

Canton speaks clearly and reverently, "The family of Reown invites you all to each come one at a time to the casket, take a handful of her tree ash, and place it inside.

We will all join in courage and help bury our deceased Sovran ruler together. After the ashes have been placed into the casket, we will process down to the water's edge where her casket will be placed on the Sovran raft, and she will be taken to our Island of Rulers Past for burial among her ancestors." He bows and, stepping back, proceeds to the casket, where he demonstrates the first handful of ash into the glass tomb.

I am overcome. I have never been a part of a grand sacred event. It may be because I did not live long enough to participate in any traditional Sovran ceremony, or because my father had not held them in Valray anymore. I cannot help but wonder what happened to my mother and if she even had a funeral. Kyrie motions for me to follow him to the large carved box of ash next to the casket, and together, we each place a handful inside. The bark ash is cool against my skin; I almost want to keep holding it. We then walk back up to our chairs, where we will wait for everyone to have a turn. I can see why the ceremonies need to be on two separate days.

I watch Deirdras take her turn, and after she opens her hand and lets the ash fall out, so do her emotions. All those years of bound-up feelings, longing, unspoken words, and a deep mother hunger, with which I can most certainly empathize. The whole crowd goes still and turns to watch; there is not a dry eye in the arena. I watch Kyrie rise and go to her. He stands tall next to her, available in case she decides she needs someone steady to hold onto. She is bent over her mother's body, and her back rising and falling with the sobs is visible to all. Her pleas for a chance to have one more minute with her alive are heard by all. I go to Deirdras' other side, place my hand on her back, and say only to myself, "I understand. I know this pain." This moment is gutting, and I never saw it coming.

She finally turns and surrenders into Kyrie's arms, and he leads her back to her chair. I follow. My attention is now captured by every member of the Kallos province saying goodbye to the ruler they have not seen in many, many years. I imagine they are also saying goodbye to the years lost under the spell, to the lives lost, and, I suppose, ready to bury the past. I understand, at this moment, how stark today will stand against tomorrow: death and life, old and new. I, too, am ready for it, as the tears escape, and there is no way to stop them, and no longer a need to capture them.

When it is time, we follow right behind the glass casket, and all the people of Kallos follow behind us, the long walk down to the water's edge. There is a beautiful hand-carved raft covered in flowers, ready to receive Reown for the small journey to the island. Kyrie tells me the man on board is the island's groundskeeper. The honor of ferrying the rulers to their final place of rest has been in his family since the first Kallos ruler, Claudegus' grandson, who died over two centuries ago. The groundskeeper carefully handles every detail of the casket as it is loaded onto his raft.

"He has already prepared her plot on the island. He was one of the first few people that Canton made arrangements with after she died. The tradition is for us to stay and watch until the raft is no longer visible. Then the family walks out to the water and releases a large paper lantern that will light her way to the realms above."

"I have never been a part of anything like this," I say. It makes me wonder what is planned for tomorrow's ceremony. I try to imagine it in my mind.

"Are you almost ready to walk down?" He asks us. I know I was watching the raft, but when I blink at the sound of his question, I no longer see the raft at all.

I look to his other side and see Deirdras standing like a pillar with a gaze that is a million miles away. He takes both of our hands and leads us to the water's edge, where Canton is holding the large lantern for us to release.

As we walk back to the arena, Kyrie asks Deirdras if she will be at the ceremony tomorrow. I listen hard to her response.

"I am sorry, but I need to get back to Clemen tonight. I have said my goodbyes to my past here and have tried to make peace with it today, but that is all that I can do. It is like mother said, "There's nothing left for me here." I wince at Kyrie having to hear that phrase again. "My home and future are in Clemen. Goodbye, Kyrie, and may the Powers Above be with you tomorrow." And with that, she turns and leaves.

Kyrie and I stand there in silence for a few moments, letting the wave of grief wash over us. Then he takes my hand and leads me towards the glider, which will take us home. As we approach the front of the estate, we pause to admire it for a moment before going inside.

"It will take some time to make this place our new home, but in the meantime, we can stay in the bedroom I grew up in. It feels safe there," he says with a boyish charm, and I smile at the idea of creating a home here with him.

As we lay quietly in bed, I realize it is my last night of anonymity. I want to remember this moment for as long as I can. Tomorrow, the public will know that I am alive.

Thirty- One

{Two hundred and twenty-five years before the present}

DEAR LASHGA AND PALLAYES,

YOUR MOTHER WAS SO GOOD AT WRITING AND SENDING INSTRUCTIONS. SHE DID NOT LEAVE ME ALONE IN THAT WAY, ALWAYS SO GOOD TO ME. TO ALL OF US. PLEASE TAKE CARE OF MY SUITCASE. YOU KNOW IT IS MY MOST BELOVED POSSESSION, SINCE IT HOLDS EVERYTHING SHE HAS SENT TO US.

YOUR DEVOTED FATHER,

CLAUDEGUS

Arden

"Good morning," I say as I open my eyes and look up at the hand-painted map of the two realms on his old bedroom ceiling. The sun has barely peaked on the horizon.

"You know," he begins, "it is funny, but every night before falling asleep all those years as a kid, I would imagine what it would be like if those two realms were merged back into one whole piece, and how the map would look different, and then how the ceiling would need to be repainted." He smiles at the memory and turns to look at my eyes.

"Knowing you now, I am not surprised by that at all." I roll over to face him and prop my head up with my hand. "It is amazing how we were chosen so long before we ever knew about the prophecy...but it is like there were signs, and that memory is one of them. Do you ever wonder how it will all play out? Like, how are you and I going to fulfill the prophecy?"

"Almost every minute." He smiles at me. "And the only conclusion that I keep coming to is that it is going to have to be with the power of love. I cannot imagine it being by force or some large battle, we have no defenses. I have seen so much death; I do not want any more people to die for any old prophecy to work. I would rather the realms stay separate than anyone else must suffer."

I love him more with each passing day. "I agree. I have been wondering about the possibility of Mentus showing up and hoping that there is a way to defeat him. I believe in love, I just do not understand how it works in battle, as a strategy, or a defense. I know it is not a weapon, I just do not understand yet how it protects the defenseless."

"I have so much hope and faith in you, and in us. Today is ours." He kisses my forehead, my nose, my lips. "It is time to rise with the dawn and go out and meet it." His words sound poetic, and they make me smile.

We each have our own dressing rooms with members of staff to help us prepare for the event. My ceremonial dress is exquisite. I have never worn anything like it. Even my wedding dress paled in comparison. It is the same fiery orange fabric as Reown's Sovran gown. The details are woven in purple-magenta and turquoise, as if they were designed to match Kyrie's eyes. I am beyond delighted when I realize it even has pockets. When I place my hands in them, my left hand brushes against a piece of paper. I pull it out and notice the familiar handwriting. It says:

"A heart led by the ego is asleep, unaware of its present reality. It is held frozen in time behind a mask and self-

protects at all costs. The ego thrives in this unconscious state, so it works hard to prevent the heart from awakening. True power only comes from an awakened heart. It is reborn without an egoic mask and stands conscious and aware in the present. As you continue to awaken to your authentic self, your true power will shine forth and lead the way. You will only need courage to allow the Powers Above to become the power within. As above, so below."

I read the words three times, letting them soak in. They both soothe and encourage me. I am not sure what is about to happen today, but I am guided. I remind myself of who I am. I am my own, and somehow, I am seen and known by a power above me that wants to empower me from within."

Kyrie knocks and enters. I know I am radiant, but he is once again simply breathtaking. After we are both completely outfitted, Canton greets us. He is holding a wooden box.

"My lord, here are the Sovran jewels your mother commissioned from Amara, they are now yours." He hands the box over to Kyrie.

"Thank you, Canton," he says, taking the box. "We will be departing shortly."

After Canton exits, Kyrie looks at me and smiles. "Let us open this box together. I want to adorn you with whichever ones are your favorite."

When we open the lid, it is as if the jewels release a minor harmonic symphony of their relief. Reown chose precious stones that are the same colors as our ceremonial attire, different shades of orange, blue, and purple stones, each piece set in gold. My eyes go at once to a mandala brooch that takes my breath away. The center is an orange stone, encircled by eight round pieces of turquoise, surrounded by eight tiny silver-blue pearls as an accent, and in between each of the eight pearls is a gold stem that leads to a cluster of three magenta stones, eight clusters in all, creating the outer circle.

"I would be honored to wear this one," I say as I gently lift the brooch out of the box. I hand it to Kyrie, and he smiles as he pins it onto my dress. "You look ravishing," he tells me, and I believe him.

After we go over some last-minute details, we board a much larger glider—I am guessing it is the Sovran one used for transporting the ruler of the province seat. It is painted in the same fiery orange as my dress.

For the second morning in a row, we arrive at the beautiful province arena, but this time, the flowers and decorations are different. The staff must have worked on this for most of the night. I am grateful for their devotion. The two large chairs are also different from yesterday's smaller, less extravagant ones. These are hand-carved and ancient-looking, like they have traveled through time and history to be here today.

We are escorted to the chairs and sit as the crowd begins to gather. There is an excitement pulsing. Today, everyone is in shades of orange. The arena looks like it is on fire. I am learning that Fiery Orange must be the Sovran color of Kallos.

When the arena is filled, and Canton gives the nod, the crowd goes quiet as Kyrie stands to address them. "Thank you for coming this morning. It is a joy to be gathered with you for this special ceremony. I am ready to take on the responsibility of this honored role as your next ruler of the Sovran seat of Kallos. I pledge to you my faith and fidelity to expand our province into a land of greater hope and freedom."

The crowd applauds, and Canton steps up with a golden circle. Kyrie sits back in the chair, and Canton says, as he places the crown on Kyrie's head, "I now crown you, Kyrie Kallos, next ruler of the Sovran seat of the Kallos province. May the Powers Above guide you." The crowd stands to their feet and claps loudly with wild approval. Then Kyrie stands and bows to them. After a moment, he raises his hand, and they sit back down, becoming quiet again.

"As promised, I want to introduce you to the woman I have made the Redamancy Vow with. She is my equal in every way, including the ruling of this Sovran seat." The crowd is a buzz, and judging by their reaction, they do not know what this means. He goes on, "I know this is unprecedented and has never been done before in the history of the realms. But even though I am starting something new, it was foretold long ago, and I tell you today, the prophecy is being fulfilled in our time."

The crowd is alert and leans forward. They ask each other questions, wild with curiosity and filled with understandable apprehension. "May I present to you my co-ruler, Arden Rose Valray, from the Valray province in Lashga." The crowd takes in the most extensive collective breath of disbelief I have ever heard. No doubt, they have heard of the corpse-bride. He continues. "With whom we are all indebted to, for without her sacrificial love, the spell would not have broken. In her choosing to live again for our sake, she freed us all from the spell that was upon us for so long. The power of love is why you are standing here today." He turns and extends his hand to me, inviting me to stand next to him.

I rise and remove the hood of my turquoise cloak as I step forward. A gasp ripples through the arena. I am not sure what it looks like to them, but a calm radiance shimmers off of me, and my skin and hair are aglow with a sparkling light. I swear I feel the brooch pulse above my breastbone.

Canton hands Kyrie another golden circle that he takes and places upon my head. "I now crown you, Arden Valray, co-ruler of the Sovran seat of the Kallos province. May the Powers Above guide you." My shadow whispers to me.

> When freedom has
> Been blown into your bones,
> Make sure you entrust
> That freedom remains
> Always inside of you.

At this moment, the sky fills with an incredible rainbow, one like I have never seen before. It captures everyone's attention. When I grab Kyrie's hand, our bracelets glow and hum together, creating a dazzling light. I knew something special would happen, but I am overwhelmed by the magnificence. Kyrie's face is a mix of fascination and confidence until the moment Earl Menstus arrives in front of us, and then Kyrie's smile crumbles.

Thirty-Two

{One week before the present}

Rexus

I am consumed by rage and despair. How could I have left her there, trapped in that nightmare? Every moment I was away, I felt her spirit slipping further from me. It haunts me—knowing now I should have done something, anything, to save her. Nulfest took everything from me, and I will never forgive him for it, and her father as well, for forcing her into a loveless marriage, shattering our dreams of a future together. She was my heart, my everything, and without her, I am a hollow shell.

I showed up that day because I knew in my soul that something tragic had happened. I felt her loss within me, as if the flame of our love was extinguished upon the wind and so my fury unleashed itself upon my arrow.

It is unbearable, the weight of this grief. But I will not stay silent any longer. I will avenge her death. The revolution is coming, and I will rise from this pit of sorrow. No more shadows. We will take this province, and I will lead these people. His grave will remain unmarked, his face forgotten, and I will boldly claim the daughter that is rightfully mine. She was always mine.

Arden

The crowd is on the edge of their seats, and their panic ripples through the arena.

"Where is Reown?" His loud question booms throughout the arena.

This moment is surreal, because although I have dreaded it for so many nights, even had nightmares about it, I do not feel fear. I am emboldened. I am sure I feel the brooch's heartbeat softly drumming on my skin. I look at Earl Menstus for the first time, finally seeing the face that belongs to the name we have spoken with dread and fear. He is not the hideous monster that I imagined I can even see the similarities in our bloodline. His black hair is parted and tied back, in contrast to his light skin, and his green eyes are so dark they almost look black. I can decipher that at one point in his youth, he was attractive. But what I mostly see when I look into his eyes is a stone-cold emptiness of all love lost. A heart frozen in time, wearing a mask of epic proportions. The moment has come, and I am ready. I step into my destiny.

"She passed away four days ago!" I loudly declare, surprising Kyrie next to me, surprising the crowd, surprising even myself, but especially Earl Menstus. His head pivots to me like a predator noticing its prey. His eyes narrow in on me. My shadow writes my reply to his gaze.

> You are smart
> And your ego is strong,
> But I have been studying,
> Patiently observing,
> And making love.
> I am learning and listening,
> Slowly
> Weaving back together
> What is mine.

"She is gone?" He becomes strangely somber, and I catch his knees buckle with my eyes. Why does he seem defeated instead of victorious?

"She was buried yesterday."

"Then how was the spell broken?"

Still hungry for the truth of my mysterious death, I decide to accuse him, to draw out his reaction, and possibly hear a confession.

"Had you not killed me, had I lived and married into the Wincot line, the spell would not have been broken by this Redamancy Vow." His eyes dart down towards our bracelets, and something like sparks fly from the gold.

"Who are you?

"Arden of Valray, the corpse-bride."

He finally recognizes me, and his eyes go wide.

"Killed you? I did not kill you. I have been looking for you. Your father tricked me, you never arrived. I needed your tears, to break the spell."

"Break the spell?" Kyrie stands and questions him before I can even respond to what I am hearing.

"If your mother would have asked me to, I would have broken the spell for her. I was waiting for her."

"My father said you were waiting for her death to take over the province. Are you not here to take the province?"

"Your father is a liar, and a thief. Why would I want to take Kallos? My bloodline is to the seat of Dashel. That is the province that I have a right to claim."

Nothing prepares us for what comes next. The loudest thunder I have ever heard moves the ground beneath us, and the trees lift their branches into a strong wind that makes us all stumble to the side. Then the voice.

"I am the Powers Above," the voice booms. I immediately remember the note in my pocket, and my hand instinctively goes to it. I am paying attention, curious about what will happen next.

The voice clearly says, "Earl Menstus, I give you permission to rebuild the Dashel province." I watch his expression change, equal parts intrigue, and confusion.

The crowd collectively says, "What?" No one expected this, especially me.

The voice continues, "You may claim the lost Sovran seat that your grandfather was denied and rebuild the strong structure that it once was, before the spell was cast by your great-grandmother." His eyes narrow and then widen as soon as the words fly across and reach the back of his mind. "However, be warned! Dashel's downfall will always be pride. You know well the story of your great-grandfather, and his father before him. It is what led to your bitter hate for the injustice done to Vera Valray and her son. So, if you do not want to repeat their downfall, and if you desire to keep your seat and your province, you will have to resolve to become something, someone, entirely different. Is this a deal you would like to make?"

The air goes still, and even the trees stop swaying, waiting for his reply.

"What are the terms?" He asks.

"You must lay down the identity of Earl Menstus, and take on the new one as Earl Dashel, humble Sovran of the Dashel province. You will need to hand-pick an heir to the Dashel line to rule after you. And finally, you must humble yourself here in front of the people of Kallos and atone for the years and loved ones lost from the spell you cast on them."

A pin drop can be heard in the arena. No one dares to take another breath until Menstus gives his answer. But before he can speak, his eyes close tight like he is in terrible pain, and then, in an instant, his hands move to his chest as he drops helplessly to his knees. It is as if the Powers Above are helping him into prostration. The pain is visible to all. It is the sound of cracking that gets my attention; it is awful. Menstus is completely slumped over, in surrender to the cracking pain in his chest, and I wonder if it is his stone heart breaking. The whole arena watches and waits. We all wait, but somehow, there is no fear.

Right before our eyes, a glowing indigo thread from the realm above descends upon Menstus, who is still slumped over his knees. It enters his back, and he lets out a loud wail, alerting us that something torturous is happening inside of him. We all watch with fascination. I am not surprised it is taking so long. It makes sense that a stone-cold heart would need extra time to be broken down and fashioned into something new. Our eyes are all on the place where the string has entered his back when my sister surprisingly appears at the front of the arena. When our eyes meet, I see the moment she recognizes me and is shocked.

"Arden!" She announces. "How are you here, alive in Kallos?"

"Aster!" I say as I move towards her and we embrace with relief. Before anything else can be said, she looks down and sees Menstus on the floor.

"What is happening to him?" She asks as she moves towards him and drops to his side.

She is kneeling next to him, trying to wake him, but he is unresponsive to her. We are all startled when Menstus begins moaning. It does not take long for the crying to become sobbing. He is entirely prostrate, face down over his knees, body quivering in painful sobs. I cannot even imagine what is happening on the inside to make this man cry right here in public, but enough applied pressure can break open an ego and release the mask from its firm grip.

"Please make this stop!" Aster begs me.

There is loud whispering throughout the crowd. The thread in Menstus's back tugs on him and pulls his chest upwards, forcing him to sit on his knees. His face is crumpled in agony. The thread yanks him as if to make him obey an invisible instruction. Then, a booming voice echoes down from the realm above, "Speak!"

Menstus's voice is shaky and gravelly. "I have seen my life through the eyes of the Powers Above. It is a vision

I cannot unsee. I am to ask for your forgiveness, and hope that I can live the rest of my days trying to make up for what I have stolen." His face crumples back up into such an ugly cry. I can see that he wants to collapse back down, but the thread is taut and will not allow it. An uncomfortable silence passes.

> True love
> Is the willingness
> To take a deep look
> Inside.
> A willingness
> to see the bare truth
> And make amends.

Thirty-Three

{Ninety-nine years before the present}

Vera Valray,

You may never read these words, I do not know how to find you, and now it is too late. I am dying the dark death you intended for me if I did not come for you. And I did not come. I was such a fool, paralyzed in fear of my father. If only my mother had still been alive to make me see the error of my ways, his ways. She would have never let you leave, especially with the baby. I do not know what pains me more, that I broke your heart, or the state of this broken province. We were known for our hospitality, and yet you, of all people, were never welcomed. I never doubted the baby was mine- I just did not have the courage to claim him. I did not dare to stand up to my father. Or to step down and disappoint him. If this letter ever finds you, give it to our son, as his right to the seat of Dashel. Whatever is left of it. I pray I find you again in the after-realm.

Earl Dashel

Arden

Kyrie steps forth and says, "I forgive you, Menstus for the lost years, and for the deaths of my parents and loved ones. You may now carry the burden of the choices you made upon my life."

Menstus falls forward with the weight, and the thread pulls extremely hard to get him back up. He is struggling under the weight of Kyrie's burden. I now visually understand the responsibility that comes with asking and giving forgiveness; it is not just an exchange of words; it is an exchange of burden. Decades-old burdens carried by all these people are now being transferred to their rightful owner. The Powers Above return to Menstus in full measure the weight of his life's choices.

I take a deep breath and look at this weak man on the ground in front of me. He once seemed so powerful, but I realize, as Kyrie told me, that Menstus's lack of love is his very weakness. All that is required to defeat him is the power of pure love. His gaping hole of lack is no opponent for our arena full of love. This has made him an easy adversary in the end. I have no fear. I look up to the sky and realize that I am no longer afraid. The prophecy has changed me. Love has freed me. I then have a strange revelation. I know that my healing is not dependent on my ability to forgive him. I have already begun the transformative process of rebirth, but there is a missing piece that I do not understand.

The Powers Above must be reading my thoughts because the whole arena freezes in time. No one around me moves a muscle—gestures are held in mid-air, and no one blinks an eye. Everything has stopped for this moment. There are no sounds from nature; I can only hear my breath. The light dims to a hazy dark blue.

Then, a clear voice rings out to only me: "The decision is entirely yours. Whatever you decide, will be honored."

"I know this is important, but I do not understand it. What is the benefit of my forgiveness?" I ask, my question dripping with desperation to be answered.

"Forgiveness is about releasing yourself from his woundedness and from your attachment to his outcome. It is the act of detaching your future choices from his choices, it is the disentanglement out of a knot. That is why it is a gift of freedom that you give to yourself. Not everyone wants this freedom. Some would rather the power that the knot makes them feel, the power of the lack can be very deceiving. It is what has fed Menstus all these years. His attachment to the painful knot of unforgiveness in his life has kept him from his true destiny, because nursing the pain felt more powerful than the release of it." The voice echoes through me.

"I want every ounce of true freedom that I can receive in this lifetime. I do not want to remain attached to this man's wounds." I say this and pause when I realize it must also apply to my father. I do not want to remain attached to his woundedness either. I do not want my new, beautiful life to be entangled in his darkness.

"The taste of revenge is sweet and intoxicating. It is the glue that keeps the knot attached in place. Most people, when they taste this sweet elixir, long for more of it, not realizing it keeps them attached to a seeping bitter wound that poisons them in the end."

I shudder as a cold memory runs down my spine. My mouth waters. I have tasted that sweetness. I know it well. I feel motion sickness as I remember riding the waves of that poison for days afterward.

"I want to be released from the attachment I have to anyone's wounds, especially the men who took away my life. I want the power that comes from release. I want the freedom that comes from detaching from the outcome." I say it clearly and with resolve. I decide at this moment that not only will I release myself, but I also decide that I will release him and will not block him from stepping into his destiny if he so chooses.

My inner flame rises, filling my body with warmth. Light and movement return to the arena, and the air awakens without missing a beat.

"I forgive you Earl Menstus for laying a claim to my life that was not yours to have. The power of love has granted you the only merciful, just, and right decision, and that is to live every day realizing that the only way to lessen the burden you carry is to carry love instead."

The way he looks at me gives me the strange sense that he has already recently seen it in a vision. Aster tries to help him stand. It seems as if she is trying to lift a thousand pounds. However, something is changing in her, too; I can see it. Love has freed her soul as well.

"I will help him." Aster declares. "I will continue the work of rebuilding even after he is gone. I will see to it that Dashel becomes a flourishing province again."

The indigo thread helps her with the lift, but he still struggles to his feet. His head hangs low, his eyes still closed. Then, the blue color of the thread ends, and a beautiful, rich green begins. Is this the color of the Dashel line? I wonder if there is a page in the suitcase that tells of all the provinces' special colors. When the green color of the thread is now inside him, his head lifts, and color begins to fill his pale face. His eyes open and change from dark green to a golden topaz. His chin softens, his nose becomes less prominent, and his hair changes from black to brown. I wonder if we just witnessed him transfer from the Valray to the Dashel bloodline.

Lastly, his overcoat and the layers underneath transform into the green of the thread. He looks noble and humble even, but he is older; this experience has aged him. I wonder what his new heart looks like and if it will be given the power of alchemy. My shadow cannot help but write a silent poem for him, and for all the parts of myself that I see in him.

> My ego caught fire
> And burned.
> There was not enough
> Water to put it out.
> My ego caught fire
> Today,
> And burned itself up.
> I surrender,
> I turn myself in.
> Lay the weapons on the table,
> No more secrets,
> No more dark closets,
> And dungeons.
> Here is my white flag.
> I lay it all down,
> The battle is over now.

Aster watches it all with a gaze of wonder, as if the birth of a baby were happening before her eyes. Her shirt and trousers are also becoming rich green, a symbol of her chosen place in the realm. She is now the heir to the Dashel seat. I am genuinely happy for her. The thread is busy transforming them both. Her natural beauty is becoming more enhanced, her face softens, and her eyes become the same golden topaz as his. Her hair becomes the same rich brown, with golden streaks, and shines even brighter next to the rich green fabric. I watch the green thread finally complete its long descent from above, ending in an intricate weaving of Aster's braid. She is dangerously stunning.

"I now declare," says the voice, "from this moment forward, that Earl Menstus is dead and no longer exists. This man who stands before us will now be known as Earl Dashel, the great-grandson to Earl Dashel, Sovran ruler of the seat of Dashel, and his new heir, Aster Dashel. May the Dashel line begin again with them."

Someone in the middle of the arena stands up and, without prompting, begins to clap. It does not take long for the rest of the arena to follow. It is a rare wave of human emotion at its finest. The Kallos power of hope is igniting around the arena—the freedom to expand is being released from within. Earl Dashel takes Aster's hand in his and nods with a long gesture of humble appreciation to the crowd. Then, the two of them fade away in our midst and disappear from our sight.

I can almost read the minds of everyone here—if this is really happening, then anything is possible. I smile, knowing that there is now a new wave of hope and faith for this province that will not be easily shaken for a very long time.

Thirty-Four

{Two hundred and forty years before the present}

My Claudegus,

What a treasure your love is- that you gave up your longevity to allow me a brief time to be with you in Olstar. What a life we created in those years! Our beautiful daughters- my beloved gifts. I am so sorry, my darling, that my body could not remain longer with you, but you know my spirit always lingers, never entirely leaving you. Oh, when I heard the fault line crack open in your grief, I wanted to find every way to console you. What a patient man you are. And your fidelity to the land and people is your legacy. I am weaving a plan to heal the land that was divided upon your death. A plan that will release you and bring you home to me.

I will see you again. I promise.

~the Powers Above

Arden

Despite the movement of the crowd, it suddenly seems that everything else in nature goes still and quiet, waiting for what will happen next. All birds cease their songs and flights. We all sense something, and everyone goes still and instinctively looks up.

The trees begin to sway slowly at first, and then more wildly as the strong wind picks up speed. Lightning strikes across the dome of the sky, followed by shooting stars. The bombastic thunder makes the ground vibrate, causing the two arc domes of each realm's sky to break open and merge into one large, unified dome, filling with rainbow prisms along the new seams. Everyone grabs hold of the person next to them for steady support as both the ground and sky shake. The bypass explodes into the air above and then crumbles down into the waters below, creating a new land bridge that now fills the space between the two lands.

Not one person in either of the eight provinces can escape the world change at this moment. No one can miss the shocking beauty and wonder of it all. It is both terrifying and magnificent to behold. When the movement finally ceases, and all feels calm again, the people of Kallos erupt into celebration, one they have long been starving for. Kyrie declares a holiday for the whole province, allowing time to celebrate renewed hope and faith. I wonder if Claudegus has been set free.

When we turn to embrace each other, sparkles fall from above and I enjoy the long kiss of my Sovran co-ruler. I can see from the corners of my eyes that my hair is shimmering, and the new colored strands are sparkling. I look down and see our golden bracelets radiating a golden glow.

"That was incredible!" Kyrie says to me.

"And terrifying!" I add, "I am so relieved it is over, and the realms have finally united just as the prophecy foretold. Life will never be the same for anyone!" I declare with awe.

He lifts me off my feet. I will tell him later that he stood frozen in time while I discussed the power of forgiveness with the voice from beyond the realm.

We turn and see Vesta and Taryn walking towards us, equally amazed, and we all embrace each other.

"Well," Vesta begins, "we would love to spend some more time here in Kallos, if you will have us."

Kyrie says with heartfelt gratitude, "Of course we want you to stay. Please, make yourselves at home at our villa for as long as you need."

"Thank you so much," Taryn replies as he offers his hand to Kyrie for a handshake on the agreement. "We really appreciate it."

"We can take you there now and get you settled," I offer, so happy that we will have friends nearby.

After we help load their suitcases in and show them around, we all sit on the terrace to visit.

"Do you really think Menstus, I mean, Earl Dashel is a transformed man?" Taryn asks honestly.

"If I would not have seen the events with my own eyes, I do not know if I would have believed it was possible for a man like him to become anything different. But I also know from today that the Powers Above is real and can make anything possible. I suppose if it can unite two realms, it can humble a dark lord. I am curious about the new Dashel province. I am also very curious about my sister. I hope she will be happy there, even though I cannot imagine how she loves him," I say to them.

A moment passes and then I have a revelation. "We need to go to Valray. The Valray province needs to be restored before it is lost."

"I agree," Kyrie replies. "We need to make things right there. The people deserve it."

"And then I need to find Aster in Dashel. I need a chance to speak to her and to make sure she is well."

"May we come with you?" asks Taryn.

"Of course!" Kyrie tells him with a smile. "We will pick you up in the morning. Enjoy your first evening in Kallos."

They wave goodbye as we leave and head back to the Kallos estate. As we arrive in front of the estate and look at it with new eyes, Kyrie tells me, "I cannot wait for this to feel like our home one day."

"Me too." I reply. I decide we need the new map of the United Realm painted on our new bedroom ceiling.

Thirty-Five

{Three days before the present}

Rae

He wakes up again with another dream he cannot ignore. But this one, he knows, is more than a dream. It is a vision. Ever since he was a child, he has had them. His parents taught him the oaths of the visionary. They are not easy to obey. For some visions, he must travel to find the person the message belongs to. This is one of that kind. And he is frightened. He has never traveled to Valray before, especially alone. Especially since the longstanding ban on passage between Valray and Zenif. Ever since Vera Valray broke her betrothal to his ancestor when she betrayed him for the heir to Dashel. Even though the Valray seat groveled for mercy, the bad blood had set. But not as much as it did for Vera, when she was rejected by her own family, for the shame she brought upon the seat. No one from Zenif has set foot in Valray, and vice versa, ever since. It had become a matter of principle. A long overdue reconciliation of bruised egos.

But he is the only one who can carry out this task. He is the only visionary left in Zenif, ever since his father died. And he has sworn an oath, no matter what it might cost him.

Arden

We pick up Vesta and Taryn in the Sovran glider since it is larger and can easily carry all of us. We are all curious about the trip to Valray. Before yesterday, the edge of each realm looked like an opaque dome. There was an opal light with streaks of prism colors, but you could not see clearly through it. Traveling through it was not for the faint of heart. As we approach it today, the view of the whole sky is breathtaking. It is clear all the way across. We can easily see the rich green land of Lashga ahead. The bypass wall became a beautiful, spacious land bridge across the blue water, allowing all to easily make the journey. The two realms now share the same vast blue sky; it is stunning. There is nothing visually or physically dividing the realms anymore. We pause at the edge of Pallayes, just taking it all in. There are many other curious people out of here as well this morning who have decided to make the pilgrimage. We all agree to move forward, slowly crossing the new land.

"Do you think this will still be called the bypass?" Taryn asks.

"What about the Great Bridge?" I wonder aloud.

"Yes, I like it," Vesta replies. "I cannot help but think of my father right now and just smile. Do you know how many ways he envisioned the two realms uniting like this? He is going to love seeing this beautiful bridge. I hope to cross it with him one day, and with my mother by his side."

"Your father sacrificed so much to make sure it happened this way, the right way. The three of you did. Your family was the protectorate of the prophecy, thank you." Kyrie says.

When we arrive on the other side of the Great Bridge, we are in the Valray province. This is the first time I have ever truly traveled across my homeland, getting to see it freely for myself. It is nothing like I remember. I can see the vision of what it is supposed to look like, but everywhere where bright greens and blues are supposed to be, there is a fog of gray sadness. The land seems hungry and neglected. It looks sick. I wonder what it would look like if the Valray power of enchantment were allowed to be released into the province. I notice a sensation inside my core. It is as if that vision caused my inner flame to shoot up and lick my insides.

As we travel through the valley, the people who are outside pause to watch us go by. Crowds are gathering, walking in the same direction as us. We make our way through the villages and finally arrive at the Center Court. Kyrie lands the Sovran glider and helps us all step out. A large crowd is already gathered. We walk up the steps to what Valray's version of Kallos' arena is. It also opens to the sky, but it does not have the canopy of ancient trees that the Kallos arena has, and if it ever did, they would have been cut down and turned into furniture already. It looks and feels completely different, but it serves the same purpose. A place for the people to gather for important provincial events.

The people look afraid. But more than fear, they look angry. I get the feeling we do not know something important, something they already know. I look at Kyrie, and he looks back at us with the same sense.

Kyrie asks aloud. "What event is taking place here today?"

A large man in the crowd, who appears to be their leader, yells out, "Nulfest Valray is dead! Now, we are taking it back! We do not want any more worthless rulers! Today, we revolt! Today, the revolution finally begins!"

The crowd rages, "No more rulers!" "No more rulers!" They are angry.

The leader continues, "The realms are united, we are free now! Our own free people! We have been planning this for a long time. No one can stop us now!"

"This should be interesting," Taryn says just to us, under his breath. His calm confidence is unfazed, but I notice the hint of concern in his voice.

I notice the winds picking up and flocks of birds flying across the sky. Things are beginning to happen. I focus my mind on the goal. I need to restore the Valray province and save it from a downfall. Before yesterday, I could never have imagined this moment. I never saw myself as a ruler of Valray, but now, I cannot imagine it any other way. This Sovran seat is my birthright, and no matter how hard my parents tried, they could not keep me from stepping into my destiny. But these people are revolting. They want liberation from the only kind of leader they have known. I do not know how to convince them that everything can be different now.

> I behold the shipwreck
> And all these dry bones
> Scattered across the beach.
> Who is the captain of this destruction?
> I am the archaeologist,
> Finding lost bones, sorting them
> Trying to identify who they are,
> And what happened to them.

The sky is also beginning to change, like a great watercolor artist dipping a dirty paintbrush into freshwater. The colors are swirling into dark grays. The rioting crowd is growing larger and louder. Sweat beads begin rolling down my back.

I feel my past embrace me
As my future gathers me
Into the spread of sky.
I look across the miles
To a wilderness of space
And a canopy of stars.

"Wait! Stop! Please stop!" A tall young man suddenly runs in front of the crowd, slightly out of breath, as if he has been rushing to get here. I do not think it is so much his words but his appearance that gets everyone's attention. They stop yelling out of sheer curiosity. He does not look like the people from this province, or any other. His light silvery-gray eyes contrast against his dark skin, and his long, dark, intricate braids are intertwined with colorful beads. His clothing is layers of bold and bright fabrics. He is from the land of textile artists, designers, and weavers. He looks majestic in a mysteriously foreign way.

"I am from the Zenif province. I traveled all night to get here in time. Please hear me out! I can see into the future!" he pleads.

"What is it man, spit it out!" Someone from the crowd yells out.

"Yesterday, I saw what would happen here in Valray if I did not intercede in time today." He has everyone's attention, especially mine. I feel another wave of heat roll over my skin. My vision is blurry.

He continues, "It is my sacred duty to come here to tell you that the future of the Valray province will end very soon if the Albatross does not rise here today."

"What are you talking about? What Albatross?" The leader asks, and the people clamor.

I watch the crowd's confusion. They look at each other, murmuring with raised shoulders, not understanding what the man from Zenif is talking about. I feel dizzy. The last line of the prophecy spreads across my mind. I see it for a second more before the gray sky spins, and I collapse.

Thirty-Six

{Presently}

Elspeth

I will never forget the day Florin walked back into the grand foyer, holding the hand of a little girl who looks just like me, and the arm of a tall scholar. I could not breathe when I first saw her; she was the most beautiful woman I had ever seen. And I knew from her long white hair that she had found true love. My eyes took in the three of them. They were clearly a family in every way. Their bond was palpable; it was something I have only ever witnessed in others but have never personally experienced. I became aware of my envy but quickly alchemized it into great pride. A fierce pride that these two goddesses had come from my own flesh and blood. I took them into my arms, and I have not let them go.

Her scholar, Mazek, is the fisherman who discovered her bones caught on his hook. There is not a day that has passed since I have not replayed their story in my mind. His terror of being "chased" by a skeleton woman, tangled up in fishing line, "following" him right into his fishing hut. That part always makes me chuckle. What an incredible man to take such great care; to meticulously untangle those bones and lay them in place, by the warmth of his small fire, not knowing what was to come. Their story has become legend.

Arden

I am gliding on top of the blue water. It is only water and sky as far as my eyes can see. I turn my head in both directions and see both of my long, strong wings outstretched. I look ahead and see the sun setting in an orange and purple-pink sky as if I am flying into the eyes of the woman in the painting. I am free. I am this powerful, soaring bird, too big to be caged. Only freedom now for my bones amidst this open sky. Only freedom to remain in flight as I cry out the salt tears before I quench my thirst. I feel the wind change against my feathers, and I let it take me, happy to follow its lead. I hear my name being called, but I do not see any other birds around me. I hear it louder this time, and I see the whole sky break open in front of me, like a large fabric tearing, leaving only the blackness that lies behind the realm dome ahead of me. I can only fly towards it to the sound of my name. When I cross through the opening in the sky and let the darkness envelop me, I feel the cool dark air under my feathers. I glide through the dark, empty space, unafraid, until I see a large, elegant hand writing on a scroll, and then I begin to slow my speed. I circle above the hand, watching it move a pen across the thick paper.

Then a voice, the same beautifully clear female voice that spoke to me yesterday, says, "Arden of Valray, your work is not yet done. Your people have lost their purpose and vitality; they have not witnessed the power of love in too long. Your father, his father, and grandfathers before him, have starved them of what they were designed to experience, a sense of wonder and awe that is passed down through the ages. I gave the Valray province the blessing of enchantment and legacy long ago. I knew the heart of this province, and took pleasure in their purpose, but their legacy has been choked. You must make things right for the people of Valray, or they will destroy themselves in this revolt, and they will never experience their true blessings again. Because you had mercy on Earl Menstus and the Dashel province, I give mercy to you, and mercy to the people of Valray. It takes all eight thriving provinces to make this new United Realm possible. No province should end in ruin, especially the first-born of Lashga."

I dare to ask her, "What am I to do?"

"You will need to use the antidotes of clarity and devotion that you possess. You must create a new legacy. Your birthright is not what you do, it is who you are at birth before the conditioning of other people's trauma and woundings. You must be willing to allow the painful removal of the false layers stitched into your being that were not in your original design. You were never designed to be afraid, or caged, or kept small. You were designed to be brave, free, and ever growing."

The salt tears release as I make another circle around the hand. I quench my thirst with her words.

"I am listening, tell me more," I tell her.

"These tattered layers get stitched into the fabric of generational lines, and form a covering that is a counterfeit, and should not exist, because it is too heavy and binding. It blocks the air and light needed for life to grow and flourish. True freedom comes only when someone is willing to endure the pain of the stitches being removed, so that the future of the line can grow without the weight of captivity. The time has come to heal the present between the past and future. Your story has given you the capacity to bridge the gap. Are you willing to make this transition between the generations? Are you willing to release the repressed anger that has held this line in fatal despair?"

I wonder about the magnitude of this assignment. Are those stitched layers going to be removed gently over time or swiftly in one movement? I cannot decide which one I would prefer. I circle back around. I need to ask one more question.

"Will you tell me why you have chosen me?"

"Because of all the soul maps written into the stars of the realm sky, yours had the signposts that told this story. Your body is designed for intercession."

I was made for this. I am nervous, but I am ready to be free. I choose this for myself, for the generations behind me, and for the generations in front of me. I decide to share my true power for this good. I remember how Kyrie worked through his pain. I can do it, too.

"I pledge my new life to you that I will make things right again in the Valray line. I want the freedom you speak of, for those who came before me and all those who come after me," I say.

"Then take this scroll back to your people, read it to them, and inspire them to open their hearts to love. Because only then can they receive their anointed blessings," she replies.

I fly closer to the scroll that the hand has ready for me. When I get near it, I slow so that the hand can put the ribbon attached to the scroll around my neck. As I circle back around, I pick up speed and head towards the colored sky of the realm. I can see the horizon over the water and, just ahead, the valley of Valray. I use my long wings to get me there faster, and then I feel it, the painful removal of stitches ripped out of the fabric layers of my being, and I can no longer stifle my screams. My voice is no longer silenced; my repressed rage is finally released from captivity.

My pain roars through the air, and it provokes the waves as I plunge headfirst into the waters below, hoping that there will be a hand to catch me on the other side. But it is a dark abyss full of suppressed generational pain. Their cries echo in the black air, and I am worried their pain is going to rip me apart. I have no other option now but to surrender to it, falling into death, unlike the one I have experienced before, because this one, I must choose.

I lay on the bottom floor under the water, undone, shattered by the revelation of secretly hidden and covered-up generational heartache, agony, loss, tragedy, neglect, betrayal, and rejection. I am alone in this watery grave, surrounded by heart-wrenching wailing as every stitch is removed. My tears melt into the waters around me. The salt of my tears dissolves and mixes into the salty water holding me. I give myself over to the Powers Above and let the expert seamstress rip out what does not belong in the future. Her hand is swift and mighty. I hear the threads tearing apart as the scraps fall away, and I hear faint sounds of her humming. What is she humming?

And that is when my ears tune into a familiar sound in the darkness. I hear the sobs of my mother. I remember it from behind the locked door that I would sit against as a little girl, hoping she would not leave me behind. Now, I lie here in another death that she could not protect me from because she was a captive in the chains of her own story. The irony is not lost on me; I can finally free her by freeing myself. I cannot help but think of the future, of the children that I might one day have. I do not want to be so unwilling to face my own pain that my child would have to plunge into this darkness to free me from this collective misery, to reclaim their own freedom.

It is as if the Powers Above can hear my thoughts. "When people cannot tolerate or process the pain of facing the truth of what happened to them, they recreate that pain for the next generation. A wounded ego that is allowed to thrive in the subconscious is creative. Unless the patterns of each generation are faced, they will most assuredly continue to appear again, however they may be disguised."

"How do I not repeat the same cycles, and create the same problem?" I ask attentively.

"You will hear my voice warn against any familiar old beliefs you consider adding back on to this new garment covering your bloodline. Most people choose a familiar pain over an unfamiliar peace. The familiar pain can be intoxicating, but it is deceiving. It is not safe, just familiar. You will feel the slight pain of fresh stitches being pulled out if you recognize your mistake in time. But if you disregard my voice, and trauma becomes conditioned and suppressed back into the line over time, it will only lead to more suffering for many. Then, someone who comes after you will be called to do again what you have experienced today. To face pain that no one was willing to feel, and it will be your wails, and your children's wails that they hear below the dark."

"I have redeemed your agony and your pain has been made holy," I hear the voice say. "Rise and go now to your people. When the cloud cover lifts, you will see with great clarity. It is time to lead without self-abandonment."

Before I can ask anything else, I am pulled out of the water by the hand and delivered back to Valray.

Thirty-Seven

{Twenty-eight years before the present}

Dear Solange,

I saw the doctor today and he advised that I start making preparations and putting things in order. I do not have the courage to tell Reown yet. I am writing to you in confidence and asking if you will be my private caretaker until the end. I cannot imagine being vulnerable with anyone else. But I understand if this is not what you want, to watch me become weak. It will require all your strength. I trust myself with you, though, as you know, over these fifteen years. You have seen me completely and love me still.

Yours,

Alton Kallos

Arden

When I slowly open my eyes again, Kyrie is kneeling over me, begging me to live, his eyes flooded with tears. I see the devastation of loss on his face. I see Vesta and Taryn kneeling on my other side; she is holding one of my hands, and Kyrie has the other. I am soaking wet, and I cannot move yet. The pain is still coursing through me, but I am not afraid of it anymore. It is mine, and I can finally feel all of it. I know where it comes from and why. I know the value of it.

"She is alive!" Vesta shakes Kyrie's shoulder. "Look, she is alive!"

I try to smile at Kyrie, to let him know I am okay, but I choke first on the salty water still in my throat. His cries are now ones of immense relief. He does not hold back or quiet them. His feelings are unleashed as his head drops down to rest on my chest. I have never seen anyone cry over me before. I do not know if anyone even cried over my first death. After I am ready, they slowly help me up to my feet.

Kyrie embraces me as I become steady on my feet again. "I thought I lost you. I was so scared. I was about to dive into death itself to find you and bring you back to me." He sobs, "Thank you for coming back to me." I hold him tight and let him settle back out of his fear.

> The power of love
> Can bring me there,
> As I also remain here.
> Love for both
> Creates one path.
> There is always a third way,
> And that is love.

The leader moves closer to me to speak to me directly. The pores of my skin release a new wave of sweat beads rolling down my neck and back, mixing with the damp saltiness of my recent ocean submersion.

"Why are you here, and what do you want with us?" He asks.

The riot is now an eerie silence, their attention absorbed by my movements. I look for the man from Zenif and find him close by. He nods to me and tells me that I need to address the crowd. I look out at their faces. They are weary, concerned, anxious, and waiting.

"I am Arden Valray, daughter of the late Nulfest Valray. You might know me as the corpse-bride." I give them a moment. There is an anxious murmuring as I try to steady myself with courage.

The revolutionary charges back, "How can that be? I know what your father did to you, and to all the women in his house. I have seen your ghost!"

"I was pulled from death and my life was restored to me, so that I might fulfill my destiny. Who are you, and what is your name?"

He is like a sturdy cedar. I study his face. There might be kindness under all that anger and sorrow. He steps up, and I dare to look deep into his eyes, not knowing why they are so familiar. He looks deep into my eyes, searching for something I hope he finds. I sense that he wants to tell me things, even bear his heart. I wish I could ask him about everything he knows and how he knows it. But instead, he says, "I am Rexus. I am the voice of these people. We have suffered for too long, and we will not give in easily."

I steady myself and feel the solid ground move beneath both of my feet. I try to find my inner balance. This feels like a reckoning. This is another moment I must step into my destiny, and the energy is both raw and euphoric. My resolve is electric, and my courage is on fire. I reach for the scroll hanging around my neck, hanging between us. I pull the ribbon to free the scroll.

"I am here to deliver the Valray province from destruction. I have a message from the Powers Above. The hand gave me this scroll, and the voice told me to read this message to you all today. Then you can make your decision."

I open the scroll. The handwriting is so familiar, I have seen it before, on the papers inside the suitcase. I read it aloud to them.

"The Valray province was originally given the blessings of enchantment, and most importantly, legacy, because this province was given the responsibility to ensure that the whole Lashga realm kept Claudegus' legacy alive and passed down through the generations."

The crowd shifts on its feet, looking at one another and agreeing.

"But you have been denied these blessings for too long, and now, the legacy has been forgotten. It has not been passed down in over two generations. The people have forgotten their stories and their purpose."

"Yeah! Yeah! Yeah!" The crowd agrees loudly, angrily, but with a tone of justice.

"These special powers can only be received through the power of love, which you also have not witnessed in a long time."

Another round of agreement shouted from the crowd.

"I have come here today with the hope to restore our beautiful Valray province, and to create a new legacy with you, one that involves wonder and purpose but can only be experienced through hearts open to love." I roll the scroll back up.

Silver shimmers float down all around them and over them. It is the Valray enchantment. The Powers Above is extending her mercies and giving them a preview, a hunger for something good. The people's faces lift to see the floating shimmers, their gazes following the silver specks around their bodies.

"I understand your longing to revolt and be free. As the daughter of your late ruler Nulfest Valray, I lived my whole life feeling the same way. I can promise that only love's power will rule this province now."

Some cheering begins to come from the crowd. I feel the heat radiate under my skin, knowing I only have one chance to get this right. Everything depends on it.

"I know you have been planning a revolution for a while, but if you are willing to change your mind and try something new with me, I would like to present myself to you as a new Sovran ruler. Everything is changing now, the realms are united, and I want our province to thrive with a new legacy that we create together. I pledge to you my undying love and devotion to making things right, to restore our province, and to create a place where everyone can thrive again."

There is stillness in the crowd. They are looking around at each other for a silent agreement to be made among them. But first, Rexus asks, "How do we know that we can trust you?"

They need a sign that comes from within me. I look up at the sky. The dark gray has cleared.

I say clearly to him, "Because I have faced the Powers Above and pledged my life to stand in the gap of this bloodline, where selfishness and neglect had been woven in and could only be removed through a painful unraveling. I faced that pain, and I felt it to the point of death. I have pledged my life to the Powers Above to create a new legacy, and I will need a trusted leader, a Regent for the people. Someone people trust because he loves and protects them. If you trust me to reclaim the Sovran seat, will you, Rexus, be that trusted Regent?"

His expression is filled with surprise at the question. It takes his breath for a second. He looks around to his companions, his people, for their consent. It is amazing to watch a crowd collectively decide without needing time for discussion. They decide with their hungry hearts, starving and yearning to be cared for, waiting for someone to take pleasure in the responsibility of serving them, no longer feeling like a cumbersome burden or an inconvenience, which becomes reinforced through neglect. With this sudden clarity, I now understand why I was chosen to stand here today. I know their heart's longings, and I can empathize with their experience.

He puts out his hand and says, "Yes, I accept your offer. Your words are true."

When the people see him shake my hand, they collectively know he has called off the revolution. Somewhere in the crowd, a slight clapping begins, and it grows into a loud sign of approval. They approve. My knees buckle with relief. I reach for Kyrie to help steady me, and when our hands clasp together, our bracelets let off the gold sparks that confirm the power of love's vow. The crowd is loud now, but it is finally the sound of celebration.

Rexus turns back to me and says, "I will meet with you in a few days, after I have had a chance to gather a list of needs and requests from the people. There is much that you and I need to discuss. Later."

I feel a jolt when I shake his hand again. I sense there is challenging work ahead on the other side of this celebration. But there is something else that passes between us that I cannot explain. Something palpable and almost familiar.

More silver shimmers fall upon the Valray people and so begins their beautiful transformations. The power of love is awakened by their readiness to consider something new, and I watch as the physical transformations begin. The crowd becomes a work of art, changing before our eyes. Streaks of new colors in their hair, eyes, skin, and clothes. As they begin to see what is happening among themselves, exuberant cheering breaks out among them. They all want a piece of this experience. They take the risk and say yes to something unknown, and they are rewarded with the power that has not been seen in their province in a very, very long time.

Enchanted fireworks shoot across the sky. The people explode with excitement, showing each other their new physical attributes. An inner radiance shines through my own skin, hair, and eyes as the old heaviness of my father's oppression melts away and a new lightness floats above, beckoning me to create something new in the land. I have never felt such inner peace as I do right now, watching these people be set free. It is like yesterday, and yet the difference, I believe, is that I have a deeper responsibility for the people now in front of me. In a way, they were left orphaned and uncared for by my father, both when he was alive and after his death…and that neglect is one that I know. I needed to come back and restore what was stolen from this province, its legacy.

Thirty-Eight

{Yesterday}

Rae

My uncle is dead. The Powers Above have shown me in my last vision where to find the pendant and what to do with it.

Arden

The man from Zenif smiles with relief that his mission is complete. I turn and ask him his name. "Rae," he replies. "I am one of the last to have the gift of seer in Zenif, so I do not take it lightly when I get a vision. It is part of our culture that if you have the power to see a future event, it is your sacred duty to bring the message to whom it belongs. The oath is to only use it for good, and so the power of seer is protected. It is a grave matter to ever use a future vision for ill intent, or to keep it a secret if it is meant for someone else." He humbly explains to us.

I look at Vesta and Taryn, "Did you all get to meet each other?"

"No, when you went down, the three of us panicked, and Rae managed the crowd," Taryn says matter-of-factly.

"Rae, these are my dearest friends, Taryn and Vesta, and this is Kyrie, my partner."

"I am so honored to know you all," Rae says as he grasps each one of their hands.

I am sure he is one of the most gracious people I have ever known. His generous warmth and honesty are like a soft silvery glow, matching the beauty of his eyes. He must be a destined ruler who possesses the Zenif power and antidotes.

Kyrie turns to me and asks, "What happened after you collapsed? Your screams were terrifying to hear, and then you just completely disappeared for a moment. Everyone heard me howl in desperation."

"After I collapsed, I had the surreal experience of being an Albatross, flying over the water. The sky broke open, and I flew behind it into the vast darkness. There, a large hand was writing a scroll and then a voice spoke to me."

"What did it say?" Vesta asks me, her eyes wide with curiosity.

"It told me that I had a job to save these people from the destruction that the revolution would bring to the province, and that I needed to inspire them to be able to receive their powers again, that they have been deprived too long. It said that the future of the United Realm depended on all eight provinces thriving and not being in ruin. It asked me if I was willing to face the pain of being restored to my birthright. When I agreed to it, the pain overtook me, and I plunged into the water below. It was like dying all over again. But when I woke up, I felt stronger than ever before. I am no longer afraid of dying of grief or too scared to feel anger. I have learned how to plunge into darkness and come out screaming. The only way across it is through."

Kyrie hugs me again, as is to make sure I am here.

"So, what happened on this side? How did you all convince the crowd to hold off the revolution?" I ask with curiosity.

Rae answers, "I told the crowd that you were the Albatross that I saw in my vision, and that if you rose, there would be a great mercy given to Valray. But if you did not, they would soon see their downfall, that the revolution would destroy them from the inside. Your screams of pain got their attention, but your body disappearing caused utter stillness, a haunting silence overtook them."

"You had the same message. Did you see the hand or scroll as well?" I ask him.

"No, I saw what would happen if the people rejected the bird and continued with the revolt. I saw the desolate end of this province, and it looked terribly similar to Dashel's state for the last century. Then I saw the enchantment that would come if you rose, and they embraced you. But in both visions, you were only a great Albatross, not a woman."

"How did you know it was me?" I ask.

"Because of your eyes. In my vision, I saw the teal with gold flecks on the bird, the same as yours when I first arrived. We seers learn to pay attention to these sorts of details. Often, the visions can use a lot of symbology and are not always as literal or realistic as you would think."

The realization startles me. "Rae, you brought a piece of the prophecy here today." I pull the paper out of my pocket and read it to him.

"When the fabric is torn

And the hand writes the scroll,

The bird will be called

To heal the present

Between the past and future.

If the Albatross rises

And only love remains,

The legacy will be restored

And the people saved."

"I am so honored. May I please read the whole thing. I will bring the memory of it back home to Zenif. I will tell my people what the prophecy says." I hand him the paper with the handwritten prophecy, and he reads it aloud to himself.

Kyrie says, "We are in your debt, is there anything that we can do for you?"

"No, you are most definitely not. I am the one who needs to clear the debt. There is another part of the prophecy I must fulfill."

He holds out a necklace, "I believe this is yours."

I am stunned. It is my Valray Oak necklace. "I do not understand. Why would you have my necklace?"

"It was my Uncle Sayszye in Zenif that sent the coachman to end your life. The coachman brought the necklace back as proof of the job done, to collect his wages. I am sorry."

"But why would your uncle want me dead?" I ask, confused. Shocked.

"Many years ago, my grandfather, a Zenif seer, had a vision on his deathbed. He said that the prophecy would begin with the death of the Valray bride. My uncle remembered his father's words and had been waiting for your wedding day since the day you were born. He began plotting your assassination when your wedding day was announced. He believed the prophecy would bring wealth to Zenif. I am so sorry."

I take a step back as if the force of the truth punches me in the gut, making me lose my balance. So, there is not only one person responsible for my death; it is now a complicit set of dominoes cascading into each other. On whose shoulders does the blame justly rest?

"I have been waiting a long time to learn the truth about my death, but his is not what I expected. Your uncle did not even know me." I can hardly make sense of it.

It is so strange that it is not personal. It is what I represent, my place of birth in a timeline, where I come from, what I possess, and what my death offered. None of which is who I am. Even though I finally have the true story of how the corpse-bride came to be, I am not prepared for the lack of solace it gives me.

"I want to speak to your uncle." The words leave my mouth before I plan them.

"I understand your desire. However, it will not be possible. His mysterious death was announced two days ago. Large tree roots came up through his bedroom floor and coiled up tightly around his body while he was sleeping. The weight of the heaviest branch was around his neck. He did not survive. If I am completely honest, I cannot say that I will miss him. His time on the Sovran seat was not Zenif's finest moments. After I take the seat, there is much that I will need to fix for the people."

"That is relatable," I say, as I try not to imagine the grisly scene as I remember the lore of the albatross. I cannot help but wonder if that tree was a Valray Oak. Enchantment is a powerful force not to be underestimated.

"Then, I want to give you a gift as the heir to Zenif, because you are worthy of knowing. We were shown secret gifts about each province, and only a righteous and destined ruler of Zenif has the power of visionary. The antidotes you must always possess are generosity and honor. And the vices of greed and envy must be avoided, so your province does not face downfall. If you succeed in this, your province will always have abundance and be rich in culture."

He smiles his beautiful smile. "In my vision, I was told that you had a special message to give to me. If I am honest, it was part of my motivation to get here in time to deliver the vision. I know I needed to hear your words. Thank you. It is not lost on me that my uncle's greed caused your death. I do look forward to seeing you all again one day. Please, if you ever decide to travel to Zenif, ask anyone there to send for me, and I will come. It will be an honored event to have a member of the Valray seat in Zenif for the first time in one hundred years. Your distant ancestor, the mother of Corin Valray, was also my ancestor. She was the last connection between our provinces."

"Rae, it would be my honor to meet you in Zenif and experience your culture and your people. Thank you." I warmly reply, hoping for an opportunity to travel to his province of color and artistry that connects Corin, the last female Valray ruler, to me. I want to learn more about this part of my lineage and the vestiges of the divine feminine that preserved the magic in our bloodline, before it was lost for a century.

"It is our hope to travel to all the provinces soon, to meet the rulers, and hopefully open the doors for new trade where it was not possible before. We are hoping that with an open bridge, there will be better communication and easier travel for all." Kyrie tells him.

He steps forward and embraces me, and a warm, magnetic peace flows between us.

"Now it is time for me to say goodbye and travel back home. I will bring some of this enchantment back with me as I celebrate, too." With that, Rae turns to leave. I know we have made an important new friend and ally, and I look forward to seeing him again.

Thirty-Nine

Menstus Valray

No daughter of mine will make me look like a fool! How dare she bring such shame upon this seat! How ungrateful to betray the carefully negotiated betrothal I made in Zenif. I cannot bear the shame she has cast upon us. Now, we are no longer welcome in Zenif. Even worse, how can one woman threaten to bring down a whole province? Dashel. Another province we can no longer enter. The Lashgan realm is now surely divided. The Wincots are now our only ally. From this day on, Vera is dead to me. Her name is erased from the line; her story will never be told!

Arden

The shimmering crowd has now dispersed into the streets and villages to begin their holiday. The sounds of singing, laughing, music, and dancing can be heard throughout the province.

"What next?" Kyrie looks at me and asks.

"I need to go to my parents' house. I need to see the condition of the Valray estate and what is to become of it since I have reclaimed the seat." I have a cold shiver run through me. "It is not what I want to do, and I know it is certainly not the best way to begin a holiday, but it is something I need to do while I am here in Valray. I need to restore the house, since we will be here often."

"Okay, we can do that," says Kyrie.

Taryn and Vesta nod yes as well. I am grateful for their continued support. We board the glider and I cannot hide my trepidation. I am afraid to find my parents' bodies still where I last saw them. I did not think I would ever return, but somehow, the enchantment offers me courage. When we arrive, the neglect is palpable. Everything is overgrown and unkept. As we walk around the side of the house, I see it first, the mound of a grave. I somehow intuitively know that my father is buried there. When I stop in my tracks, Kyrie follows my eyes out to what I am looking at, and he knows instantly.

"Are you okay?" he asks me.

"I just need a minute to adjust. I am almost relieved to see the grave...I was afraid his body was still inside. Although, I have no idea who buried him or killed him." The image makes me shudder. This scene is so different from the elaborate Sovran funeral rite we just experienced for Reown in Kallos. My mind barely knows how to balance the disparity.

A part of me rises above the scene and watches from below. It watches this restored version of me staring at the grave, holding the person who broke me. My shadow writes a poem of vindication in honor of the wounded healer who now lives inside my body. This wounded healer is me, and I have become mother and father to myself. I have become my own child.

> To the victor
> Go the spoils.
> The winner takes it all.
> You will never know how
> The depth of love's victory
> Over the torment turned,
> And how my wound
> Became wisdom.

"Would you like me to go walk through the house first just to make sure there are no other surprises?" Taryn asks me, his question bringing my awareness back into my body.

"Yes, would you? I really appreciate the offer. I do not know what happened to my mother. I do not know if she is still here." I quickly reply.

"I will go with you," Kyrie tells him. Vesta and I watch them walk through the side door. It was left unlocked.

We both turn our heads towards a sound I cannot quite place. Coming down the property's lane is a type of transporter I have never seen before. It is not like the glider where you climb into it and sit. For this type, it is a single seat that you straddle, holding onto handles to steer. There are three of them approaching. Vesta's eyes narrow in on the group, and then she asks aloud, "What is Barrow doing here?"

The small band of three men slows their speed and comes to a stop near us. Barrow is about to speak to us when Taryn and Kyrie come out of the side door, and I watch the surprised confusion appear on all the male faces at the same time.

"Taryn? What are you doing here?" Barrow asks his brother first as he dismounts the transporter and dashes towards him.

"Me? What are you doing here?" Taryn replies, receiving his brother's exuberant bear hug.

"The Wincot seat received a letter from Nulfest Valray. Nulfest had an investment he wanted to make into another invention, so father sent me to collect it and sign the terms," explains Barrow.

Part of me wonders what my father was angling for this time, but the other part of me does not really care anymore. That part of me is tired of trying to solve the unsolvable riddle that was my father.

"Nulfest Valray is dead," Taryn says as he points to the grave.

"What? How?" Barrow asks, his face paling a bit. I can tell he is afraid of being taken for a fool, not knowing whether to believe it as fact or fiction. "Well, shoot, this is bad luck! It just seems like every time the Wincot seat tries to make a deal with the Valray seat, a member of the Valray family winds up dead," he says anxiously.

We can all agree that he is not wrong. I try to remember the list. Wincot is not having good luck and cannot move forward with its innovations. I follow the strand back to Taryn's parents and realize their prejudice against Vesta is evidence.

Taryn answers Barrow's question first, "It is a long story, for later. But this is his daughter, Arden Valray, the new ruler of Valray."

"Arden? The daughter you were supposed to marry? I thought she died...her ghost was at your wedding." Barrow's confusion is understandable.

I step forward. "It is a long story, but I am back from the dead. It is nice to meet you," I say playfully, trying not to make the moment more awkward.

Kyrie steps forward, "I am Kyrie, from the Kallos province, nice to meet you."

Barrow shakes Kyrie's hand. I can see that he genuinely does not know how to connect all the dots dangling in front of him. It just does not make sense for all of us to be standing here together today. He does not know whether he is being pranked.

Kyrie senses it, too. "Let us all go inside and try to quickly recap the story for Barrow so he can be at ease."

"Hello, nice to see you again, Barrow," Vesta says as she walks up to him. Barrow dips his head as a sign of respect. "Vesta," he replies, and then he gives her a gentler hug than the one he gave Taryn.

I look at Kyrie with one question on my mind. "Did you find my mother?"

"Arden, there is no one inside. The house is empty." He says sympathetically. I nod that I understand, even though there is still so much that I do not. I am terrified of never knowing what happened to my mother.

I dread having to enter this house again. I step in, remembering the last time I left, hoping it was going to be my last. It is dizzying seeing it all again. I ask Taryn to lead everyone to the main den. As we pass the doorway of my father's study, I pause to look. There are still blood stains on the chair and floor. The windows are still broken but temporarily covered. It seems as if someone cleaned up most of the wreckage. That day feels like a hundred years ago.

We all sit in the front den. I am happy to let Taryn explain the story of my second life to his brother. I sit back and listen, impressed by his attention to the critical details. Barrow does not move an inch. Only his eyes shift from me to Kyrie, to Vesta, and back to Taryn, depending on which one of us he is talking about at the moment. Even his two companions listen intently as if their future depends on it.

I look at these two brothers. They could not be more different. Taryn is tall, dark, and handsome, with emerald-green eyes, short dark hair, a clean-shaven face, and a quiet, reserved, but strong nature. Barrow is a bit shorter and stockier, with lighter skin, wavy brown hair tucked behind his ears, a well-groomed beard, and piercing blue eyes. He is outspoken, upfront, and casual, with a boyish charm that is surprisingly disarming. It is obvious that Taryn was the one groomed and polished to be the next ruler, but I bet Barrow is beloved by all of Wincot. When Taryn reaches the end of our story, Barrow exhales deeply and finally sits back. We sit in silence for a minute, letting him decide whether he believes it.

"It is just all so incredible. Almost too good to be true." He looks at all of us with the awe of a younger brother and says, "Man, you all have had such a cool adventure together. I have just been running errands for my parents. You are so lucky, you have each found your person and you have been doing all these epic things…like changing the world. I wish to have that someday."

We all laugh and feel relieved to break the ice.

"Taryn, I just want you to know that I do not think it was right what our parents did to you, I am sorry. You too, Vesta. You were not treated as you should have been." Barrow admits. "I was ashamed of them when they refused to come to the wedding."

"Thank you, Barrow," Vesta says, followed by Taryn. "I was hoping they would come, so that I could finally meet them."

"So, what now?" Barrow asks.

"It is a good question. It is already evening, and I cannot imagine staying in this house for the night. But I need a little more time in Valray to arrange for the repairs to be done here before it gets worse. I also want to check on Aster before we go back home."

Vesta looks at me and says, "I know it is hard for you to be back here with the memories, and it may not be the best night sleep, but I think we can all manage staying here for the night. There seems to be plenty of empty rooms we can use."

"I am all in! This beats whatever father has in mind for me to do." Barrow exclaims.

Vesta says to Barrow and his two companions, Scout and Rim, "You three are welcome to join us tomorrow, if you want to go to Dashel, you can follow us there."

Barrow says, "We packed food that we can share. It will give us a chance to catch up!" He smiles at Taryn as he heads outside to get their bags.

Vesta turns to me and says, "Do not worry about any of us, we will be fine. We will get ourselves settled into some rooms. You just try to get some rest now; it has been a long day."

"Thank you." I tell her, more grateful than she could know, but somehow, she knows. She always knows.

Forty

Vera Valray

Truth be told, I took his hardened bones in hopes of conjuring him from death, but he did not return to me. At least not yet.

But the Powers Above whispered to me that she is weaving a plan for our future reunion. One of our descendants will show us the way. Agreements are always made in the after-realm, and I am anticipating the complexities of ours.

Arden

Deciding to stay here feels like staring down a fire-breathing dragon. Even reaching for the sword to slay it feels impossible. The sword is heavier than I can lift. I look at Kyrie. I need his help to get through staying here.

He walks over to me, puts his hands square on my shoulders, and locks his eyes on mine. "You are not alone. I will be with you. We can do this together."

> I do not want to
> Carry the past within me
> Anymore.
> I do not want
> My cells to remember
> The haunting
> Memories.
> I have been trusted
> With a beautiful
> Weapon,
> And it is time to use it.

I try that sword again in my mind, and this time, it is lighter. I grab it with both hands and slay the invisible dragon that always seemed to lurk within these walls. I take a deep breath of relief. Kyrie and I head upstairs to my old bedroom. It was truly another lifetime ago that I slept here. This was the only place where I felt safe. The irony is not lost on me now. A slight shudder goes up my spine.

"The girl who used to live here is dead," I say to Kyrie.

"I know. I would have loved her," he replies.

"She was put in an unmarked grave on her wedding day," I say.

"I found her grave."

"And then what happened?" I ask.

"She brought me back to life," he says, with tears in his eyes.

I go to him and hold him tightly.

"I was so scared today when I thought I lost you. It was terrifying to feel it all this time. After your father was killed and you went into that unreachable darkness for days, I did not have access to my feelings yet. So, I logically understood that it was a terrible situation, but I could not feel the fear and cry the tears that I had today. Your screams of pain touched a part of me I did not know existed. What happened to you? Where did you go?" He asks.

I tell him the story of the bird, and the hand, the voice, and the scroll. Then I tell him about the terrible agony and the searing pain, the plunge back into death, and the abyss of cries that were never allowed release. I tell him how the memory of him facing the painful breaking of the spell inspired me to face the painful ripping of stitches. I tell him everything I learned on that flight into the unknown. I tell him how I have seen what happens to the body when the ego prevents the spirit from healing the soul.

I let him carry me to the bed of my past life, and we travel together into a time and space that is our own, no longer belonging to the past or future but something that is only ours in this present moment. He found the realm within me that fate had always intended for him to travel, as I lose myself in the faraway galaxies hidden in his eyes. Sometimes, love is palpable, and sometimes it is cosmic.

Thankfully, it was a short night, and there were no hauntings. My relief is palpable. I did not realize until now how much I was afraid of encountering either my mother's or father's ghost during the night. I thank the Powers Above that it was not on the agenda as another next-level experience to navigate. But I did have a profound dream, one that I will think about for as long as the memory lives in my mind.

The enchanted woman standing behind Claudegus in the family portrait comes to life and steps out of the canvas. She has the same beautiful voice that I have heard before, and she calls my name. When I approach her, she holds out an exquisite quilt and tells me to step inside. The moment the quilt is wrapped around my shoulders, I open my eyes and wake up before I can ask her name. I lay there quietly for a long time, letting myself linger on the memory of it until I see Kyrie wake up.

I smile and say good morning.

"I cannot wait to get back to mornings that have coffee," he says sleepily. I smile with agreement, remembering the smell and the pleasure of each first hot sip.

"Before we leave here, is there anything from your room that you would want to bring back to Kallos with you?" He asks thoughtfully.

I look around, and I see it on the bookshelf. My journal. It is where I wrote my thoughts and feelings into lines of poetry. I smile and go to retrieve it. I open the last poem and read aloud,

> "I followed that love
> Like a thread on fire.
> A spark running down
> The untouched fibers.

Leaving nothing but
Ash behind me."

"Did you write that?" Kyrie asks.

"Yes, it is my poetry journal. I am so glad it is still here. This paper has always held my pain. It holds all my secrets, my thoughts. It knows my darkness. It is where my shadow lives. When I was alone here, with my journal, was when I felt safe. This paper soothed and comforted me when my body could not hold any more pain, the paper cradled it all."

"Are you telling me that I made a vow with a poet?" He asks, smiling.

"Yes, you did." I grin back at him. "I am sorry I never told you. I am always drafting poems silently in my head. I have written so many since you found me, I just did not have my journal to write them in. It is how I process my emotions when I am flooded. The words just come to me; it is how I have always self-soothed the pain."

"Can you read it to me again?" He asks, so I do.

"It is haunting...it is as if you wrote about your future without ever knowing what would happen. When did you write that one?" He asks.

I look back at the words. I suddenly remember the day I wrote it. "It was the day before I died." I reply and shiver at the realization.

"Can you read me another one?" Kyrie asks.

I flip back a few pages.

> "Your love is a suffering
> I have learned to load on my back
> And carry uphill.
> Learning to tolerate the pain
> Of it pressing into my skin,
> Bearing down into my bones.
> I carry it like a fresh
> Leather backpack
> That wears over time.
> Every touch making its mark.
> Every passing glance leaving
> Its bruised indentation."

I look up at Kyrie, and his hand has moved over his heart. He is clutching it like he is in pain. He looks stunned.

"I felt your pain inside of me. You have suffered so much. Come here," he says as he puts both arms out and draws me into an embrace of safety and comfort. "You do not have to carry that load anymore. I want to take it from your shoulders. Let us leave it here."

I agree and imagine setting it all down.

"I want to check on my sister, I need to know she is okay, but I am so nervous about facing them again. I am holding a tension of trying to trust that this is all real, and yet, I am still afraid of betrayal. I have both courage and terror all at once. The pain of the past is still as fresh as the recent beautiful-fantastic. I hold my experience of past reality in one hand, and my present mystical wonderment in the other. It is like being both above and below the water at the same time."

His warm embrace feels like the beautiful quilt from my dream. He whispers, "You are not alone, I am with you for all of it." I let myself melt into it until I am ready to face the day ahead.

Forty-One

Barrow

I can only follow my heart. It is how I am made, although my parents would be utterly disappointed to know this about me. They believe I am malleable, easy to control. But they do not know the real me. I have been docile, dutiful even, but after I saw what happened to Taryn, I have made up my mind to set my own course. They do not know this, of course. They think I am ready and happy to claim the seat, but it was never mine to claim. I am looking for true love. I am looking for true happiness. I am looking for my freedom. And I have never seen anyone have both a Sovran seat and true love, well, until today.

Last night I dreamed I was flying on the back of a majestic bird above the old Dashel province. We circled it three times, and on the third lap, it landed. When I unmounted and stood on the ground, the most beautiful woman I have ever seen approached and took my hand. She led me into a labyrinth of gold walls overflowing with honey.

Arden

After I find a contractor and arrange for the repairs, we pick up breakfast at a village cafe before our journey.

Barrow asks Kyrie and Taryn, "Do either of you know the way to Dashel?"

They both answer yes. Part of their education as heirs was studying the maps of the two realms. I never had those lessons.

Kyrie says, "I know where the pass is through the mountain range, we will just need to head south just a bit before we can cross over the hills."

"We will be right behind you," Barrow says.

The journey gives me plenty of time to think and wonder as I take in the new scenery around me along the way. The green rolling hills soothe me. I think back over the paper from the suitcase that lists the provinces' attributes. One of Dashel's province's blessings is hospitality, which means that at one time in history, people loved traveling there. I wonder how Earl Dashel will manage this new humble version of the power of hospitality. I also wonder if there will be an opportunity today to ask Aster about our mother's death.

"We are close," Kyrie tells us.

There is a slight change in the atmosphere, as if the abandoned, untouched province has been in a deep, century-old sleep and has suddenly awakened to daylight. I can sense that this raw nature is ready for human connection again.

"I will head towards the center of the old province, and we can start looking for them there." Kyrie offers.

We agree it is the best plan. We slow our speed and pay closer attention to the details. It is impressive to see how much is still standing today after all these years. So many of the buildings are constructed in stone, so the foundation of the past is still in the present. This will make their restoration work here easier.

When we arrive at the old arena area, we park the transporters and decide to walk around. It is easy to see that the old town was primarily designed for walking and was not planned for the new types of transport used today. Many quaint stone alleyways spiral out from the center, leading to what would have been a bustling market area of shops and cafes. I see the vision of both the past and the future. I am not sure whether it is just my imagination or a touch of the Valray enchantment within me, but I can see the alluring charm and magical draw of this place.

"I wonder if they are at the old Dashel residence?" Taryn asks and then continues. "Usually, the province estate is near the center…so it should be around here somewhere."

We decide to head east, and sure enough, as we come around the other side of the arena, there is a sprawling stone estate up ahead. We all pause and take in the size. The style is so different from what I have seen in Valray or Kallos. Its footprint makes the Kallos estate seem small, and the Valray house seems even smaller. It is not fancy or ornate. It is grand, in a masculine way. As we approach the property, I see movement under a large shade tree.

"Is that them?" I ask as I point to the shade under the largest tree.

We all squint and focus, hands over our eyes to see better without the glare. "I think so," Vesta says.

A gentle wind picks up, and I hope to the Powers Above that it is a good sign. Kyrie looks at me and smiles as if my thoughts of hope catch his attention. All the rest of nature becomes wide awake as well. I take a deep breath, and we walk forward. Aster notices us first, and I see her surprise. She stands to get a better view, but the new Earl Dashel remains sitting a bit longer. When we get closer, she bends down and helps him to his feet. It looks like they found a walking cane for him; he is still bearing that very heavy weight.

I wave my hand, hoping to send a friendly message, and thankfully, she waves back. It looks like they are having a picnic, making the best of what they have here. As we approach, I watch her slowly drop her arm and notice that her expression changes to a blank seven-mile stare. I check my body to make sure I did not unknowingly change into my ghost form. I turn around in case someone else unexpectedly arrives behind us.

Then I look to my left and notice Barrow has slowed his pace with a similar gaze upon his own face. It takes a moment, but everyone else finally sees what I am seeing. Vesta smiles, but Taryn's reaction is more complicated. He is working out the calculations of what this would mean from five different directions. I am learning that he is always quietly a few steps ahead in his mind; it is what makes him a great leader. Kyrie chuckles, along with Barrows' two companions. It looks like love at first sight has struck our younger siblings hard. I cannot help but wonder if Earl has noticed as well. Vesta laughs lightly when she realizes that Aster is so striking to Barrow that he stopped walking a few steps ago. We would all agree that our journey here is worth every minute witnessing this moment.

"Hello!" I say first as I walk up. Aster's eyes are fixed on Barrow's. She walks right past me, past all of us, and straight towards him. We are all transfixed by the two of them.

She offers her hand to him, and he takes it in both of his hands. Then, her loose hand soon joins in. Their eyes are still only on each other. Kyrie looks at me with raised eyebrows. He is a romantic at heart, so I know he is captivated by this new story. Taryn is astonished but concerned. I look at Earl, and he has a faraway gaze, like he is remembering a moment like this from his own past many years ago. The silence is not awkward yet, but any longer, it will be.

"I am Barrow Wincot, Taryn's brother," he says first, bringing relief to all of us.

"I am Aster Dashel, Arden's half-sister," she replies. "Let me introduce you to the new Lord Dashel, my guardian," she says as she leads him back towards the group, back to Earl.

I cannot think of a better personality than Barrow's for this first introduction of Earl Dashel as the new humble ruler of a province purposed with hospitality. Barrow's casual, genuine charm puts everyone at ease. He shakes Earl's hand like he is meeting Aster's real father for the first time and wants to make a good impression. I watch the whole interaction and am impressed. He must be beloved by the people of Wincot.

"So, what are the plans for Dashel?" Barrow asks Aster and Earl. "I would love to hear about what you two have in mind." He adds, with enthusiasm, an invitation with his hand to all of us to sit down and listen. Barrow is enchanted.

The grass is soft, and the shade feels cool. I watch Aster come to life as she begins explaining the vision for the new Dashel province. She has captured the essence of the power of hospitality without ever having seen that paper. She has thought of clever ways to draw people in to visit and to entice enough entrepreneurs to stay and make Dashel a new home. I look at her. She is even more stunning than when we first arrived. Something is glowing from within, lighting up her topaz eyes. I have never seen her this animated. Barrow is putty in her hands.

When she is finished, I ask, "Aster, can I have a moment to talk to you in private?" She nods and stands up, and I rise to meet her. I hear Barrow continue to ask Earl questions as we walk away from the group.

Forty-Two

{One hundred and ten years before the present}

My beloved boy, Earl Dashel,

I never thought I would be the first to say goodbye. No mother ever plans that. What a beautiful boy you are- a fine young man you are becoming. I see so much of myself in you, and I fear for you once I am gone. I will not be there to protect your sensitive heart from your father's fits of anger and bouts of pride. I wish I had more time with you to help guide you through the upcoming years.

What a force your father can be. He was not ready to rule the province. The duty was thrust upon him when his older brother Rex fell in love with a young villager from Valray and gave up the seat to marry her. Your father never forgave Rex for leaving Dashel; for leaving him unprepared to rule.

I do hope you are able to have both one day- love and the Sovran seat. Not many people do. I have heard stories from long ago, but I have not seen it yet myself. I am not sure why it is so hard. Do try to be strong and become your own man. Follow your heart. I believe in you.

Your doting mother,

Bess Dashel

Arden

"Aster, we have so much to catch up on. I was there when mother took her last breath. Her last words were 'Find Aster, tell her.' And then I saw Nulfest shot with an arrow, but I am not sure who did it." I cannot get all the words out fast enough when she calmly interrupts.

"Rexus told me your ghost was there that day he shot Nulfest. He was spooked by your presence and did not know what it meant. There have been so many stories told about your ghost."

"Rexus? The revolutionary leader from Valray?"

"He is my father."

"What?" I am shocked. "Your father killed my father? And I just made him my Regent? How long have you known about him?"

"Not long. When news traveled to Vaxxa that your ghost appeared at Taryn's wedding, Earl Menstus and I traveled to Valray to look for any signs of you. Menstus wanted to question Nulfest, to find out about your death. He was deeply grieved about the news. And infuriated with Nulfest. When we went to the estate, Nela and Rexus were there, cleaning up the disaster in father's study. Rexus buried Nulfest, but he took mother's body for a proper burial on his family's property. That is when Nela and Rexus told me everything."

"Menstus and Rexus met each other?"

"Yes, Menstus told Rexus he would help him lead the people to revolution if Rexus would help him reclaim Dashel. And Menstus would have gone to Kallos sooner, but he stayed longer in Valray to make sure I was okay. I was feeling so ill after learning that mother had died. I was so mad at myself for staying away so long. Earl had offered to bring me back many times, but I chose to stay. I loved it there in Vaxxa. He was worried about leaving me in Valray, but he said he knew that something had happened to Reown. He said his heart had an ache he had not felt in twenty-six years. I decided to follow him even though Rexus did not want me to leave. But I felt this powerful sense that I needed to go to Kallos too. Now we know why."

"Can you tell me the story about Mother and Rexus?"

"Rexus and mother were in love since they were teenagers, but her father forced her to marry Nulfest instead for her family's rise in social status. However, they never stopped seeing each other. They found a way to stay together. Nela is Rex's sister. That is how he and mother exchanged messages and stayed connected."

Nela. She was like an older sister to me. She taught me about my monthly cycles and what would happen on my wedding night. My mother and I never had these conversations, but with Nela, I could safely ask her anything.

Aster continues the story. "After I was born, they started planning for the three of us to leave Valray one day and run away together. Their plans became finalized when mother arranged your betrothal."

"Is that why Mother was sending me away to Wincot?" I ask, trying to make sense of it all. Trying to hide the blow to my heart, unable to decipher if my mother was trying to get rid of me so she could start her new family or send me to safety? I am guessing Rexus is where all her affection went; there never seemed to be any leftovers. I always felt greedy, trying to gobble the crumbs when I found them. I wonder if she despised me because she hated my father. Or loved me just enough to not leave me stuck with him.

"I do not know," Aster replies. "They were planning to take me with them, start again as a family, but Nulfest destroyed their plans when he used me as bait and sent me to Menstus. Nulfest lied to her about where I was and when I would be back. And he lied to me about where I was going. He said he had a special provincial job for me to do, and if I went, I could be rewarded with more freedom to travel."

"That bastard." I let the words fall out. "Aster, I was so sad when you left. I did not understand what lies were being told and the betrayals that were happening. Everyone stopped talking to me when I told him that I would not call off the wedding. After you left, I spent my days alone, waiting for the wedding."

I watch the heat rise in her cheeks as she admits, "I would never have left if I had known about mother and Rexus' plans. Rexus told me that mother did not want to leave without me, that they should wait for my return. I would have happily gone with them. I hate how I was so easily manipulated by everyone. Even Menstus got in my head when I first arrived. While he thought I was you, he treated me like a queen. I had never known such attention, it was intoxicating. I know it sounds crazy, but I did not want it to end. I did not want to be me ever again."

"How did Menstus find out the truth?" I ask.

"Your wedding was the first alliance between two Lashgan provinces in a long time, so it garnered attention. When it was called off because you went missing, he did not think anything of it, other than that I was you. But when the story of your corpse-bride appearing at Taryn's proposal reached Vaxxa, Menstus knew something was off. Nulfest had already admitted to him that he only had one legitimate daughter, and it was the one marrying Taryn Wincot. So, Menstus demanded that I tell him the truth of my identity. When I found out that Nulfest was not my real father, and that he had lied to me and used me, I chose allegiance to Menstus that day. Luckily, Mazek was there to help us through it."

My eyes are wide. I can hear my heart thrumming in my ears. I see the fierceness in her. It is the same force of power I saw yesterday in Rexus. They have the same eyes and the same spirit. I finally understand something I did not before. We might have the same mother, but our noticeable differences come from our fathers. When I compare Rexus and Nulfest in my mind, I notice a strange sense of envy rise in me. I look at my sister. She has such an honest boldness that I will always admire. She has become the dark horse.

"Did Menstus ever tell you why he cast the spell on Kallos?" I take the risk and ask a question I have been wanting to know.

"Yes, he told me the story of him and Reown. They were once in love," she says.

My eyebrows rise. That is not what I expected her to say.

She continues. "When he was still a young boy, he and his mother fled to the Pallayes realm after his father died unexpectedly working in Valray. His mother heard about the opportunities for work in Kallos, so she took them there and got a job on staff at the Kallos estate."

Menstus' mother worked in the house that is now my home. "And then what happened?" I ask.

"He and Reown grew up together. His mother Solange was a beautiful and kind woman and Reown's father, Alton, a widower, fell madly in love with her. It was a private love affair, lasting seventeen years until he died. On the days when his mother brought Earl to work with her, he and Reown would sneak out and go on adventures together across the estate. Even when they were teenagers, they saw each other every day when Earl would drop off his mother and pick her up from work, still sneaking away for time together. They were secret childhood friends who became secret teenage sweethearts."

I do not know how to tell Kyrie about this.

"When she turned twenty-one, Reown's father became gravely ill. He wanted to make sure the Sovran seat was secure, so he made an alliance with the ruler of Teahn for one of his sons to marry Reown. She was conflicted between her heart and her duty because Earl Menstus had already asked her to make the Redamancy Vow. She told her father about Earl, but he said it was forbidden to form a Sovran union with anyone outside of the Pallayes realm. He told her that if she ran off with Menstus, she could never come back to Kallos. So, she reluctantly obeyed her father and accepted the Teahn betrothal instead. Shortly after the betrothal, her father died. Reown was crowned and then married Juris Teahn."

I think back to the scene at Reown's death. This is why she reacted the way she did. This explains her outrage and her hidden shame. Hearing this story helps me no longer feel a misplaced guilt for her death. It was not my fault. I refocus. I need to know the rest of the story. Kyrie will need to know all of it, too.

"And then what happened?" I ask.

"When Earl Menstus came to see Reown one last time, Juris refused. Instead, Juris aggressively attacked Menstus and left him for dead outside the estate. Solange was immediately let go and told not to return. No one knows if Reown ever found out what really happened."

I swallow. My throat is dry. I never met Kyrie's father.

"A member of the staff, a friend of his mother, found Earl, had mercy, and had his severely wounded body sent to Clemen to be treated by a specialist. While Menstus was away in that long recovery, his mother died at home alone, unbeknownst to anyone. When he returned home after those years in recovery, he found her corpse in that awful state. He alone buried her. His body may have recovered but, on that day, his heart had turned to stone."

The memory of those stone pieces breaking flashes through my mind. "Did he ever tell you about the spell?" I ask.

"Yes, he grew up hearing the story about his great-grandmother's desperate cry for the return of the love she lost. So, in his agonizing heartache, he cast the spell of the Veiled Heart. He hoped that Reown would remember her first love and find him, to break the spell. That is why Menstus wanted to find you, for your tears. He always hoped that Reown would come to him to break the spell. He wanted to be ready. When he heard you were getting married, he was anxious to get your tears before you were no longer a Valray maiden. He did not know if they would break the spell after you married."

This is such a strange turn of events and I may never fully understand my place in all of it. Or Aster's.

"Are you really happy here with Earl Dashel? Is he truly different now?" I ask curiously, still unable to grasp it.

"Yes, he has always taken care of me, better than Nulfest ever did. But now, there is just a peace about him, he is not as anxious. He does not say much anymore, I think he is trying to bear the heavy weight he feels. He just has a far-away look in his eyes, like there is a vision he cannot unsee."

When the ego dies
There is an actual death
With a season of grief.

"I know I am where I am supposed to be, like everything has led to this moment of today."

"What do you mean?" I ask.

"Because I had a dream last night...there was a man flying on the back of a giant bird, circling the sky above the Dashel province. I was watching to see what would happen to him. When the bird landed in front of me, the man got off and came towards me and said, 'I am Barrow Wincot. I have been sent to you.'"

I cannot hide the surprise on my face when I ask, "You dreamed about Barrow coming to Dashel? Does he look the same in person as he did in your dream?"

"Yes, exactly him, that is why I was so stunned when he walked up. But the strange part is that, in my dream, the bird was you. You smiled at me, and then you grew wings again and flew away."

I hide my shock but say, "You are not the first person this week to have envisioned me as a bird."

"And there is something else. Rex's great, great, grandfather was the heir to Sovran seat of Dashel, before he renounced it for the Valray woman he loved. He was the older brother to the Lord Dashel of Menstus' family line."

She waits for me to connect the dots of what she is saying. "You are part of the Dashel lineage. Not just by appointment, but by blood. This is your destiny." I am genuinely amazed. "And, strangely enough, that means we are both related to Earl Menstus. I mean, Earl Dashel."

She smiles softly at me. I see the complex dimensions that have layered her perspective. She has found her own ways to survive in a mad existence of family and betrayal. She went through it like a fearsome warrior but came out with empathy like no other. She will be an incredible ruler one day, formidable and benevolent.

Forty-Three

{Twenty-three years before the present}

My dear son Earl Menstus,

I am writing this letter as my goodbye, since I no longer believe that I will get to say these things in person. I am dying, and I do not know when you will return. I am too weak to travel back to Clemen to try to see you again.

What a long road we have traveled together. You were such a devoted son, always taking care of me, especially after your father died. You became the man of the house at such an early age. I am sorry I could not give you a better life. Your father would not have approved of the move from Valray, though. He told me to keep you near Dashel in case the fates finally turned in our favor. You have read Vera's letter, of course. I am sorry I did not listen.

I blame myself for what has happened to you. I should have never let you return to the house to plead for my job after Juris fired me. There were so many good years there up until Lord Kallos died, and then what heartache we both endured. He was so good to me and loved me in his own secret way. It broke his heart that he could not give Reown his blessing to be with you. He knew of her great love for you. He was afraid that none of the Teahn brothers were not going to be a good match for her, but he had an even greater fear of breaking protocol. We would speak of these things in his last days as I fed him and cared for him. He worried that you and Reown would run off together and leave the seat vacant without an heir, or worse. I always tried to understand his great fear of a union across the two realms, but I never did. I always believed Kallos would have been a better province with you by her side, but I know our family's history makes it hard.

And now, you have nearly lost your life, and I am near my own end, here alone. I know the necklace is the only thing of value that was passed down to you. At least I kept that promise to your father and made sure you got it. Keep it safe in case it serves you in the future. I love you beyond time.

Your loving mother,

Solange Menstus

Arden

"Aster, do you think we can start over." I begin, my voice shaking. "Neither of us are the same as we were, we have both been altered by trauma but also transformed by love. Even though we may never completely understand each other's pain, I wonder if we can somehow reconcile the past for the new future we have together. You will be the ruler of Dashel sooner than later, and I would love for us to be trusted allies. Would you be willing to trust me?" I put my whole heart into this question.

She stares right into my eyes with her inherited fierce strength that I do not possess. "Yes. Of course I want to be allies, but more than that, I want to be trusted sisters. And now I have one question for you. How *did* you die?"

I tell her the strange story of Nulfest hiring the Zenif coachman who had already been hired by Rae's uncle to end my life that day and how the tree ended his. I tell her about Rae and how I met Rexus.

As we walk back to the group, she says, "I invited Rexus to come to Dashel to invest in a shop here, to sell some of his furniture."

"That is a great idea. Aster, the original Dashel province thrived in the industry of tourism and hospitality. There were hotels, cafes, and fair-trade markets that people traveled from the other provinces to experience and enjoy. They also mastered the art of beekeeping and harvested honey that was famous and highly sought. If you can think of ways to use alchemy, where it is a mutually beneficial exchange, you should find great success. And to avoid the downfalls of pride and foolishness, cling tight to humility and the inseparable pair of justice and mercy."

I have a genuine desire for her to thrive here and a hope to come back and experience the fruits of her success. When we approach the others, they are discussing ideas for reviving the Dashel marketplace and making it bustle with business again.

Kyrie looks at me and says, "We should get back to Kallos soon." I nod yes, I agree.

Barrow looks at all of us and says, "I am not going home. I am staying in Dashel…" Then looks to Aster and Earl and asks, "If you'll have me?" I see the future hanging in the balance of his question…this moment will be another new beginning in the story of the United Realm, and it is another domino in the unfolding prophecy.

A week ago, no one could see this coming. I smile at the Powers Above, saying silently, 'You are so clever in sending Barrow as their first permanent guest,' and I chuckle quietly to myself. Even Barrow is part of this great prophetic unfolding, this epic adventure, and he is finally getting to jump in and have a turn. Everything he wished for yesterday at the Valray house is coming true for him right now.

"Of course…that would be great, thank you," Aster replies with a softness I have never known her to possess. I wonder if she will tell Barrow about her dream. She looks to Earl Dashel for permission and reassurance that he is willing to let another male into their small circle. He gives her a knowing smile and nods to Barrow. Aster looks back at Barrow and adds, "We would love to have you join us here…there is a lot of work ahead."

I have seen enough of Kyrie's smiles to know that the large one on Barrow's face means he is diving all in, and nothing will deter him from the future he has in mind. Thank the Powers Above, no one will ever have to defeat the old Lord Menstus for Aster's hand…but if there was ever a man brave enough to do it, we are looking at him.

Barrow looks at his two companions. "Will you please bring a message to my parents for me?"

"Anything for you, Barrow," Rim replies.

"Please tell them I am not coming home. They have another son who would rather have love than power."

I look at Taryn, and his expression says he is already imagining his parents' reaction to this.

"Yes, Barrow," Scout replies. Then he looks to Aster, "If we are able to return, is there anything you would like us to bring back to Dashel?"

"Good people who are ready to create a new province...one that has never been seen before," is her only reply.

They both smile at the imagined adventure ahead and turn to leave, each giving Barrow a firm shake that turns into a bear hug. It is obvious these three have spent their youth together, and their bond is thicker than blood. They will be back.

While they are still in earshot, Taryn yells out to them, "Please tell my parents that I am currently serving as an Ambassador for the Kallos and Valray provinces. I can be found traveling between the two." His grin is one I have not seen on him before; it is as if he is enjoying his own sort of revenge, serving it sweet and cold. Vesta shrugs with a light chuckle of her own.

After our final goodbyes, the four of us walk back to the glider in a comfortable silence, each of us processing the day's events. Then Taryn asks, "Do you think Barrow will be safe here?"

I almost want to apologize just in case it all ends in tragedy. But then I remember Aster's dream and say, "I am confident that everything is as it should be now. I think the Powers Above have a hand on this one."

We climb in, Kyrie turns the glider towards home, and I cannot decide whether to tell them everything I learned today from Aster or wait until a better time. The inner conflict gnaws at me. I am not ready yet to tell Kyrie about the other version of his parents' story. I know it will be incredibly hard for him to hear it. Would there have even been a dark lord without the ways in which they broke him? He needs to hear this later, in private. I think about Rexus and remember his eyes; familiar because they are Aster's. I wonder if when he was searching mine, he was looking for my mother. I wonder if he saw her. I tell them about how Aster found her real father, which answers our questions about my father's death.

When we arrive back in Kallos, the people are still celebrating and enjoying the holiday. I long for that weightless joy of hope again, the one I see tonight in the people of Kallos. But right now, there is a heaviness that only true grief can weigh as I remember all of Aster's words. Tonight, after Kyrie falls fast asleep, I go out alone to the top balcony and face the moon. I let myself face the painful truth of all that I learned today.

I look at the story of my old life, and I say to my past self, "It is all so sad. What happened to you, your mother, and your sister, is all so tragic, and it is going to take some time to grieve it. It is going to involve some pain when the memories wash in like waves, but your pain makes sense, and I will be here with you, you are not alone." I cry for my younger self.

Then I think of my new life, and I say to my present self, "I am so proud of you, you have done some incredibly brave things in this short amount of time. You have faced grief and death, you have experienced the immense power of love, you stood in the gap of time and became a bridge while the realm around you changed, and you trusted the Powers Above, surrendering the entirety of your whole life." I take a deep breath of gratitude and feel myself bowing in reverence.

Finally, I think of my future self and smile. I tell her, "I have not met you yet, but I already like you. I trust you because I know your story and your capacity to love; I have seen it. I already admire your bravery because I know you will amass the courage to do even greater and harder things than you ever have before. Because more will be asked of you, and I know you will follow love wherever it leads you." With this, I let my heart wring itself out with tears of awe and wonder at the person I am to become.

I wait until this moment to put my necklace back on. I realize that, unlike me, it was never buried underground. My destiny did not die. It stayed alive the whole time. I feel the warmth of the metal against my skin. As if it were a light glowing in the dark. After the tears of true release fall, my heart feels so alive again, but this time, it is full of a wholeness that comes when all truths of a story are accepted: the loss of the past, the courage of the present, and the hope for the future. I decide to let the great tailor use a fancy double stitch in this beautiful new layer now that I know there are two sides to love: death and life. I imagine her smile with pleasure at her handiwork. She has not been able to embroider love in a long time.

I fall asleep with immense gratitude for my new life. I am free, and my voice has been unlocked. Somehow, in a mystical way, there is a woman in the outer realm who knows me and has claimed me. I am seen, known, and heard. I am cared for and understood. I have the safety and security that comes with a wiser woman guiding, teaching, and leading the way. I receive this gift of the divine feminine mothering me and let it wash over me. I fall asleep with a peace I have never known and an understanding that it will always be inside of me now.

Forty-Four

{Presently}

Dear Taryn,

It is time for the lyrics to be transformed. I am enclosing the new ones. You will never have to sing the original ones again. Let them go. Everything from the past is being made into something new. I think you will come to love what the power of this new song brings.

~ the Powers Above

By your love
I am purified
No longer lost down
Deep inside

I am free
I am free
My Love

Now that you
Are here with me
Life is just
As it should be

Come and see
Come and see
Our Love

You're my hope
And my fire
Fan the flame
Of this desire

I am free
I am free
My Love

With this vow
As our guide
I'll be always
By your side

We are free
We are free
My Love

Arden

"What if we just keep today to ourselves?" Kyrie asks me this morning, still holding me tightly.

"Yes," I say as I roll over and kiss him softly. "We can lay out by the pool and swim and remember how this all began." The private pool behind the estate is extraordinary, and it is all ours.

"That sounds wonderful. But I do not need a pool to remember," as he rolls me back over, kissing my neck and making me laugh. "But, before we do go down to the pool, I want to show you the whole house so that you can decide which rooms you would want to be kept private for just our use," Kyrie says as he continues to kiss me softly. "I can start lining up the renovations soon."

"I would love that," I reply. "The days have been going by so fast with so much change. We are finally having a chance to catch up to the present moment."

After we eat breakfast together, Kyrie makes us each a cup of coffee to bring on the tour of the sprawling house, and we sit in the middle of every room, deciding what purpose it should have. Most of these rooms have not been touched in years. We choose the bedroom with our favorite balcony. I look up and imagine the map of the United Realm painted across the ceiling, and smile.

"What do you think we should do with my mother's old bedroom?" He asks me and continues before I can reply. "I do not know if I can go back there. That room feels so dark and heavy."

I think of Earl Menstus as a young man in love with her, his heart crushed. I remember Reown's anguish before she died. I replay their conversation. Her reaction to Kyrie's defense of choosing me makes sense, considering the new information about her and Earl Menstus. I think her unprocessed grief of choosing another man over her true love was what began her frozen resignation, and I believe that same realization is what stopped her heart at the end when Kyrie said, 'I did what I hope you would have done as well.' I know I need to tell him everything soon.

"We can have it cleared out to become a new space, fresh walls and floor, lighten it up. And then, in some way, honor her when we decide what to do with it." It is the only thing I can think of offering now. "Maybe we can do something special with the dresser from Valray."

He smiles with appreciation, and I decide it is better to tell him now.

"Kyrie, I have to tell you something really important, but I am nervous, because it is going to be pretty difficult for you to hear." I try to sound brave.

Worry crawls across his face. "Arden, what is it? Please, do not be afraid. I need to know the truth…whatever it is." He turns his body around to sit and face me; our knees are touching, and he takes my hands into his.

I begin. "Aster told me yesterday about the history between Earl Menstus and your parents. I am sorry I did not tell you last night, we were both so tired. But I knew that I needed to find the right moment, one where we both have the emotional energy, because it is not the same story that your parents told you."

His eyes widen. As I open my mouth to form the next word, a staff member steps in and alerts us to the guests in the front den…Taryn's parents, the Wincots, are downstairs. I guess we should have seen this coming. But we did not. I take a deep breath and try to tap into the inner strength that saw me through the last few days.

We look at each other. He squeezes my hands and says, "I want to hear everything. Can we try again after they are gone?"

I say yes and kiss him, reassuring him.

Then he adds, "Remember, we are not responsible for their situation, and you do not need to try to please them."

I take a deep breath and exhale, letting go of the old notion that I need to people-please the older adults in the room. When we walk into the front den, they stand to greet us. But the pleasantries do not last long.

"Where is our son?" Taryn's mother, Berel, asks.

"And what is the meaning of this?" His father, Mavis, asks, motioning to my presence with his arm. "Your crazy family is what started all of this in the first place. First, your mother pays us to let you marry our son, then you end up as a corpse-bride and she ends up dead. Next, your father asks us to build a transporter that can take him beyond the realms, and he ends up dead. Thanks to you, we have one son disgraced and married to a foreign villager, and the other son is in love with your illegitimate half-sister and wants to help the dark lord rebuild a ghost town. Now, the Wincot seat is left without an heir."

This is not going to be the afternoon I had in mind. As much as I want to defend myself and clear my name, I realize that I do not owe them an explanation. I am not the cause of their own downfall, as convenient as it is to peg it on me. I will not take the bait. I have learned the importance of protecting my power and not giving it away.

"All I can offer you is to arrange a meeting with Taryn and Vesta. You are welcome to wait here while we pick them up. They are our beloved guests, and their privacy and protection are our utmost priority." I reply kindly but firmly. It takes everything in me to remain calm.

I can see this is not how they expected me to respond. They were ready to keep an upper hand and control the encounter. Before my death, I would have eaten out of their hands and played right into their trap, just like my parents taught me. But after walking into the pit of death, facing every horrible truth, and then watching the power of love bring me back to life. Well, it has given me clarity that no one can easily manipulate anymore.

They agree to wait. When we arrive at the villa, Taryn and Vesta seem to be having a day like ours began, relaxing together.

"Hi! What brings you two out here?" Vesta asks warmly.

"Your parents." I reply, looking straight at Taryn with a friendly grin.

"My parents are in Kallos?" Taryn asks.

"They are sitting in our den, waiting to speak with you," Kyrie replies, with a chuckle.

Taryn and Vesta look at each other wide-eyed.

"Well, knowing my parents, they will not leave until they get what they want," Taryn says.

"Taryn," I say directly to him, "What do you want? Because you need to know for sure what that is before you sit down with them."

"I refuse to be their puppet. I am a grown man. They still see me and Barrow as belonging to them like small boys. They see us as an investment they want to make a return on, and that we owe them. They are upset that they have lost control."

"So, what are your terms?" I ask.

"I refuse to be under their rule or control. I would rather have nothing than any part of their controlling hand on my life. They were so quick to discard me and Vesta without ever taking the time to know or understand what we have together. They did not even come to our wedding."

I flashback to their wedding and scan my memory, looking for the Wincot family. I realize now it was only Barrow and Vesta's neighbors in those front pews.

"Okay, are you ready to face them?" Vesta asks Taryn.

"Yes, and they will not like it one bit." A smile of equal parts, satisfaction, and nervousness.

Forty-Five

{One hundred years before the present}

Lord Dashel

I should have burned that witch, Vera Valray, while I had the chance. Vile woman! How dare she think she can lay a claim on this seat? I am not a fool; I see this ploy for what it is. That insufferable father of hers must be scheming to increase his wealth and power. Trying to manipulate the feelings of my son, tempting him to give up everything for a baby!

I have seen this all before with my brother Rex, blasted fool! Fell for a villager and left it all for me to pick up the pieces. Bess, it is a good thing you are not here to see this. You would have fallen for the whole trick. You would have taken both the girl and baby in and called them family.

Arden

The Wincots are pacing around the den when we return. I wonder how many laps they have made while we were gone. Hopefully, the lovely pieces of art around the room gave them something to focus on.

"Hello, mother, father," Taryn says as warmly as he can manage, then slides into sarcasm. "You remember Vesta? Or maybe not since you were not willing to meet her."

I watch their faces as Vesta steps up next to Taryn, taking her place by his side. Her rare beauty is the kind that requires a moment to adjust to when you first behold it. Earlier, when they spewed out the word villager, I knew then that this moment would be satisfying to witness, and I savor Vesta's silent vindication with great enjoyment. They are caught off guard by her regal beauty. I do not know what they were expecting, but it was not this. Both of their bottom jaws drop down, and I work hard not to laugh aloud.

"Hello, it is nice to finally meet you," Vesta says with sincerity.

"I apologize for the gawking; we just did not expect you to be so...beautiful. You can imagine our surprise." Taryn's mother awkwardly admits.

I insert myself into the moment. "How about we all sit down and get a little more comfortable," I suggest, since we might be here longer than any of us wants to be.

"Mother, why are you here?" Taryn looks directly at her and asks boldly.

"Well, you can imagine our shock when we found out last night that your brother has decided not to return to Wincot, but to rebuild the abandoned Dashel," she dramatically explains.

"That is not my problem to solve," Taryn says dryly. "You discarded my leadership abilities when you questioned my choice of who to love and marry."

"Well, what did you expect us to do when you decided you would rather give up your duty to marry a villager from Valray?" She asks impatiently.

"I had hoped you would have an open mind and be willing to learn the truth. You had so much prejudice that you refused to meet Vesta and find out who she really is. Your ignorance is the cause of the problem you are in, and if you do not change somehow, it will lead to your downfall."

The noble ruler is shining from within. He is becoming his own man with each passing minute here, and I am honored to call him my friend. Vesta has obviously taught him the secrets of the provinces as well.

The Wincots have the wind knocked out of their sails. There is an awkward silence, and then his mother narrows her eyes and asks, "Learn what truth?"

A distinct kind of smile appears on Taryn's face...like he is about to enjoy their reaction to the answer to her question. Like he is the cat who ate the canary. Taryn and Vesta look at each other with a secret knowing only between them, and then she nods to him, like she is ready to answer this question.

"The truth is," Vesta begins, "my grandmother is the Sovran ruler of Amara, and I am her heir."

His mother whispers, shocked, "What? Your grandmother is Elspeth of Amara?"

"Yes." Vesta beams. "As long as my father was away in Vaxxa, and my mother and I were on mission in Valray, we could not risk anyone knowing my identity and location. My parents wanted to keep it that way, for my safety and protection."

"But, but...not even us?" his mother replies.

"Especially you, mother," Taryn says to her. "You would have announced it to the realms for your own benefit, not thinking about the possible danger it would have put Vesta in."

"But Taryn, you gave up everything, and you would not have had to if you would just been honest with us." His father arrogantly states.

Taryn tells them firmly. "You are missing the point entirely. No matter how many times you flip it, I will not take the blame for how you treated us."

"The point is," Vesta begins again, "the very fact that Taryn was willing to give up his seat for my hand is what made me choose him. It is how I knew it was worth what I would have to give up in exchange."

His parents tilt their heads to the side, not understanding where she is going with this.

"In the Amara bloodline, if a destined ruler is given the power of longevity, there is no more aging past the age of twenty-four. If the ruler has a pure heart, and finds true love worthy of sacrifice, the longevity can be given up, to age naturally with the chosen beloved. When I discovered that Taryn is my true love, I exchanged my power of longevity, so that I can now age at the same rate alongside him. I am not sure how else to say this, but I am much older than I look. I have been looking for true love for a long time."

I look at Vesta with awe. She is from Amara. I always knew there was something hidden about her, something remarkable. I cannot believe I did not see the resemblance to the girl in the painting sooner. It just makes our intertwined story so much richer. We are each from the lines of the only two granddaughters, the bookends. Then I remember what happened at her wedding when she made her vows, when her hair turned pearl white. I wonder if that was the exchange of her longevity for true love, happening before our eyes, the Powers Above sealing the bond with an outer sign.

They blink several times, readjust their bodies, look at each other, and look back at her.

"But what about your parents? Where are they now" His father asks.

"He and my mother are now safe in Amara, recovering together."

"But why is your mother not the next heir?" she asks.

"Because longevity has given us all a bit of added wisdom, it comes with living for so long. She was next in line for a long time, but after many years of building a home and family with my father, and raising a strong daughter, she asked for permission to step down and let me take her place in line. She saw what was destined for me. My mother's heart is so pure, there is no pride...she did not need to rule others to feel powerful or fulfilled.

Her love for my father and I gave her that fulfillment, and she received our love in return. It is the power of love."

The Wincots sit in stunned silence. This goes against everything they know to be true. I try to imagine Vesta's mother, even more mythical than the last time I imagined her, and I know I cannot wait to meet her one day. I wonder if she has pearl white hair like Vesta's. I scan my memory of her wedding again. Was her mother there? A faint image floats to my mind's eye of an ethereal woman with a lovely headpiece that had an attached light blue veil covering her face and hair. That must have been her. I look at Vesta again and realize she was mothered. We do not share the same hunger; she was fed the love she needed to know her true worth.

"Do you have any more questions before you go?" Taryn asks.

They look at him, trying to figure out who should say it.

"We want you to be next in line to the Wincot seat. We raised you for that role, and we all know your brother is not the right choice, especially now. Will you come back to Wincot?"

"I am sorry, you really should have thought that through before you made your decision to discard me so easily."

"Oh, are you going to make us grovel?" His father asks.

"No, I do not want your insincere apologies. If you cannot understand my heart, I at least want you to understand my terms."

"Well, just spit it out already," his father says impatiently.

"I no longer live under the power and control you believe you have over me, and I am not going to be your puppet while you dangle the Sovran seat in front of me. I am free. If I come back to Wincot, it is not as your heir in waiting, it will be as a Sovran ruler. Those are my terms. If they are not acceptable to you, then you can beg Barrow to come home."

I look to his mother for her answer. She looks as if she has been slapped unexpectedly.

"Well," Berel begins with indignation, "I am sorry if I am not as wonderful and beautiful and humble as Vesta's mother."

Then she stands and says, "After all I have done for you, this is how you treat me. Unbelievable." She barges out the front door. Taryn's father follows close behind, stopping to give Taryn a glare of disappointment before his dramatic exit. The door slams behind him.

Forty-Six

{Presently}

Rexus,

You took someone's life with your own hands. Even though no one has accused you, the scales of justice are off set, and I see the debt that hangs in the balance. Much will be required of you. Prepare. In the days and weeks ahead, you will begin your amends and learn to forgive.

~ the Powers Above

Arden

"Well, that went better than I expected," Taryn said aloud.

We all sit in silence for a minute. I look at Taryn and Vesta with compassion. They have given up so much to have a life together.

"I want you all to know, this visit does not change anything for me," Taryn begins. "This is why I needed to leave Wincot, and this is why I had to set those terms to go back. What I have learned over the past year is that a cage is not worth it. I have an amazing future ahead full of adventure with the love of my life, and the best kind of friends I could have ever asked for." His eyes well with tears, but his big smile breaks through first and overcomes them. "It is not lost on me that it seemed easier for Earl Menstus to humble himself before all of Kallos more than the current ruler of Wincot could in front of her own son."

I think about it. He is not wrong, but there was extreme help from the Powers Above that day.

"Yes, but the humbling downfall of Earl Menstus was written in the prophecy. I am not sure he would have chosen it freely on his own. Your mother just might need some time to think everything over," I offer, and then have another sudden realization. "Because Taryn, you have the power of song, which means that you are a destined ruler."

He smiles his perfect smile. He already knows this. This must be why he has that calm inner confidence since he has married Vesta. She told him the truth. This must be how she knew he was worthy of exchanging her longevity. She saw the power of his song bring me to her proposal. She could accept love from someone who has a heart of gold. I am lost in my discovery when I realize he has been talking. I tune back in.

"Either way, I do not think we will be back to Wincot for a while. Which gives us more time to travel." He looks at Vesta, "Maybe we will finally have a chance to go to Amara, and I can meet your grandmother," Taryn says.

Vesta replies cheekily, "She has a weakness for tall, dark, and handsome, so I will need to protect you. She is a spry young woman, despite her years." We all laugh, happy to break the tension.

"She looks as young as ever, despite her long life, but unfortunately, she has never known true love. One day soon, we will all need to visit Amara together, and you can meet my family." Vesta adds.

"I would love that," I reply.

"I look forward to meeting them." Kyrie comes up behind me, wraps his arms around me, and nods yes in agreement over my shoulder.

"Vesta, was the moment your hair turned pearl-white at your wedding a sign of the exchange of longevity for true love?" I ask.

"Yes," she says, smiling. "This is the unique power the Amara line received from Claudegus. Did you notice his white hair in the painting?"

I nod yes. I look at my friends standing there together, and it suddenly occurs to me that Taryn and Vesta were originally from two different realms before they married and before we made our vows. Their new union would not have been recorded yet in the suitcase genealogies. I am excited for them, like I have just uncovered a mystery no one else has—that the prophecy is about their union.

"Vesta, Taryn…Kyrie and I went through the eight genealogies of the Sovran seats, and there were not any other unions made across the realms. So, we thought ours was the first. But it just occurred to me that yours is the first union made across the two realms. Your story is the beginning of the uniting of the realms, the prophecy spoke of your true love finding each other."

They look at each other with that same knowing smile and back at me. I pull the prophecy out of my pocket; I have kept it with me every day since Vesta gave it to me.

"It finally all makes sense. It tells the story of everything that has happened since my corpse-bride first appeared at your proposal. But I hear it differently this time. It is not just about me, it is about all of us, and your love story came first, it united the realms." They both smile, but it is like I am missing something. I look back at the poem, looking for what they obviously know that I do not.

Vesta says, "After my father arrived at our cottage, we told him about everything that had happened so far, then he went through the poem line by line and explained it all to us, about all that would happen next."

"He knew? Even about our Redamancy Vow?"

"Yes, that was an easy one for him, but he told us not to tell you and Kyrie about anything that had not yet happened. That it would not be right to take from you the surprise of your own story happening organically. He explained it all to us, my mother, me, and Taryn."

I look over at Taryn, grasping that he knew my love story before I did. I remember how well he told my story to Barrow, and I understand now how he knew.

"Even the part about Earl Menstus?" I ask, bewildered.

"Yes, even that part. He understood that the void within the dark lord would be transformed by love's power. It is why he agreed to go to Drauge. He knew he was looking at a man who would soon face his death, and my father felt compelled to help protect us all so that you, Arden, and you, Kyrie, could find one another."

She has known all along.

"I am sorry we could not explain everything to you the day that I called you, but it has been an even more incredible experience watching you, both of you, carry out the lines of the prophetic poem from the power of your bond, from the goodness within each of you, that only gets stronger each day that you are united."

I understand now why they were packed up and ready to come to Kallos for the ceremony. I smile when I remember that dinner.

"It must have been hard keeping this to yourselves and not telling us when we were at your cottage. I do not know if I could have done it."

"It helped that we had each other to talk to about it," she says as she looks at Taryn, and he smiles in agreement.

"We had plenty of time to go through that suitcase before we handed it off to you guys." Taryn admits coolly, "So there was a lot to talk about."

He knows it all, too. She trusted him with everything. So did her parents. How did he go from being so scared at the proposal to this confident knowing, this peaceful understanding? He has become an open-minded leader. He is no longer the same guy who wrote me letters; he has become a new man. And I genuinely admire him for it.

"Vesta, how was I your sentinel?" I ask.

Vesta looks at me and says, "A sentinel is a guard who keeps watch over someone. You are the one that led me to find Taryn at the search party. Looking for you is what led me to true love, and without you guiding me, I might have gone another one hundred years without ever finding a love worthy of the exchange. You even watched over the proposal and the wedding, ensuring that a union of true love took place."

That is not what I thought I was doing, but I appreciate her perspective.

"But you were also my sentinel. You marked my grave and guarded me, and then helped Kyrie find me. Without you doing that, I would have never lived again…would have never known true love either."

She walks over to me and says tenderly, "You said, 'Take my life and let it be yours." She takes my hands in hers. "That kind of sacrifice, a love like this one," as she squeezes my hands so that I know she is speaking about us. "These two created unions that pulsed with a power of love more extraordinary than any others before it—a love that would unite realms."

I see a different interpretation of true love, a new understanding of the prophecy. I look into her eyes and realize that she is speaking about the two of us finding each other, our deep bond formed from our lives intertwining and unfolding into each other's stories. My mind expands with a new world of possibilities. All my tunnel vision is breaking open, and a greater understanding of love is being planted in its place.

I blurt out excitedly, "The realms could not unite until Vesta and I found one another, and then we each created a beloved union with a power that had not been known before!"

She smiles happily and adds, "Yes, we are the union across the realms! I wanted to tell you, but my father said you would come to understand it. And you are right, the lines in the prophecy are about all of us, everywhere true love finds the other across the realms, which is between all of us right here. But...Claudegus saw you on his deathbed, the one that made him smile with relief. He saw you cross from death to life, even had a poem written about it, and sealed it in deep magic, to ensure it happened just like that."

I do not know why, but after all that has happened and all that I have seen, I am still surprised to hear it. I do not think it will ever be anything but surprising.

Then Vesta says, "Crossing the forbidden divide is not about the bypass."

I look at her, hoping she will explain what I cannot quite grasp yet. I can sense that she already understands things that I do not, and that she is being very gentle with me. But I do not know how it can be anything other than the bypass.

"Crossing the forbidden divide is the line between life and death."

This new thought feels like the missing puzzle piece turning up just in time, but I need help clicking it into place. I look at her with trust.

"The prophecy says, 'The bird follows true love's power, and crosses the forbidden divide to find the other.' You crossed from life into death when your life was taken from you. But you crossed the forbidden divide back into life when you followed the power of love in Taryn's song and let it take you to its source. You found him, but you also found me, and it is how I found you."

The memory comes back to me.

"Then, you crossed back into death when you gave me your blessing to marry the man you loved. The man who loved you before he loved me, the power of love in the song proves it. When Kyrie dared to stand at that great divide and dig past the line of life and into death to ask for your help, you crossed that forbidden divide back into life again. You have been willing to cross over that forbidden divide wherever love's power calls you. Even when you were alive again, you crossed back into death, becoming a ghost, when you heard the song again at our wedding, and when I called you to my cottage, because you cannot help but willingly follow the power of love that has always been leading you. It is the very thing that gave you the power to face Lord Menstus, whose spell represented death itself, and bring him to his knees, never to return. The power of alchemy was returned to the Dashel line when he was transformed from death to new life. It is because you had already harnessed the power to cross the forbidden divide for true love's sake, many times over. You crossed the divide again when the Powers Above called you to retrieve the scroll and save the Valray line and its people. We were there when your screams rang out, and we were there when your breath went still and silent."

Forty-Seven

Elspeth

I need to send word that Vesta will soon be required here in Amara to rule. I know she is ready; Florin believes it, too. I remember the day Florin came to tell me that she was stepping down as heir and passing it on straight to Vesta. I heard her out and soon came to agree. Even though Florin did not raise Vesta solely inside the Sovran estate, she was able to impart everything she knew about life here. Florin has prepared Vesta well, and I am grateful for her loyalty.

Besides, it allowed me more time as Sovran, the true love of my life. I have always held tight to my purpose. My birthright. I may not have any breath left within me by the time they arrive, but I have memories that I take with me. They will know what to do. I have passed on my strength and fortitude, along with my beauty.

Arden

It is the first time I feel known from the inside out, finally understanding a truth about myself that I could only know from her explaining it to me. I am finally getting to see myself in a way I never have. A truth that rests deep in the core of all that I am, deeper than my flesh and bones. These new tears feel heavier and saltier, as if they come from my inner core. I look at Taryn. Our betrothal was written into the prophecy. My mother had no idea she was orchestrating the beginning of its unfolding. I remember the power of love in his song. It pulled me out of my grave so that Vesta could find me. I look at Vesta and remember surrendering my life to her, trusting her, and allowing her to experience the joy for me. I look at Kyrie. The image of him beckoning for me at death's door, and me taking his hand and crossing that threshold into a new life with him.

Vesta softly puts her hand on my cheek and, with her thumb, gently wipes, and says, "The tears of the Albatross are very salty because they do the impossible. They spend many years flying over ocean water, so they must filter the salt out of the water before they can drink it. They have a special place on their beak to cry the salt tears while also hydrating themselves with pure water.

They were designed to live like no other bird can. The Albatross is the master of water, land, and sky."

I will never know how she knows everything. I just know I can trust it. I remember the feeling of flying over the water and crying out the salt on my way to meeting the Powers Above.

I look back to Vesta and ask her, "You knew who I was that day, at your proposal, when you called me the Albatross? And you spoke the line of the prophecy to me before you buried me."

She smiles at me and says, "Yes, I did. I knew who you were."

"But how? You said that you just knew what to do. How did you know that my corpse-bride showing up was the beginning of the prophecy unfolding?" I ask, feeling a little desperate to know how she always knows what is happening.

"Because my father taught me to be ready. He told me that whenever your ghost appeared, to know that it was my good omen. He said that it would mark the beginning of everything, and to not be afraid. He told me to treat your bones with the utmost care, because we would come to share a life. He said that when we found each other through the power of love, it would be the sign of the realms soon uniting."

Her words strum through my body. Her father taught her to be ready. I have never known that experience.

We would come to share a life. We would share a life. Unite the realms. True Love. Taryn's and mine. Hers and Taryn's. Mine and hers. Hers and mine. Mine and Kyrie's. Every piece was needed and has been woven together.

"You knew everything all along. You even promised that I would be free again one day, and I am."

"Yes." She nods.

"Was there anything that you did not know about?" I ask.

"We did not know who caused your death, or that Kyrie's mother would die when the spell broke. We did not know that Rexus would be the one to put the arrow in your father's chest, or that Aster would want to stay with Earl in Dashel. We did not know Barrow would get involved. We did not know what was going to take place in Valray, until Rae showed up, then I recognized the last line of the prophecy as it was happening. Before my father left the cottage, he told us that we needed to be in Pallayes before the realms united."

"How did he know everything?" I ask.

"My father was the first and only person to translate the prophecy, because he began to understand it was about the power of love. A love pure enough to cross from death to life, having the power to heal and unite. When he met my mother, the Powers Above taught him how to truly love a woman, and that lesson has guided everything else in his life, even his work. The Powers Above showed him how to carefully untangle my mother's bones and piece her back together with love. He saw your foretold resurrection and understood it because he witnessed my mother's. It was the Powers Above who gave him the suitcase full of papers. The Powers Above assigned him the sacred task of translating and interpreting the ancient poem."

She was raised by a man who knew how to love a woman. She was both mothered and fathered within a bond of devotion. This is our whole difference. I look to Kyrie and hope that our children will be raised with the same knowledge. I think of the suitcase. It came straight from the Powers Above. Mazek was chosen for this task.

She picks up the prophecy and says, "See this line here, 'New life has been given in retribution.' It was the very first line he was able to translate. That is when The Powers Above returned the power of longevity to not only my mother, but to my father as well. He is the only person outside of the Amaran line to receive this gift. The Powers

Above said they would need both time and love to fulfill the task they had been given."

My eyes widen. It all feels so enchanting. I wonder how old they all truly are.

"The next line he translated, 'A protection, and then freedom,' he understood was about his call, his life's work. It was from this conviction that he felt safe on the day he agreed to find Earl Menstus in Vaxxa. He trusted that he would be rescued and returned to us without any harm coming to us. Because my father would do anything to protect us."

Her last sentence strikes me hard. I will never know what that is like. My father fed my sister and me to the wolves.

"That is incredible," Kyrie says with awe. "I cannot wait to hear their story. It somehow feels strangely relatable." He looks at me with tenderness, and I see the copper glimmer on his skin. I remember that I still need to tell him the truth about his parents.

"Thank you both for everything you have shared with us. So, what is next?" Kyrie asks. He must be as curious as I am about the unknown yet to come.

"Well, if it is okay with you Kyrie, can we borrow your glider? I would love to take my beautiful wife on a sunset tour of your province before we head back to the villa. I will return it to you tomorrow." Taryn asks.

"Of course, that is a wonderful idea. Please enjoy yourselves," Kyrie replies and tosses him the keys.

We hug them goodbye and see them out. Then, we finally make our way down to the pool's edge. The sky is singing. We sit back on the steps, letting the cool water have its calming effect.

"Will you tell me now?" Kyries asks.

"Yes," I reply. So, I slowly and gently tell him about how his mother and Earl Menstus grew up together, falling in love, and the unmade vow. I tell him about his grandfather's relationship with Earl's mother. I tell him about his father's aggressive attack and the long recovery of Earl Menstus. I tell him about how Earl found his mother's body years later and his heart turning to stone at the devastating sum of all his losses. I tell him about the unraveling of Earl Menstus, the making of a dark Lord Menstus, and the spell that was the hopeless act of both love and hate, both a desperate cry for help and revenge.

I tell him everything I know, and then I make space for him to process the new story. We sit in silence for a bit while he gathers his thoughts and feelings.

"I always knew there were things my father was not telling me. The conflict that always stood between us makes more sense now. He carried repressed guilt for the spell and the lie he crafted to protect himself. The flash in my mother's eyes right before she died also makes sense. It was not about me; it was about her past. She felt shame for not choosing love. But with all that we have learned about the prophecy, I know that no union across the realms was going to be allowed before the chosen time. My mother and Earl were from two different realms. Is it weird that I am having compassion for him? I cannot imagine what it would have been like if after I asked you to make the vow that you would have chosen someone else your father picked for you. I cannot imagine living with that kind of heartache, and then to be physically broken by the man you chose instead of me. I am not saying I would have cast a spell on the province, but I cannot imagine not being permanently altered in some way."

He lets his thoughts pour out as he stares far into the early sunset. I can sense there is more.

"If I had known this before we went to Dashel, I think I would have asked Earl for forgiveness as well, on behalf of my parents, for the harm that was done to him. It feels one-sided."

I cannot hide my expression. It is a mix of surprise and awe. He looks at me, tears now in his eyes, a light quivering in his chin, and humbly asks, "Will you use your power of travel and take me to Dashel? I need to make this right."

"Of course I will. We have time, let us do it now," I say tenderly, and he nods in agreement.

Forty-Eight

{Yesterday}

Dear Kyrie,

I am writing to celebrate the good news of your place in the Sovran seat of Kallos. I have heard that the spell has finally been broken, after all these years. What a relief you all must have. However, I do send my condolences on the recent passing of your mother, Reown, my dear aunt, and for Juris, my father's younger brother.

I apologize that there was nothing we could do to help Kallos during the years under the spell. As you know, I was struggling through my own transition to the Sovran seat as my beloved father fell ill and recently passed as well.

I would like to invite you to visit us in Teahn and share your experience with us in person. There are many scholars here who are eager to write the most accurate version for the history books. I hope you can make the journey; we have so much to catch up on.

Your cousin,

Saladin Teahn

Arden

We stand, and he holds onto me tightly as I close my eyes and envision the Dashel estate. It only takes a moment to arrive at their doorstep. It feels different without having to go through the bypass anymore. Now I realize the true gift this power gives me, especially as I will often need to travel between Valray and Kallos.

Kyrie rings the bell, and we wait a bit. I can see his nervousness. In the next moment, Barrow opens the door. The exuberant joy on his face is contagious, and we cannot help but feel the excitement in his energy as he embraces both of us with his signature bear hug.

"What are you doing here! This is such a surprise!" He asks excitedly.

"I wanted to speak with Earl, if that is okay," Kyrie replies. "I am sorry it is late and unannounced."

"Please do not ever apologize for showing up here, we love it when friends visit! Come in! I was just making some evening refreshments as we watch the sunset."

We follow Barrow straight through the large foyer that connects to the back patio of the sprawling estate. I have never seen anything like it. It is big enough to get lost in for days. Aster and Earl each look so comfortable in their patio chairs. There is a small fireplace for a cozy effect, warm lighting, soft cushions, and blankets. It looks magical against the backdrop of the evening air's golden glow. The view of the mountain range is spectacular. Barrow announces our arrival, and they look up in surprise. I wonder for a minute if there is a future ahead where Aster and I visit one another like this.

We all say hello, and Aster settles us in chairs while Barrow places glasses of cold tea in our hands.

"I am sorry this is unexpected," Kyrie begins, "but I needed to come speak with Earl before the sun set today."

"Do you need us to leave you in private?" Aster asks.

"No, please stay. I want all of you here," Kyrie says. Then he faces Earl and begins. "Earl, I needed to come make things right with you. I have just recently heard the story of the heartache you experienced being rejected by my mother and beaten by my father. I heard of your long recovery and your mother's tragic death. I know you have already asked forgiveness for the spell on Kallos, and the deaths of many, including my parents. But until now, it has been one-sided. I have come to ask you forgiveness for the many ways in which my family wounded you and your mother. I can now see the part my parents played in this story, and they are not without fault. They too, have a hand in the tragedy. On behalf of my parents, Earl Dashel, please forgive me for the trauma you experienced at the hands of the Kallos family. You and your mother were not treated with the respect and dignity you both deserved. I need to take the burden of that loss off your back."

Kyrie then pulls the Valray Oak necklace from his pocket and hands it to Earl. "I believe this belongs to you."

The oaks are returned. There was not a sound heard in that moment of silent stillness.

Earl Dashel lifts his topaz eyes to Kyrie's, and small pools of tears form. If humility and gratitude could meet in an electric spark, then the patio would be on fire. It is palpable.

"I gave it to your mother long ago. It was the most valuable thing I possessed until I could buy the gold bracelets for the vow that we planned to make."

"She never took it off. She was wearing it when she died." Kyrie replies and Earl lets out a surprised gasp.

I remember my mother said a new one had to be made for me since it had been so long since a daughter was born into the line that no one knew what happened to the last necklace. The necklace that was meant for me has been on Reown's neck this whole time.

Earl carefully takes the necklace into his hand and gently opens the pendant. He carefully draws out a small, folded paper. Once he opens it, he reads it to us.

"When the two oaks are returned,

The true heirs will claim

Their Sovran seats,

And the salty tears

Will become diamond dust."

He pauses before he continues. "After Reown married, I had a dream about the pendant opening and the lost words of the prophecy falling out and bringing me back to Dashel. It is why I went back to ask Reown for this necklace. And when I was recovering in Clemen after the attack, I had a recurring dream about losing the last piece of the prophecy and not being able to return home. This is why I was obsessed with the prophecy and needed Mazek's help. It is why I thought I would get Dashel back if I could understand what words were lost in the necklace. But the Powers Above showed me yesterday that this last piece of the prophecy is not about me. It is about both of you, Arden and Aster, and the new generation of heirs in each province seat."

I am speechless. We all are. My hand finds my own necklace on my chest, and I wonder if my pendant opens or holds anything special. I have never thought of opening it.

Earl draws the necklace towards his heart and says to Kyrie, "I forgive you. Thank you, I did not know I had been waiting decades to hear those words. They are a balm. The acknowledgement of my pain is what I was so desperate for. I regret the way I handled that pain; I know now it was all so wrong. But I did love your mother more than I ever loved anyone before or have ever since. I admit that I hated your father, and I ended his life the same way he nearly ended mine. Except, the irony is, he could not feel the pain. When your mother chose him instead of me, it crushed my heart, but when he took away my manhood, it crushed my soul. I buried him in Vaxxa. The Powers Above showed me the whole story of my life, including this moment. I did not know when it would happen, only that it would, and then I would know it was time to say goodbye."

"Wait, what do you mean? Say goodbye to who?" Aster asks, panic rising in her voice.

He looks at her and lets himself weep. She goes to her knees in front of his chair and grasps his hands, which hold his walking stick.

"It is time for me to say goodbye to you, my darling heir. Thank you for saying yes to saving the Dashel province. You are going to be a worthy ruler; it has been destined for you. And you will not be alone. The Powers Above showed me Barrow arriving, it was part of the deal. I knew I could never leave you abandoned here. You deserve to be loved and cherished for the rest of your long life. The Dashel line is in your blood. You are the rightful heir."

We all look at each other, and Barrow's eyebrows are raised in surprise. Earl Dashel knew about future events while silently waiting for his release from this realm. The Powers Above arranged it just so.

Earl looks back at Kyrie, "Thank you for your humility, it is a gift that I wish I had possessed earlier in my life. Your people will be blessed under your guidance."

Then he turns to me and says, "You have more power in your tears and in your bones, and now also in your blood, than I could ever hope to have in my lifetime. Thank you for the mercy you showed me and thank you for not being afraid of me. Somehow, you saw the remnants of my humanity."

My breath catches. My heart swells.

Next, he turns to Barrow and says, "I entrust you with the heart of my heir, and the heart of my land. The Powers Above could not have sent a better man for the tasks ahead. If you ever doubt your place here, just remember that you were handpicked by the Powers Above. Your enthusiasm is going to animate the Dashel province and bring in new life to the village market square."

Finally, he says to all of us, but looking out into the far sky, "It is time for me to keep my end of the agreement with the Powers Above. I can finally handle the weight of my faults. I am to travel out into the realm beyond and arrange the reunion and reconciliation between my great-grandparents, Vera Valray and her Earl Dashel. And now I have her necklace to return. I am the one to go to my ancestors because I have lived both sides of their experience, the egoic pride, the bitter heartbreak, the desperate cry to be loved, the revenge, the apathy, and the foolish lust for power. I have been transformed by the power of love so that the Dashel line can be fully restored down to its roots. You will know it here, when I have become the bridge that they can finally cross to heal the bloodline in this province. You will see it when the people arrive, and when the land is again filled with life. This sacrifice that I have agreed to is part of my own repentance. It was only right for the Kallos province to receive healing first, and then the Valray province, before Dashel could flourish in its transformational healing. There is still one more part of this story that needs a transitional character, and the Powers Above, even after all that I have done, has let it be me."

We all hang on to his every word, stunned and not expecting this event to unfold. When he finishes speaking his last word, he looks out to the setting sun with a faraway look in his eyes, like he can see something that we cannot, and then he simply vanishes from his chair. All four of us jump back in our own chairs, completely surprised by his unexpected departure. I almost hear his goodbye carried on the wind that blows through the patio, strong enough that it extinguishes the fire.

"What just happened?" Aster asks aloud, her hands visibly shaking. "Where did he go? Is he coming back? Does anybody know what just happened?"

Barrow gets up and goes over to her, picks her up, and holds her shocked body as she lets herself cry the tears of complex grief. I look at Kyrie, and I can see he is also shocked by what just happened. He had no idea his apology would set in motion Earl Dashel's departure from this realm. Or that every minute before it was holding Earl from his destiny into the unknown.

Kyrie walks over to Aster and says with the utmost compassion, "Aster, I am so sorry for your loss, I had no idea that was going to happen. I felt so compelled to apologize for what my parents did to him, but I did not know it would mean that he would disappear. I am so sorry Aster."

She lifts her wet face and says, "I know Kyrie, there is no way you could have known. No one knew. He has been so quiet since the day we left Kallos. This is the most he has said since we arrived. I just did not think he would ever not be here. I am not sure what to do next."

Barrow softly says, "Somehow, this moment was a gift, already planned and foreseen. He was ready to go wherever he was being called to. He was at peace, and he was ready to say goodbye, ready to begin his next journey."

Kyrie says, "No one can deny the power of love's alchemy after watching the darkness become light, the lack become overflowing, and the stone become flesh."

"He came to somehow understand that the power of love beckoned him to sacrifice for the sake of others. He chose the harder burden to carry because of the love he experienced internally from the Powers Above. He wanted to return it in full measure, like he was finally able to enter the power of the Redamancy Vow that he always longed to have but was denied." I offer these words that roll out, and they press on me deeply as I wonder in awe of the mystical levels that love can reach without bounds.

"Thank you all for your words, I appreciate them," Aster begins. "I know we will be okay. I know he is going to help heal the Dashel line, and this province is going to flourish again. Barrow and I will be ready for it." She wipes her eyes, and a soft smile arrives on her lips as she looks at him.

Barrow kisses her forehead and draws her into another hug.

"Do you need anything before we leave?" Kyrie asks.

"Only a promise that you will come back and visit," Barrow replies.

"We promise," I tell them, and I give my sister a hug. We both hang on tight for a while.

"You are the Sovran ruler of Dashel now," I say.

Her eyes widen with the delayed revelation. Then she looks over to Barrow, grabs his hand, and says, "We are going to figure this out together."

His response is pure joy as he lifts her from her feet and spins her around. We watch their happiness one minute longer before Kyrie and I grab hands and instantly travel back home.

Forty-Nine

Vesta

It is time for you to travel to Amara. The Sovran seat is awaiting your arrival. And yes, you may crown him your co-ruler. I have a special surprise planned for you both. I have decided to change part of the Amaran power. True love deserves more time, not less. I am certain this is true. So, I am returning your power of longevity to you and giving it to Taryn as well. It will happen when you renew your vows inside the Redamancy ceremony I have planned for the two of you once you arrive in Amara. I know you have always dreamed of this ceremony, and no one is more deserving of it than the daughter of Mazek and Florin.

~the Powers Above

Tonight, we lie in bed, both feeling the immovable weariness that comes from being emotionally poured out. We process our thoughts quietly and peacefully, not even having the energy to speak them aloud. We both know there will be time tomorrow, and it will even be better over coffee. We are both still stunned by what we experienced today.

I dream again of the woman in the painting, Claudegus' true love, the mother of Lashga and Pallayes. She steps out of the painting and comes to me with the same exquisite quilt. She wraps it around my shoulders, but this time, she stays and looks into my eyes. This time, I remember to ask her name.

"I am the Powers Above. That is my name. I am the one who wrote the prophecy, and it is my handwriting in the suitcase full of papers. I am the artist who painted the family portraits, and I am the weaver of this whole story. Everyone has been chosen by my hand. When I saw how the grief of the living was going to break the land in half, I knew I needed to find the counter-grief, the righteous grief of the beloved corpse, to unite it again. I am the one who chose you to help unite the realms and release Claudegus so that he might return to me in the realm beyond. I knew that I could trust you to trust me. It is my voice and my hand that has guided you. I am the master seamstress that you have entrusted to design the mantle over your bloodline. You have done well, and I am very proud of you."

Before I awaken, I ask, "Is there more for me to do?"

And she says, "Yes, there is more to come. You will hear my voice and find my writings. When I draw up plans, I always leave them where they will be found."

I open my eyes to the smell of fresh-brewed coffee and the realization that I know the author of love and that she is my divine mother. She has known me all along and has called me by name. She read my map in the sky, saw my story written in the stars, and decided it was good. I finally remember to open my pendant. There is a small, folded paper inside. So, I take it out and unfold it. My breath catches when I realize that, somehow, my shadow has saved the best poem for last.

> Watch me glow and rise,
> And come to know my power.
> All my beauty and strength
> Will rise within me like the sun,
> To greet the light pouring out,
> Like Psyche holding the lantern
> Up to the god of love.
> Kissing the moon and stars above,
> This is how Pleasure is born.

I smile and treasure this moment of feeling fully alive and deeply content.

"Good morning, I have coffee ready." Kyrie chimes in with a smile.

"Let's bring it to the balcony," I reply, as I roll out of bed, ready for that first sip.

After I settle in, I tell him about my dream. "Kyrie, the unknown woman in the painting has not been forgotten, because she is the Powers Above. It was her the whole time. It is her handwriting on the papers, and her voice that I heard. She visited me last night in my dreams. She told me there is more to come, and that she would leave notes where they can be found."

He pauses and brings his cup to rest on the table so as not to spill it as he takes in my words.

"Well, I found one this morning on the coffee tray." He says, almost chuckling.

"A note?" I ask, feeling my heartbeat quicken. "What does it say?"

He carefully pulls the handwritten note out from under the coffee pot. I notice her familiar handwriting right away.

"Now that the legacy has been restored, it is time to expand it and bring a new freedom to all. It is time for

the old ways to evolve into something new. Prepare for many journeys ahead. Love has returned home, the realms have united, mercy has been granted, bridges have been made, and the land has awakened. But the people need to be enlightened to the changes, so the inside can match the outside. The Albatross will fly far and wide, and she will bring her home and family with her, as she masters both land and sky. She will commandeer the waters above and below, protecting all under the shadow of her wing. Your journey to Amara is soon upon you."

We just sit in awe and silence, looking at one another.

"Wow. That is incredible. I am excited about our future. And it looks like we are traveling to somewhere neither of us have been!" I say.

"This is just the beginning," Kyrie replies, letting out his beautiful, hearty laughter as he comes over and wraps me up in his arms.

"It means we have a whole future ahead of us, and I get to feel all of it with you. It means there are more adventures ahead and new people to meet. It means we have more time to let the power of love strengthen our vow, as we return to each other the full measure of our love." He has the strength to hold me up as he softly spins us around in delight as he speaks.

But I know his true strength comes from his ability to be vulnerable, to share his feelings honestly, and to trust me with his tears.

"I want to do all of that with you," I tell him as I kiss him, the man who whisked me from my grave and let my tears heal his heart.

I notice him notice something that I cannot yet see. He leans forward, puts a finger on my cheek, and catches a tear. He lifts it to show me; it looks like it is filled with diamond dust. It is one of the most beautiful things I have ever seen. Then, I watch him lift it to his lips.

His eyes close in wonder, and he savors it, then says, "I claim all these tears of joy for myself, and I will happily spend the rest of my life making sure these precious tears are part of our life. They are my treasures because your joy is my joy."

I remember Earl reading the last words:

And the salty tears

Will become diamond dust.

What a journey we have had. Not too long ago, my salty tears of grief were sought for. But now, my grief has been transformed into a kind of love that can make tears of crushed diamonds. True tears of joy. I have discovered my own alchemy of love, and I cannot help but make more tears for him to enjoy.

Epilogue

{One week after our story ends}

Arden

I arrive at their new grave site with anticipation and relief. I have come to pay my respects and honor my parents. The headstones that I commissioned are finally installed, along with the new landscaping around the area, which is now designated as a memorial at the Valray estate.

This was not an easy conversation with Rexus. He was not willing to let my father's grave be identified or my mother's grave be disturbed. I am coming to learn the great lengths, good or bad, that people go to when their heart is broken, when they are torn from the ones they love, and when all hope feels lost. Somehow though, the Powers Above persuaded him, although he did not tell me how.

It was important to me that I honor them in this way before we begin our travels to Amara for Vesta and Taryn's Sovran ceremony, along with our visits to Clemen and Teahn on our return home. Before I can welcome the future, I must begin to honor the past.

After we return, Aster and Barrow plan to travel with us to Vaxxa. Aster promised to show us her favorite spots and tell us the history she learned while living there. But most importantly, we have the location of Juris's grave, and we have made arrangements to bring his bones back to Kallos, where he can rest in peace next to Reown.

I am ready to forgive and release them all. I am ready to share my blessings with those I came from as well as those that will come from me. The knot that formed over generations and tightened from unmet, unrealistic expectations, when there was a need for others to behave, believe, and be for the sake of another's comfort and happiness has finally been untied.

I am learning how to create my own happiness without anyone else being responsible for it. I have learned that true freedom is an inside job and it cannot be taken away when the power above becomes the power within.

Afterword

My dear Reader,

Even after this book ends, there is still so much more to tell you because, as you see, it is only the beginning. I trust that we will one day meet again, maybe across the Great Bridge, or somewhere under the United Realm's lavender-blue sky.

Ever so I am,

~the Powers Above

Author's Notes

Six years ago in 2020, I spent most of my Covid quarantine hours listening to Dr. Clarissa Pinkola Estés tell stories on Audible. The one that captured my whole attention was her retelling of the corpse-bride tale. I kept coming back to it. I pondered it and let it seep deeply into my psyche, where I imagined possible back stories for the characters. I was turning forty-three that year and processing the new experiences of midlife. Something about the relationship between the corpse-bride and the living-bride impacted me.

I wrote poems about those two brides for the next four years. I saw myself in that symbolic relationship between the corpse-bride and the living-bride at the midlife point that shows up when our buried past begs to be awakened and healed for a better future. I longed to unravel the complexities packed into that small tale, and it led to a cathartic, transformative discovery in the writing process as this imaginary story uniquely came to life.

The other story Dr. Clarissa Pinkola Estés tells that lives rent free in my mind is *The Skeleton Woman*, with the fisherman who is chased by her bones that are caught on his line, and how he devoutly untangles them the same night her soul is revived by his tears. I decided that if I ever wrote a book, I would somehow find a way to connect those two beloved tales and then add in a sprinkle of *Baba-Yaga,* another one of my Dr. Estés favorites.

Acknowledgements

The beauty of self-publishing is the author's liberty and agency to make changes in the manuscript when needed. (It is the upside to wearing many hats on the job.) This aspect was appreciated when I realized (after its original publication and subsequent printings, even a Pie Lady commission) that this book wanted to be told in a completely different way. So, I unpublished the original, went back to the drawing board, and started with a different perspective. Suddenly, new characters came to life while old ones wanted a new storyline. The characters inspired me to take new creative liberties, and I began to have more fun with the story. A year and a half later, a new revised and expanded version of the original book was born. I am thankful for these new friends that live extravagantly in my imagination. They seem to show up each day asking, "what if?"

Like most books, this one was many years in the making. After taking on the job of writer, editor, designer, and publisher, I now understand why there is a team of professionals behind most books. Grateful for this opportunity to self-publish, I now have an ever-growing set of skills that I never imagined acquiring before this challenging yet empowering endeavor. I am also grateful for a husband who said yes every time I asked for extra help with formatting, kids who would not let me quit when another round of edits felt impossible, and friends who texted encouraging words after reading. I am grateful for this team of love. Thank you. If you enjoy this book, please consider recommending it to a friend. There is nothing like a book that finds its readers through word of mouth.

About the Author

In 1999, at the age of twenty-one, Courtney G. Hamilton graduated Magna Cum Laude from the University of Southwestern Louisiana (now the University of Louisiana at Lafayette) in the College of General Studies, concentrating in Arts and Humanities, and received the honor of Outstanding Graduate in her graduating class. Two weeks later, she got married.

Courtney exuberantly used her education, skills, and talents to successfully home-educate her five children for over twenty years, along with teaching art lessons and creative writing classes. She had the honor of presenting her three oldest children with their high school diplomas. When her last two teenagers enrolled in a local high school, Courtney retired from education and began compiling her poetry, writing a backstory for the corpse-bride, and learning to self-publish her first book.

She currently enjoys growing Monstera plants, taking meditative walks, mastering dairy-free and gluten-free baking while listening to jazz, and watching Psych reruns with her family. At this moment, she is probably either hanging wallpaper or sipping coffee with her husband while looking for edge pieces on the puzzle spread across their table. You can email her at ardenofvalray@gmail.com.